BROKEN DOLLS

a Joi Sommers Mystery
by Susan Peters

Sunrise Consulting
Chicago, Illinois

Broken Dolls. Copyright © 2014 by Susan D. Peters

All rights reserved. Printed in the United States of America. No part of this book may be used or reproduced in any manner whatsoever without written permission except in the case of brief quotations embodied in critical articles and reviews.

ISBN: 978-0-9827125-1-1 Trade Paperback
LCCN: 2014937173

Cover by J.L. Woodson www.jlwoodson.com
Interior Design by Lissa Woodson for www.macrompg.com

Second Edition

Manufactured and Printed in the United States of America

BROKEN DOLLS

Broken Dolls is dedicated to the members of my family that have served in the Chicago Police Department.

My late, beloved uncle, Robert "Pete" Peters, formerly one of Chicago's elite Regal Theater ushers, became a cop in the old days when the Police Department had a height requirement. Not to be discouraged, my resourceful uncle had himself "administratively stretched" a half inch to meet that requirement.

Besides serving as a Regal usher, my Uncle Pete was proudest of having served on security detail for the late Harold Washington, Chicago's first African American mayor.

To the memory of my cousin, Devon Anderson Jr., a Chicago homicide detective who sacrificed

to ensure that his children, Devon III and Ariel, got the best educations possible.

Lastly, I salute the resourceful and dedicated professionals that have the unseemly job of working backwards to figure out who committed the murder, why and hopefully bringing the guilty to justice.

"We are all wonderful, beautiful wrecks. That's what connects us--that we're all broken, all beautifully imperfect." — Emilio Estevez

CHAPTER 1

The five o'clock news predicted a major thunderstorm, but the evening began with a deceptive soft summer breeze. Barely an hour later, the willowy trees in the home's back yard seemed to suddenly sweep forward, bowing their heads to the west. The decorative chimes began to tinkle furiously with a light discordant melody.

The top of the wood-grained rain barrel was blown across the yard, landing against the fence with a hard clash. Thick sheets of rain cut slices through the air. Soon it saturated the pavement, showering the vegetables and flowers in the lush garden. Though the rain beat itself into the ground with unrelenting and thunderous strokes, still the smell of fragrant but battered roses wafted into the study.

Dennis Gregg regained consciousness on the floor of his study. The last thing he remembered was sorting through August accounts payables—and his unexpected visitor. His head throbbed with an ache that would probably last longer than the storm.

How long have I been unconscious?

He barely noticed the crimson drippings from his nose as he pulled himself up on unsteady feet. He scanned the room, feeling it pitch and roll as the images of his surroundings stared at him from blurred edges.

If I can get some fresh air.

Dennis trudged toward the open garden door and ambled a few steps from the threshold. Still dazed, the icy rain pelted him as the last words spoken to him reverberated in his ears. *You're a goddamned liar! You aren't healed. I saw you ... I saw you ...* The steady progression of cold rain plastered his shirt to his burly frame, sending a chill rippling through his body. By the time he made his way back inside, he was breathing heavily and had to lean on the desk to steady himself.

Then there was a voice, almost an echo, which asked, "May I come in?"

Dennis grinned inwardly in relieved anticipation of the sympathy and support he would receive from the familiar voice behind him. Before he could turn to receive the embrace of his rescuer, a deafening sound ripped through the air. A flash of fire was followed by a whisper of smoke.

In the next instant, the immortal soul of Elder Dennis Gregg was set free.

CHAPTER 2

BOOM!!!!

The first explosion snatched the middle-aged Nancy Gregg from a drug-induced sleep. She glanced out of the window, trying to decide if that uncanny sound was thunder or something else. Before she could make up her mind …

BOOM!!!!

The second blast propelled her from the bed. She was groggy and shaken, but mustered enough strength to yank a pink satin robe over her frail frame then stuff her narrow feet into pink and white satin bedside slippers. She clutched the spiral staircase railing and was instinctively drawn toward her husband's den. The lights glowed as an ominous sign that something wicked had happened right in the comfort of their home.

Nancy made her way past the hallway credenza and a mahogany bookcase filled with collector vases. She placed a hand on the half-opened door to her husband's study. A chill rippled through her and she took a long, slow breath. She recoiled at the fetid smell of blood, but she was not deterred.

There was a lifeless figure sprawled out on the plush beige cut pile carpet!

Fighting to hold down the small amount of dinner she managed to force down, she inched back until her body pressed against the door. Nancy stared at the mass of tattered flesh that had been the face she had adored most of her adult life.

She panicked when she remembered the sound of her son's voice calling up to her as he had come into the house earlier. *Marcus? Sweet Jesus!* Was her baby son capable of this?

She cursed herself for not coming down when Marcus had called out to her. There had always been undisclosed tension between her son and husband. Nancy's incapacitating physical pain had kept her from coming downstairs when Marcus stopped by this evening, but she secretly had hoped that by staying in her room, father and son would take the time to sort through their issues.

Tonight she regretted abdicating her role of the ever-present mediator; the stabilizing force between the two men.

Nancy inched forward, her heart slamming against her frail chest. Denny was unrecognizable in his current state. Lifeless. Mangled.

Ever since Marcus had moved in with his best friend Scott's parents during his sophomore year in high school, every encounter between her husband and son had been filled with anger. Marcus' connection to the family was held together by the tenuous thread of his afternoon visits with her while his father was at work. She wished she had worked harder to bring them together. Unfortunately, the easiest way to avoid the inevitable conflicts was to see Marcus on Friday afternoons and tactfully share his progress with her husband when they were alone. In hindsight, not the best idea, but it was what it was.

Nancy clutched at her robe. Every nerve ending in her body tingled. The painkiller's potency was ebbing, and the pain that stalked her was now slowly overpowering her. She knew that calling the police was the right thing to do. But she also knew that while the pain was in control, she couldn't think straight. Now was not the best time to talk to the police. She might give away too much.

At the moment, the one person she needed to protect was her son, despite the fact that he apparently was the one who had taken away the man she loved more than life itself. Marcus stilled deserved to be shielded, and for that she needed to have her wits about her.

Staggering backwards through the den door, she shuffled into the hallway. Blinded by tears, Nancy Gregg grasped the staircase railing, hand-over-hand hauling her feeble form up each step.

What she wanted right now was freedom from the pain and time to think. She screamed inside her head for help. There was no help for her and there was no more help for poor Denny. And truthfully, with the way she had handled things in the past, there might not be any help for her Marcus.

She would call the police in the morning.

CHAPTER 3

Inside a small bungalow on 107th and South Parnell, Marcus Gregg lay wounded and prostrate across a king-sized bed. A brown Army camouflage tee shirt was wrapped around the swollen knuckles of his right hand. His guts were whirling.

How did I let the old man get the best of me again? It never, freakin' fails. Every single time!

His anger raged to the point he could barely remember the details of what happened in his father's den. *How would his mother take what he had done?*

Marcus sat up and lit a Salem. He took a long, slow drag, then released the tendrils of smoke to curl around him. Spotty images of his father flashed before him. Angry. Falling. Bleeding. On the floor. Marcus had never been so enraged.

Sure, he had been angry at his father for most of his life, with good reason. Now that he knew the truth, a lot of people had a good reason to hate his father. But rage, the type that made him want to smash his father's brains in and to see him dead, had never overtaken him. Until tonight.

Marcus sat up on the side of the bed and inhaled deeply. That seemed to calm him a little. He took several more deep pulls, feeling the warm smoke in his nostrils and concentrating on controlling its exit from his lungs.

Corey. His mother. All victims. And he suspected there had been others. Perhaps many others.

Pausing a moment, the tip of his tongue registered the taste of tobacco mixed with the saltiness of blood. In the scuffle he'd cut his bottom lip. He noticed stains on the cigarette paper which oddly mimicked the kind of cheap lipstick that a hooker left on a married man's collar. This telltale sign symbolized his complete loss of control.

What have I done?

"I was healed of my affliction by the grace of Almighty God," his father had said. "And if he doesn't judge me, *who* do you think you are?"

Where was God when I needed him? Where was God when Corey needed him?

"I'll never address *that* subject with you or your sister again, not today, not ever!"

No, it's quite possible, that he never would. Neither would Marcus set foot in that house again. Ever.

He could never understand how his sister Kelly managed to stomach their dad, especially after what she had been through.

The mirror on his dresser gave a more complete story of the evening. He stared at the small gash over his right eye from where the old man had clipped him. It was close to his brow and had swollen to a deep magenta. Had it been an inch or two lower and had he been a few shades lighter, he would've have had a shiner. For once he was glad that he wasn't as light skinned as his sister. But he still looked a mess.

Marcus stubbed out the cigarette in an empty Coke can and lay down, imagining the side-eyes he would get when he picked up his service truck from the dispatch center in the morning. He had been working at SBC for several years and had a good relationship with most of the fellas.

As long as none of the guys say anything to me, I'll be fine. Them damn customers don't care if you've been in a train wreck; they just want their service restored.

The rain pelted his bedroom window as though asking to be let into the house. There were so many important things he had tried to keep out over the years. Especially his dad. The memories were a much harder pill to swallow. Those he couldn't keep out if he tried.

The bedroom phone rang, interrupting his struggle with a barrage of mixed emotions. He looked across the bed to the wrought iron nightstand and wondered if now he would have to listen to his mother berate him for mixing-it-up with the old man. He loved his mother, but he would not listen to her explain Daddy to him another time.

No ma'am. Not tonight mother!

The phone rang seventeen times before it finally stopped, rattling his frayed nerve endings.

Damn that woman is persistent!

Marcus grimaced as he twisted his sore body to switch off the bedside lamp. Losing himself in the darkness, he laid back to rest his body and his mind. Tomorrow would take care of itself. It had to.

CHAPTER 4

The phone buzzed on Joi Sommers's wicker nightstand. She forced one eye open and then the other, to find that the digital clock glowed 1:45 a.m. Fine time for some ass to call. Especially since she was consummating the most deliciously wicked dream.

"Damn!" she sneered through her teeth. She picked up, then cleared her throat, managing a raspy, "Hello?"

"Hey beautiful," the voice crooned on the other end.

She sighed with impatience. "Uh, hey yourself." Turning on her side, she settled back among her pillows. "Do you know what time it is?"

"I do," he answered smoothly. "But ah…"He paused as though gathering up some courage. "Is it too late for company?"

"Yes," she responded quickly, then the delta between her thighs did its own talking. It throbbed with the need for a man; a need that grew with every passing day. Never mind that he was someone she didn't see herself with on a long-term basis. She quickly added, "But it's never too early."

"I'm on my way. You want something?" he chuckled. "I'm stopping at Wendy's."

Suddenly her taste buds chimed in. "A chocolate Frosty. A *big* one."

"Got it," he crooned, and she could practically hear the relief in his voice. "I'll be there in fifteen minutes sweetheart."

"I'm unlocking the front door, 'cause I might doze back off."

"You sure you won't get raped or something?"

She swept a look across the room at her holstered Glock. "Um, not likely," she replied and disconnected the call.

She sat up and stumbled sleepily past the treadmill that was a quasi-clothes hanger on her way to the bathroom. A quick steamy shower stoked her growing desire. She considered slipping into a negligee, but reconsidered. She had no need to impress her lover. He had already explored every inch of her 5'4" curvy frame.

Joi had been so relieved to end this stress-filled day that she tumbled into the bed without showering. Despite trying to leave the tension of the job at the station, she wasn't always successful. She also felt saddled with the periodic dramatic episodes that sprang from the fact that her mother, Maze Sommers, always plucked her lovers from the pool of losers with heavy hands, light pockets and bad ass tempers. Joi, at sixteen, had run away from a home that was a revolving door for Maze's trifling boyfriends.

Spraying a double shot of Red Door perfume on her pulse points, Joi looked in the mirror at her dark brown skin and silently cursed the blackhead taking up residence in the middle of her forehead, a signal that it was time for her period. She would deal with it some other time—when she was fully awake and ready to take on the world. Right now, she was only ready for rough sex on satin sheets, and she could do that with her eyes closed.

After brushing her teeth twice, she bent at the waist and shook her heavy, chin-length locked hair into place, more to awaken herself than for vanity.

She had barely slipped her shapely, fragrant body under the pale green comforter when the call of the perfect dream became more powerful than the man she expected to soon walk through her bedroom door.

CHAPTER 5

The rain was unrelenting as it punished the windows of the South Holland Police Station. The abnormally gusty winds pummeled the streets, causing soggy paper to litter the grass and stick unattractively in the street gutters as the world outside of the station ground to a temporary halt.

This was the type of weather where people who hadn't intended to fall asleep found themselves dozing; and partiers planning to rock the town on a Friday night were forced to rethink their plans. Drivers began to act like they didn't know how to drive in the wet stuff. Fender benders comprised the bulk of the calls to the police station on a night like this.

At 10:45 p.m. the phone rang at the front desk.

"Detective Wilkerson speaking," came the terse response from Russell Wilkerson, weary and kicking himself for not leaving the station the moment he had finished his shift. The voice on the other end of the phone was slurred, barely intelligible. "Speak up, Ma'am, I can't hear ya," the detective said, angling the receiver closer to his ear.

Hearing a click on the other end Russell slammed down the phone, muttering, "Freakin' drunk!"

The station door opened and a gust of wind blew in an undercover officer holding onto a hot, big-bootie blond chick who could have profitably worked a stripper pole, but unfortunately had offered him more than a lap dance.

The undercover officer smirked at the 6'4" Russell and said, "Booking."

Russell nodded as the undercover cop walked past him to charge the bombshell. The tired detective had covered the front desk to allow Officer Martin to drop his wife at her third shift job as a server at I-Hop. As soon as he was relieved, Russell was headed home to Helen. His wife and high school sweetheart was bravely fighting multiple sclerosis. He marveled that no matter what type of day she had, she never complained and somehow always heard his key in the lock of their apartment and sat up in the bed to greet him. He picked up the phone and dialed. "Hey baby," he said, "I'll be leaving here in ten or fifteen minutes. You want me to pick you up some ribs or something?" He knew the answer was going to be 'small end, extra sauce' and smiled when she told him. "See you soon. Love you too."

Ten minutes later Officer Martin relieved him.

"Thanks man," Martin said, breathless from the sprint. "It's a mess out there."

"No problem, I'm out," said Russell wasting no time. He exited, opening his black golf umbrella and heading into the heavy rain. Tonight his commute was shortened by the fact that he didn't need to shower first to make sure he didn't smell like sex before he got home.

CHAPTER 6

Blocks away, a trembling female hand unsteadily replaced the receiver onto on its cradle. She continued her vigil under the cover of the darkness.

Mattie Wilson sat on the kitchen barstool shivering as the shadows of the night swirled around her. The shots still reverberated throughout her brain. The gory scene in her good friend's den was forever etched in her memory. Mangled face. Blood everywhere. Flashes of thunder loud enough to make her heart stop beating.

"Dennis Gregg was an evil man," she whispered, rocking to console herself. "He deserved what he got."

She froze, remembering her terror at the sound of footsteps moving towards the other side of the closed door while she was still at the scene of the crime. Mattie had been relieved to slip out through the garden before anyone else spotted her.

Mercifully, her son Corey wasn't home. At nearly half past midnight, total darkness was reflected through the windows in the small two-story, white frame home.

Her brain had turned to jelly while she drove the three blocks from the Gregg's house, but somehow she'd managed to activate the garage genie to lift the door at her own home. After pulling recklessly into the junk-filled garage brimming with Corey's bike, skateboard, roller skates and unruly boxes of Christmas ornaments, Mattie had collapsed over the steering wheel, sobbing, finally pressing the button to lower the door behind her. Safe.

Her stomach suddenly exploded. She staggered zombie-like towards the guest bathroom. Fumbling with the waistband of her slacks, she was mortified by what filled her underwear and ran down her legs. The middle-aged woman wretched at the stench that was evidence of her own fear. She had heard stories of people being so scared they "shit their pants." She had officially joined their ranks.

"Oh my God!" she shrieked, disgusted by her loss of control. As a woman who never lost control of anything, and even lined up her canned goods and jars in her cupboards so that all the labels faced forward, this loss of control was unthinkable.

Once inside the privacy of her shower, the hot spray pounded her face, neck and shoulders. She lathered again and again, not realizing that she hadn't removed her white lace underwire brassiere. Her normally "every-hair-in-place 'do" was now a puffy mass of dyed auburn and gray wool. Her heartbeat was so erratic she felt light-headed.

She reflected on her last call to the Gregg home. "Honest Nan, you know boys, but Corey … I don't know … he's changed. Something's different and it scares me."

Corey was her heart, so she'd be the first to notice that something was off. CD's and video game cartridges all over the floor, empty pop cans under his bed and on the window sill, and clothes strewn all over, just where he stepped out of them. This was becoming his frustrating new norm.

She went on to tell Nancy, "I was changing the funky sheets on his bed when I saw something sticking out from between the mattress and box springs."

"What was it?" Nancy asked, her tone a mixture of concern and impatience.

"I grabbed it and it turned out to be a pair of Corey's boxers. I didn't pay them much attention until I looked at a stain in the back and noticed it was blood … bright red blood."

"Blood?" Nancy replied, "You sure you weren't just seeing skid marks? You know these kids don't take time to wipe themselves right."

"No, it was fresh blood." Their conversation had continued in hushed tones until Mattie made a suggestion of what might have transpired.

Nancy's voice erupted with, "Corey, gay! No Mattie, you have to be kidding! He's constipated or something. Why would you jump to that conclusion?"

While Mattie sobbed on the other end of the line, she understood very well that there are some things you just 'know by knowing.' The blood in her son's underwear signaled something dark. Something he was too ashamed to tell his mother.

Mattie dropped like a crumpled weed to the base of the tub, sobbing in a supine position as the steamy water continued to pummel her and the evidence of her fear gurgled reluctantly down the drain.

CHAPTER 7

SATURDAY, AUGUST 14, 2004

Joi lay basking in the afterglow of the kind of sex that only certain women relished. As R&B legend Tina Turner said in her iconic song "Proud Mary", "Some people like it nice and easy, and some people like it rough." Joi liked it rough. Her bed had just been vacated by a man who knew how to seriously 'do rough.' She closed her eyes, her body pulsing with soreness and satisfaction. With her current work schedule, she didn't have sex nearly as often as she liked. Soon she drifted off.

❖ ❖ ❖

Her cell vibrated and for the second time that morning. Joi was jolted from a deep sleep. Expecting a wake-up call from her lover, she cringed when she heard Sergeant Rimmer's coarse voice on the other end. "Detective, you need to haul ass to a crime scene. You're the Lead detective on this."

Dammit, I overslept. So much for easing into the day. When Rimmer roared, everyone moved. And because this call came directly from the Sergeant and not the dispatcher, there must be some political connection to the victim.

"What's the address?" Joi asked.

"16707 Elmwood Avenue."

"Copy that," she snapped, committing it to memory.

"Thanks."

She placed a quick call and found that Russell had gone to pick up medicine for his ailing wife. He would drop off the meds and meet her at the crime scene.

Although Joi and Russell were both detectives, Joi had taken a different path that finally led her to South Holland. Originally becoming a beat cop after the police academy, she moved into Crime Scene Analysis to get off the streets of Chicago's Westside Lawndale District. After a few years she got restless and thought life in the south suburbs would suit her better.

Unfortunately, crime was increasing in the south suburbs; not as much as in Lawndale, but enough to justify adding another two homicide detectives. She was paired with Russell, and between the two of them, they had cleared more cases in six months than their predecessors had in a year. They got along well, except for the fact that she was more cerebral about police work. He was taller than her by a foot and well-muscled. A self-professed gym rat, he spent eight or nine hours a week weight training and was just as ripped as a detective as he had been as a Chicago Police Department Tactical cop. As a younger cop, Russell had been described as a cowboy, thriving on the adrenaline rush of chasing dope boys down dark alleys and kicking down doors, not knowing who or what was on the other side.

He'd had to kill a few men in the line of duty and been in a few scrapes that he barely got out of alive. These days his main focus was getting home to his wife at the end of his shift.

There was no one at home waiting for Joi.

Joi was dressed and strapped within minutes. As she rushed out the door, she scooped up a package she needed to drop off at the post office.

CHAPTER 8

En route to the crime scene, a scant three and a half miles from her apartment, Joi stopped at Dunkin' Donuts to grab a cup of Joe. When she got back in her car, fellow officers were warning her and Russell over the radio that this was a particularly grizzly murder scene.

The victim, a black male, was a church elder in the large and powerful congregation of Christ's Victory Apostolic Church. Several of the officers knew Elder Gregg personally for his work with children and families in the community. He had a reputation for being hardworking and caring.

The driveway was full of white police cars so Joi parked in front of a beautiful two-story Tudor brick home next door to the Gregg dwelling. She walked twenty feet up the winding rust cobblestone path toward the Georgian home set graciously back off the street. She made it into the foyer and was directed by a cop into the victim's den.

"How come the crack heads don't all get blown the fuck away like this? Why a nice family guy?" she overheard one of the white officers comment. She turned the corner to see him pouring himself a fresh cup of coffee from a silver coffee urn on the portable teacart someone had wheeled just outside of the den.

Russ arrived moments later and was visibly unprepared for the mess he walked into. A uniformed officer, motioned for him and Joi to join the ranks of those milling about the coffee urn.

"No thanks, I brought my own." She pointed to the large cup she had placed atop a ledge that held five or six family photos of obviously happier times.

He waved her and Russell into the den. "The first shot entered his back, dead center, exiting his heart," Enrique Ramirez, a stern-faced Latino veteran who at 5'2 was two inches shorter than Joi. He commented, "The second shot blew the victim's face apart."

Joi nodded, sweeping a gaze across the area and resting her right hand on her ample hip. Rique continued his analysis. "It's as if the killer intended to kill with the first shot; wanted to make sure that he had the nerve to do the damn thing, but with the second shot, he wanted confrontation."

"I'd betcha a week's pay that this joker knew his killer," Russell commented, stepping over an overturned chair as he tried to keep up with Joi.

"Probably someone he didn't have a clue would kill him," Enrique responded.

When she looked over the notes that her fellow officers had taken before she arrived, Joi learned that folks in South Holland considered the Greggs to be a close-knit family. Dennis and Nancy Gregg had raised their children, Kelly and Marcus, in the quiet upscale south suburban community.

Joi had always wanted to move into the area, which had been settled in the mid-1800s by immigrants from the Netherlands, but her money didn't stretch that far. Although the historic and cultural influence of the conservative Dutch Reform immigrants was still tangible in community life, South Holland had become a village of middle-to-high-income people of diverse ethnicities on the far south side. She enjoyed her work and wasn't ready to move up the chain to a desk job so she settled in a part of South Holland that she could afford on a detective's salary.

Joi took a moment to study the photos that Officer Enrique had shoved in her hand shortly after she had arrived. Even the handsome Latino, a family man himself, had to shake his head at the senselessness of it all.

The photo of a smiling older couple was a depiction of the all American Black family. The wife was attractive, shapely and very-well groomed. Her perfect smile was broad and welcoming. She came across as an open-faced woman who genuinely liked people.

The contrast of Elder Gregg's light colored eyes against his dark skin and perfectly groomed hair made Dennis Gregg striking. Rique pointed out his only physical shortcoming, a noticeable height difference between him and his wife. "Wonder if he was bossy the way they say short men are." The Latino officer's accent was subdued after years on the police force, but his heritage always came through in times of sadness or anger.

Other photos in the pile were of their children at various stages in their lives. Joi flipped through each one. The cap and gowned photo of the girl with her mother was a bit larger and was framed more elegantly than the others. Was it a high school or college graduation photo?

She reflected upon the cop's earlier remark. "Why all the crack heads don't get blown the fuck away."

It pissed Joi off when she considered how ridiculous they sounded discussing the value of one human's life over another's. All life was sacred. At least it was supposed to be. It alarmed her that some officers would discount the deaths of hookers, pimps, and the homeless, all because they were not so called "upstanding" citizens. Joi never saw life that way. One would think that the good Christians—which the majority of the officers proclaimed to be—would get that. But contrary to what they thought, this crime wasn't committed by a crack head. Of that she was certain.

As she continued to sweep the house, she listened to the conversation volleying back and forth. It only confirmed that she had made the right decision to avoid becoming a regular churchgoer. She tried to keep an open mind before this job totally made her a pessimist. When it reached that point for her, as it had for so many officers who had been on the force long past their expiration date, she would leave the force altogether rather than become a jaded representation of "protect and serve."

"Russell, you identifying the neighbors?" she asked.

"Yep, I'll get the names of the families on the left and right of here."

"Remember Russ, the houses behind too."

"Same process as always," he sighed turning on his heels, simultaneously pulling his notepad from his jacket pocket. "This isn't my first rodeo, Partner."

In the next moment, Detective Sommers winced, surprised at a sudden flash of light in the room. By the second and third flashes she turned to acknowledge Crime Scene Investigator Mario Tyler photo-documenting every facet of the dismal scene.

She turned to the short, curly haired Italian, his Nikon moving in a circular motion as he squinted and squatted his way around the room. A minute later, Mario hung his camera on his shoulder while he pulled a stick of chewing gum from its wrapper, folded it and popped it into his wide mouth.

Noticing Joi he offered, "Gum?"

"No, but thanks."

"Damn Detective, this is a far cry from taking glamour shots," he commented, placing the gum paper in his jean pocket.

"Hair and makeup definitely won't' make *this* better."

Mario adjusted the focus of his lens. "How you doin' today?" he asked.

"Can't complain, as you see, we have our hands full. You?"

"Believe it or not, I'm doin what I love." Raising the camera over his head, he photographed splatter on the neutral colored ceiling.

She pointed at the camera. "When will these photos be available? I want—"

"Stop Joi." Mario held up a thin palm with long artistic fingers. "You know how I roll, two day turnaround. Day after tomorrow."

"Okay. Gotcha."

Her colleague moved across the room, stepping around the police presence to continue getting his shots.

Detective Sommers brought a reputation from the Chicago Police Department for her painstaking evaluation of the smallest clues, clues that other investigators often overlooked or in some cases clumsily contaminated. She labored over the investigation of crimes against crack heads and prostitutes as painstakingly as she did in the investigation of the so-called pillars of the community, like Elder Dennis Gregg. That was her job and she took pride in doing it well. Sometimes the more you dig into the lives of those pillars, the more they seemed to be the ones on the flip side of the law.

Behind her back, the other detectives nicknamed her Ms. Turtle Shell, a handle she earned when she had first arrived in the South Holland unit. Joi was one of a few special women who chose homicide as a career. Women, it was thought, tended to be better in units where they could actually help the victims—such as sex crimes and juvie. In homicides, the victim is beyond help. But this is where Joi flourished. Details. Details were her thing.

She knelt to the floor and put eyes on the victim, taking in the way the body had fallen, looking at the destruction the bullet had caused and checking for gun residue patterns.

"Don't get too close." Russell said, rejoining her, but on the other side of the body. The scent of Russell's Joop cologne mingled with the distinct odor of death rising from the victim almost made Joi gag. The hazing ritual for new dicks was to dispatch them to the most physically difficult to stomach crime scenes. So as not to choke, Joi developed her own coping mechanism.

As her male colleagues anxiously waited for her to wretch or turn away, she could only be seen stretching her neck forward, as though trying to get a closer look and then rotating her head to the left and then to the right. They joked that she looked like a snapping turtle about to retract its head into its shell.

What they didn't know was that she had been seasoned for gore as a beat cop in the Chicago Police Department on the West side. She had worked the mother of all hellish homicides—and one in particular she would never forget. So the Gregg murder might be gruesome, but it wasn't the worst she had seen, not by a long shot.

"What do you think Joi?" Russ asked, a look of utter disgust on his face. She suspected he was trying to hold his cookies down.

"The killing smacks of passion. There's bound to be mistakes. We're gonna find them."

The first case she worked as a dick was of a headless homeless man found in a dumpster in River Oaks Shopping Mall. The other cops thought she would fold at that first sight, but after the Red Sandal case, she was unflappable.

Dennis Gregg. Pillar of the community. Perfect wife. Perfect children. No obvious motive.

Joi had a feeling that this case was one that would equally test her mettle. She remembered the parcel on the front seat of her car that needed to get into the mail before this case consumed her day.

"Russ, I've got a quick run to make. I'll be back in a few." She didn't wait for his response, but she could imagine the perturbed look he shot her way as she left.

❖ ❖ ❖

It was mid-morning when Joi pulled up at 162nd and Louis, stopping in front of the South Holland Post Office. Joi grabbed the parcel containing her well-read copy of Donna Hill's steamy novel *Sex and Lies.* She was sending it to her potty-mouthed niece Ayanna. Ayanna was twenty-four and feisty by her own definition. She was ambitious and so determined to become a registered nurse that after working third shift at minimum wage in a Kalamazoo, Michigan nursing home, Yana, as she was nicknamed, would grab a large black coffee and hit the highway for the Bronson School of Nursing. Joi hoped the romance novel about a female crime-fighting cartel was just the thing to show the serious minded young woman that there was a little more to life than work. Besides wanting to take her niece's mind off work, Joi had placed five one-hundred dollar bills in a sealed pink envelope at the center of the book. Dennis Gregg was deceased. Yana, was alive and needed her help, and that trumped all.

After stuffing the parcel into the mail slot Joi reached into her pocket, and fumbled briefly for her keys before spying them in the steering column of the locked car.

"Damn, what the hell!" Her shoulders sank in defeat.

Traffic whizzed by at a steady pace as she thought of her best move. She pulled the flip phone from her back pocket and dialed her partner.

"Russ, I'm at the Post Office up the street." She grimaced at how careless she had been. "I locked my goddamned keys in the car." She grabbed the two locks of hair that fell into her face and planted them behind her ears.

Laughter erupted from the other end of the cell. Joi's irritation ramped up a notch. She held the phone a few inches from her ear and yelled, "Hey, can you stop laughing and get over here!"

She disconnected the call, tucked the phone into her pocket and waited beside her vehicle.

An elderly blonde with a dowager's hump, wearing a stylish pink jogging suit and white sneakers, got out of a 1993 electric blue Ford Probe GT holding a cache of letters. The wrinkled woman pushed them through the mail slot, then gave Joi a quick once-over and frowned as if the fact that her pinstriped shirt wasn't tucked into her blue slacks didn't quite meet with her approval. Joi, turned away, wondering why the old broad was driving a muscle car.

She spun around to see Ms. Jogging Suit speed off and cut a tight turn around the corner. "Damn! I wanna be like her when I grow up."

The post office was only a few block away from the crime scene. Russell pulled up several minutes later in his own car.

He frowned. "Whatever you had to do here, couldn't it have waited?"

Joi snapped, "I'm not your wife. Don't question me."

His eyes widened, but he didn't speak. Instead her partner of four years pulled out a red and black case containing his Swiss Army pocket knife and worked the rubber rim of the driver's side window.

"No, you're not my wife. Aren't you glad?" He gave her a sideways glance, frowning as he asked, "How many times you gonna hammer that in, Detective?"

Joi sighed. Her partner's wife was chronically ill, she regretted her lapse in sensitivity. Her own personal issues were less obvious, mental, but distressing nonetheless. She should never have come at Russell that way. "Sorry, I didn't mean that."

Her partner gave her a faltering smile with his mouth that didn't reach his dark brown eyes. She translated that to mean that her words were forgiven, but not forgotten.

A petite female postal worker came out and pivoted when she scoped Russell, causing Joi to bristle. There was no denying that her partner was fine, but right now Joi needed Ms. Rain-or-Shine to keep it moving. "Hey! Don't you have some mail to deliver or something?"

The woman gave Joi the evil eye and continued toward the parking lot. When she got there, she looked over at Russell and Joi once again before taking off in her truck. Russell laughed and Joi gave his shoulder a not-quite-playful punch.

Joi supposed that Russell had weaned himself from the adrenaline rush of tactical to the predictability of knowing that he would only meet dead guys. There was something to be said for the patience required to work backward from that certainty to the "whodunit." It was probably comforting to his wife Helen, a woman afflicted with multiple sclerosis, that even if he worked long hours trying to close a case, eventually he was coming home to sleep in bed next to her.

Joi didn't have anyone but her Maze, and she doubted that Maze worried about anyone but herself or whomever she was sleeping with at the time. That sad fact was the root of Joi's current sex life, but she was too busy, or scared, to do anything about it. The men that graced her bed from time to time were as forbidden to her as that apple was to Adam. And look how that turned out.

Russell struggled with the effort to get Joi's car door unlocked. A few bystanders began to crowd around and Russell gestured for them to move on. Most of them ignored him until Joi flashed her badge.

She rolled her eyes at her partner. "I thought you had a Slim Jim."

"It's at home," he replied, working the knife inside the rubber rim and trying to get to the infamous "click" that popped the lock.

"That's a nice place for it."

Russell leaned in and pressed the handle downward. "I cleaned the trunk out when I had the car detailed last week; forgot to put it back."

"Well, you'd better do something," she said dryly. "Cause I'm not going back to the station to ask Sergeant Rimmer for a Slim Jim. Shit, I called myself just taking a few minutes to drop this off. We're working an active crime scene." She leaned on the driver's side door, keeping her eye on his hands. "Rimmer can't stand me as it is."

Russ slid the knife back into his pocket and whipped out a phone and dialed. "Right on both counts. Listen, I'm calling Snake."

Joi groaned. "Not your bad ass cousin?"

"He's a tax paying citizen now," Russ grinned, showing pearly white teeth. "He'll get us in this car in a flash."

Joi had to admit that Snake had mad skills. He had done time for having one of the largest chop shops in Chicago. Now he appeared to be content operating a mid-sized towing/body-and-fender repair company.

Well, she hoped that was all he was into.

❖ ❖ ❖

Ten minutes and a cigarette later, Snake pulled up across the street from them in a maroon SUV. He was a brown-skinned edgy-looking character, with a nicely trimmed beard, short hair, a black hoodie, and sagging Roca wear jeans atop a pair of black Timberland boots. He reminded her of famed rapper-turned-actor Ice Cube, only with a major gap between his front teeth.

"What up?" he asked Russell, giving him "the handshake" and giving Joi a head-to-toe once over and a grin to acknowledge her presence.

"Damn key got locked inside the car."

Russell didn't attach her name to the key being locked in the car, but Snake probably knew. Both snake and Russell wore the smirk men tend to get when they have one-upped a woman. Joi planted herself on the driver's side of Russell's ride while the two men focused their attention on the driver's side of her car.

Snake strolled to his truck and returned carrying a long, bent up Slim Jim with a bright pink top. He slid the tool between the rubber and the glass around the window, and with a quick jerk, pulled up the lock. "There ya go." He gave her a gaped-tooth grin.

Russell held out a hand for a shake. "Hey, thanks man."

Although pissed, Joi managed to growl, "Thanks Snake, glad you were around."

He gave her another thirsty once-over before saying, "No problem. Glad to be around for ya, Miss Lady." Snake couldn't seem to take his eyes off her thick 5'4", 168 pound frame. He appeared to appreciate the riveting quality of her dark brown eyes and the mid-length brown dread locks with tinges of burnt auburn that crowned her like a lioness.

Russ cleared his throat.

Snake's legs started moving, but he looked over his shoulder at her and wisecracked, adding, "These days a brotha is always happy to be on the right side of the law."

Then he climbed into his truck, gave her a signature "deuces" salute and sped off.

Joi's eyes narrowed on Russell, who was trying to hold in a laugh at the sensual exchange between his cousin and his partner.

Instead of saying thank you, she flipped him the bird and walked away.

Russell followed her to the squad car.

CHAPTER 9

YEARS EARLIER - MAY 15, 1985

Diana Gregg had returned to her town home from her teaching job as a special education teacher at Berkeley Middle School, in Saint Louis County. The children's laughter rang in her ears long after she left the grounds of the dark red-brick building. She loved her job. Teaching was the only thing she had ever wanted to do in life. Well, that and to marry a God-fearing man and push out one child.

She parked a stack of ungraded papers on the entry way table and sauntered straight to the bathroom to don her silk print caftan before heading to the microwave to load it with a Lean Cuisine entree for dinner. She was breaking iceberg lettuce for a salad when she received the emotionally charged phone call that would forever change her life.

She had smiled at first, after snatching the receiver from the wall phone, expecting small talk with her sister-in-law, but soon after "Hello,

Di," Nancy had launched into an intense, almost unintelligible tumble of words. "Di, I need to talk to you and you can't tell a single soul on earth what I'm going to say. Do you swear?"

Diana put the knife on the wooden board and leaned back against the counter. "Of course. But Nan, I can barely hear you. What the heck is going on?"

"Denny has been—"

"—Oh God, has he been hurt?" Diana asked, her heart constricting in such a way that it hurt to breathe.

"No Diana," came the stern but soft whimpering voice on the other end of the phone

"Well tell me, what *is* it!"

"Denny's been …. he's been … messing with Kelly," said Nancy, her voice trailing.

Diana turned to face the window. All thoughts of dinner vanished. "Messing with Kelly? How?"

"For God's sake, don't make me say it." Nancy cried. "He's been … he's been … molesting her!"

The view from Diana's kitchen window of the small bungalow across the street suddenly blurred. "Whaat! How in heaven's name can you say something like that about my brother, Nan?" Diana snapped. "That's your husband and your child!"

"As God is my witness, I would never say it unless it was true. It's true. On the blood of Jesus, it's true!"

The microwave beeped and Diana let the receiver dangle while she retrieved the entrée she now had no taste for. She grabbed the receiver and pressed her shoulder against the wall to steady herself and to calm the quivering in her gut. "How did you…?"

"I *keep* finding blood and something crusty in Kelly's pajamas, and on her sheets."

Diana closed her eyes, trying to keep the nausea at bay. "That could be from riding a bike, or maybe her period started early or some—"

"She's been acting so, so quiet," Nancy whispered. "She tenses up whenever her daddy comes into the room. *She's a different little girl.*"

Flashes of Denny and the aftermath of his trip to Provident Hospital's emergency room over four decades ago suddenly flooded her mind. Diana fought to push them away but could not.

"He's a different boy. He's not my son. He's different," her daddy had said. "He should have fought harder."

"You know our pediatrician, Dr. Oliver," Nancy continued. "He grew up with Dennis. The real friendly light-skinned guy in the choir with the shiny bald head—"

Diana's heart was pounding a hole in her chest and a little man with a hammer was doing a number inside her head. "Get on with it, Nan," she snapped. "I have a vague memory of him going into the Army and then on to medical school. That's all. What does that have to do with anything?"

"That's him," continued Nancy. "He diagnosed Kelly with a raging bladder infection, but then he caught me at the door and took me aside. He asked me if any male relatives had been over for a visit. When I said no, his eyes … I'll never forget his eyes. They were accusing me of some unspoken crime," she said between sniffles. "He wrote a prescription for Kelly and gave me some salve to put on her bottom."

Both women were quiet, then Nancy whimpered, "Some things you just know by knowing. When I first looked at my girl's vagina I knew, but Dr. Oliver's look was confirmation. He knew. And he wanted me to know that he knew."

Diana reflected back to the emergency appendectomy their father announced to his congregation to explain her brother's hospitalization and the night crying she often heard from her brother's bedroom. But it wasn't until that moment so much later that she realized just how damaged her brother might have been.

Diana talked to Nancy that night until she was exhausted. The pink silk caftan was wet with perspiration under the arms and her slippers were damp from sweat.

"Nancy, you have to go to Reverend Pate!" Diana had pled time and time again.

"That's easy for you to say," Nancy replied in a hushed tone. "But I just can't bring myself to tell our personal business to Pastor. What will he think of Denny? What will happen to our family?"

"What will he think of Denny? *You should be thinking of protecting your daughter!*"

Eventually Nancy agreed.

A week after the gut-wrenching disclosure, Diana received a call from Nancy that Reverend Pate had called her while Dennis was at work and assured her that he and Dennis were having ongoing private counseling sessions.

"Reverend Pate understood and urged me to trust *him,*" Nancy gushed. "He is personally going to work with Dennis."

"Oh Nancy I'm so relieved," Diana replied. "Will you be in joint counseling or—"

"—No! He said not to say a word to Dennis myself, but to consider that my concerns are left upon the altar of the Lord."

"Oh Nan, this is wonderful news!" Diana was relieved at the news of personal support from their Pastor, even though the "left upon the altar of the Lord" part did not sit as well with her. Diana was also worried about the backlash Nan would face from her an exposure and humiliated Dennis, even with their pastor as a cushion. She was concerned for her brother's healing, but most concerned about Kelly's well-being. "Listen Sis, I'm not sure how long the counseling with Pastor will last, but I've been thinking that in the meantime I want Kelly to stay with me. Let me take her for a year, to give things some time—"

"But you teach—"

"I know. It'll be hard taking care of her myself and teaching full time, but you know I want to do anything I can to help."

"Oh Di, thanks. We—" Nancy corrected herself. "I appreciate you so very much."

Diana realized that her brother would never know that his wife and sister-in-law had spoken.

"But that just isn't necessary," she said. "Trust and believe me, we have our situation under control."

For several months, she and Nancy continued to have periodic telephone conversations, always in the predawn hours—never when Dennis was within hearing range. During each call, after their small talk, Nancy assured her that things were going along just fine. Then, without warning, the calls stopped.

Diana prayed faithfully that there was truth to the saying that no news is good news. Whenever disturbing thoughts about Dennis harming her niece came to mind, she inwardly shouted out the holy chorus, *the devil is a lie!*

But there was some consolation for Diana. Nancy always made sure that Kelly spent her entire summer with Aunt Diana. Diana used those summers and their special time together to fill the loneliness in her own heart and to pour her love, like warm oil, all over her niece. She always prayed that what she provided for her niece was enough. May God forgive her if she had been wrong.

CHAPTER 10

Joi shook her thick tresses as she headed back into the den of the Gregg home. This day had gotten off to a rough start, from her oversleeping, to looking into the face of death before finishing her first cup of coffee, and then locking her damn key in the car and having to be rescued by Russell's low life cousin. Things had to look up. With the post office escapade behind her Joi, was ready to focus on the Gregg case. Experience had taught her that every murder has its own logical origin—at least in the killer's mind. So rather than judge the killer, she found it wiser to follow the perp's logic. Entering the den at the Gregg's home, Joi nodded at Officer Enrique Ramirez before finding the starched white shirt of Sergeant Cecil Hanks.

"Looks like we have some work to do here," Joi said, half-joking.

"Oh yeah, glad it's your case," said Hanks, looking at her through strained gray eyes. His know-it-all back of the yards voice irritated her. Cece, as he was commonly called, was 6'2", nearly as tall as Russell. He wore a short buzz cut under his uniform hat and had such thin beak-like lips that she often amused herself wondering how he could even deliver a righteous kiss.

She moved closer to her partner, who was standing over the corpse. "Russell how long you been back?" she asked, looking around the room at overturned chairs, a broken lamp and blood and brain splatter along the baseboard and gauze inner curtains.

"A few minutes," he replied, running a gloved hand over the lamp base. "I just can't get over this mess."

"Looks open and shut to me," Hanks shouted from across the den. "I bet a crew rolled in here and the old man tried to fight back. Damn shame how they did this guy." He took a quick breath and pushed back his bibbed hat. "Young thugs movin' into the village from the city."

"Yeah that's kinda what I was thinking," said Russell, looking at his partner for confirmation.

What idiots! Things are rarely what they appear to be. "Sarge, how are you so sure it was a crew?" Joi asked, tilting her head to avoid looking directly at Hanks.

"That's how they operate."

Joi sighed. *They?* Her trained eyes scanned the room for clues she could connect to the crime. She asked out loud, "They? Nothing here points to anything but one person."

Joi took several steps back to put the room into perspective. The sliding doors were wide open and she walked over to a smudged panel. If this was the exit, there's probably prints, this doesn't look professional.

Hanks continued, "Lookit, I seen Mr. Gregg around the village. He runs a computer repair shop in River Oaks. He was a real nice black guy."

"As opposed to a real nice *white* guy?" she said, giving him a lopsided grin.

"Aw Joi, don't gimme that race crap," he snapped. "You know what I mean."

"I do." smiled Joi, glancing over at Russell, who made it his business to focus on taking measurements and looking around the victim's desk.

Then Hanks spoke again, this time with more conviction. "Geez I don't know what they was thinkin' down at City Hall. Bringing all those people from the city out to the 'burbs."

"Being stacked like rats in Chicago Housing Authority projects is a better plan?" she quickly injected. "Don't answer that or you gonna make me *and* Russell real mad," she laughed, trying once again to bait her partner into their repartee.

Unfortunately, he didn't bite. Usually, he stayed out of office politics because it was a no win proposition.

Joi refocused on the task at hand. *No lie, this is a mess.*

Time was valuable, considering what was left of Dennis Gregg and the fact that they would be removing him fairly soon. She narrowed her field of vision and trained her laser beams on the physical evidence.

"Looks like they fought first and then the killer pulled out a piece and shot the vic," she said.

"Uh huh," Russ said, narrowing his gaze on the victim. "So was the perp getting his ass kicked and then he decided to finish it?"

"Beats the hell outta me. Who says it was a he?"

Russ cut his eyes her way.

"Only the top drawer is open," Joi continued. "Messy, but not the kind of mess that happens when a crew ransacks a place. Check for his watch."

Russ placed a white handkerchief over his mouth and lowered so he could lift the lifeless arm four inches off the floor.

"He's wearing that $1,500 Wittnauer wristwatch. I'd like to own this bad boy myself," he remarked, his words partially muffled by his handkerchief.

"I'm sure he'd be delighted to own your Timex at this point. Focus please."

"I'm just saying," Russell replied, stuffing the handkerchief into his back pocket.

Drawing a shallow breath, Joi covered her mouth slightly to avoid gagging at the fresh smell of the mass of ragged flesh that had once been a human face. Pulling on blue latex gloves, she began her own painstaking examination. Joi leaned forward, turned her head to the left and then the right, and heard the familiar crack signaling the release of tension.

She glanced at her partner, who gave her a knowing grin. Ms. Turtle Shell. Yes, she had earned the nickname honestly.

Russ, usually hardened to the face of death, finally pivoted away from the gruesome scene, saying, "What a goddamn mess."

"Oh yeah, this killer wanted the victim to be surprised," Joi said, cautiously scanning the area leading to the desk. "Lots of pent up rage here. The killer *had to know* that simply shooting dude in the back at close range would've killed him."

Joi lifted a flap of skin on the front of the face and exposed a shattered cheekbone. Her efforts exposed something shiny that barely caught the light. Carefully lifting the blood-covered particle, she placed it in a small vial of containment solution and then in a small plastic bag from the toolkit she kept in her handbag.

"The overkill was an act of defiance," Joi whispered, causing Russ to move closer to hear her musings.

Joi held her breath before leaning into the mess before her. She rotated her neck once again, trying to focus. *Damn, now I'll be waking up in the middle of the night thinking about this shit.* She blinked, acknowledging that familiar thread of anxiety that ripped through her when she first landed a case. And it had been that way since day one.

She would never forget the 911 call that got her dispatched to an apartment building where neighbors had called because a couple of known dope fiends had been fighting.

The first officers on the scene had entered the apartment with their guns drawn. A tall dude wearing a number 23 throwback basketball jersey had leapt over the second floor back porch banister into the alley. The fat ass cop covering the back door was too lazy to pursue. He fired a couple of warning shots but the perp wearing Michael Jordan's number kept moving and got away.

The apartment stank so bad that after they called the paramedics to transport the injured woman, they followed the scent to a junk closet. Under the clothes and broken appliances they found a thick wad of black plastic that was tattered. The stink intensified.

None of the other officers spoke about what they knew they were about to find, but Joi knew intuitively that they were damn near choking on the stench of human decomp.

Carefully unraveling the withered plastic, what remained of the couple's toddler came into focus. She was not only dead but had been hacked to pieces. The horrific sight of the child's rotten flesh was debilitating enough, but the kicker was the tiny skinless human foot that was still covered by a red patent leather sandal.

Joi had an instant flash of a little girl taking some of her first steps, heart open and loving toward the animals that would kill her and quarter her like a hog, then wrap her in plastic. The baby shared her last bit of humanity with the detective.

It was then that Joi summoned all her strength not to turn away or wretch. Instead, she chose to lean into the tragedy, took a deep breath, swallowed the hot fluid that gurgled in the back of her throat, and tilted her head from side to side. It was then that she earned the turtle moniker. She remembered over hearing her Grandma Dot, a wash woman from the Mississippi delta, saying more than once, "You can git thew anythin wit a deep breath n a sip a whiskey." She'd had the whiskey later.

Something about that little red sandal woke Joi up in the middle of the night for weeks. After that, she placed her flat feet firmly on the path to earn the detective's shield. Considering the long line of veteran cops with connections applying for an upgrade to detective and the way things worked in Chicago, she left CPD for the suburb of South Holland, where it would be easier to move up. And a lot fewer murders to deal with.

Or so she thought.

She looked down at what was left of Dennis Gregg and asked, "Now who would want to kill you, Mr. Gregg?"

CHAPTER 11

Nancy Gregg lay across her bed waiting. The OxyContin was finally dulling the physical pain, but not her grief. She could almost see Denny sitting across from her on a stool at the breakfast snack bar. She would have just served him two eggs sunny side up, runny, two strips of bacon and two slices of burnt toast with butter and Smucker's grape jelly.

"Nan, if you want to economize fine, but don't do it on my jelly. That starts my day," she remembered him saying once when she tried out a generic brand of jelly. Her husband always completely finished his breakfast before asking for his coffee, as though it were dessert. She closed her eyes and smelled his Old Spice cologne, the only product he ever used. Nancy Gregg felt alone, like a ship without a rudder. She buried her head in the oversized down pillow and wept. She thought back to barely a month earlier.

❖ ❖ ❖

MONDAY, JULY 6, 2004

The minute Dennis Gregg's black Mercedes cleared the driveway, Nancy picked up the yellow kitchen wall phone and placed a call to the clinic. "I need an emergency appointment with Dr. Angela Crawford. Can you fit me in?"

The soft, empathetic voice on the other end asked, "Are you able to get here by noon?"

Nancy peered at her watch and winced as another painful spasm shot through her. It was exactly 11:00 a.m. which gave her only four hours to get into the city and back to their two story, four bedroom home in South Holland. Her left eye twitched uncontrollably and she finally squeezed both eyes shut. "I'll be there," she whispered, praying that this could all be taken care of quickly. By the time he returned home from his computer repair business, she would have dinner on the table and a smile, or what passed for a smile, on her face.

One hour later as the taxi left the Dan Ryan Expressway, the sweltering July heat took its toll and her energy was even lower than when she had awakened that morning. Her soft pink sleeveless dress was plastered to her skin and she didn't bother to wipe the sweat that peppered her perfectly arched brows. The taxi turned north on 87th and drove two blocks up State Street before stopping at her destination. The meter read forty five dollars, not including tip. Expensive, but necessary.

Stepping from the taxi, even with the bushy-haired driver's assistance, was hell. The 85th Street Clinic was located in a small, modern tan brick building right near the Dan Ryan expressway. The elevator opened on the third floor into a waiting room, which was especially crowded at this time of day. When she saw the overflow of women and children spread around the room she wondered if she should have called an ambulance to take her to a hospital's emergency room, instead of gambling on the fact that Dr. Crawford could finally put an end to her misery. Fear had kept her away from her gynecologist, who she saw for most ailments, but she could not bear this torment another day.

Nancy sighed, wincing inwardly as she ran a trembling hand across her tender belly. She had postponed this appointment far too long.

Six days a week, after she got her husband of twenty-nine years out the door, Nancy collapsed back into bed and endured agonizing pain until the early afternoon. Eventually she would summon the strength to drag herself downstairs to wash the breakfast dishes and begin dinner. On Sundays she barely made it to service. They ate brunch out afterward and she retired as soon as she could. She had abandoned her weekly bridge game and systematically excused herself from all volunteer activities. Now only three things filled her day—the morning routine, a painful existence, and a loving husband, who didn't have a clue that his wife was going through a lot more than she let on.

Nancy had convinced Dennis that moving into the guest bedroom, which had been their daughter's old bedroom, was her attempt to allow him a comfortable night's sleep during what she had told him was increasing menopausal hot flashes and sleeplessness. The truth was that she lay helpless in the guest bedroom gritting her teeth and surfing the mounting waves of pain.

A short redheaded nurse motioned Nancy into the outer exam room. "Mrs. Gregg, right this way please."

Nancy struggled to stay focused as the woman weighed her, checked her blood pressure and temperature, and asked a few preliminary questions while Nancy continuously adjusted the short brown human hair wig that thankfully concealed her matted hair.

Once prepped, Nancy waited only a few minutes before Dr. Angela Crawford entered. She had known Angie since her residency. She was a no-nonsense, hard-playing bridge partner. Ken, her quiet husband occasionally golfed with Dennis.

The doctor greeted Nancy with a warmer-than-usual smile, Nancy instantly felt grateful for the familiarity.

"It's good to see you. I've had no time for bridge lately, you still playing?"

"No, not so much these days," Nancy said nervously with a quick look of longing toward the exam table.

Angie frowned as she peered at Nancy. The doctor washed her hands then sat her portly 5'6" frame on a small black stool near the writing desk. Nancy cringed at the realization that two women that were once considered hot were both now middle-aged broads. Angie scanned Nancy's chart. "Hmmm, your pressure is slightly elevated Nancy, and you're having a lot of stomach pain. Tell."

"It's very intense," she whispered, shifting her body in her chair in search of a more comfortable spot.

"How so?"

"Angie, I hurt so bad I can't function."

Her friend looked up from the chart and focused her gaze directly on Nancy.

"On a scale of 1-10 with 10 being the most painful, what level is your pain?"

Nancy closed her eyes as though checking with her body before responding, but she was already certain of the answer. "It's mostly between nine and ten."

Angie shook her head slowly and squinted. "Really? For how long?"

"Ah," she exhaled, riding another wave before saying, "about six months."

"Naaann," she sighed. "Why didn't you come in sooner? Six months?"

Nancy read Angela's look as one of annoyance. She knew Angie was a champion for everyone having access to quality healthcare and here she had suffered in silence rather than see a doctor that, for Christ sakes, was also a family friend.

Nancy's face twisted with pain, causing Angie's eyes to fill with empathy. "Let's get you on the table Nan." She moved to Nancy's side, helping her remove her shoes and slide back on the paper-covered examination table.

Angie pulled on a pair of blue gloves and began palpating Nancy's stomach region, watching her grimace in response to pain heightened by the lightest touch. Moments later, the doctor snapped off the blue latex gloves and reached for the phone.

"Radiology scheduling, this is Dr. Angela Crawford at the outpatient clinic. I'm sending a patient over for upper and lower GI." She paused for a moment, then said, "Yes, I want a full set of X-rays." Angie looked over to Nancy and asked, "Have you eaten anything today?"

"Only black coffee."

Angie grimaced and repeated that information to the person on the other line. Suddenly her tone became stern, "Listen, I understand that patients are stacked but I need these x-rays completed today!" She gripped the edge of the chart. "Excuse me, I am well aware of your procedures and the fact that you have some discretion. I'm requesting that you use it." She listened and slowly toyed with the telephone cord until finally a slight smile graced her full lips.

"Thank you very much. No, Mrs. Gregg has not eaten. And no, she does not mind waiting." Angie breathed a sigh of relief. "I'm sending her over right now."

❖ ❖ ❖

Since the day she first acknowledged just how sick she was, the days that followed had been one big blur at times.

"Mom, the police are here," her daughter, Kelly whispered.

"I won't be able to speak with them right now," she slurred. With that, Nancy Gregg drifted into a medicine-induced sleep, sweeping all memories of that day and her husband aside.

CHAPTER 12

Joi crouched down near the victim. "Who would want to kill you, Mr. Gregg?"

"On the way in, a neighbor told me Gregg's an Elder at Christ's Victory Apostolic Church," Russell replied, as if answering for the deceased. "Evidently, he's highly respected."

Joi thought that over for a minute. "An Elder, huh? Isn't that the mega church with eight thousand seats?"

"It is," said Russell raising his left eyebrow in a way that made him look rakishly handsome. "Bishop Pate. That's where the wife and I go to church, that is when we go." Congregation's so damn big we're lucky to find a seat. I never knew him."

"Yeah?" came Joi's biting reply. "Hell, if I was going to a church, which I'm not," she said, wagging a finger to shut off his never-ending protest, "I wouldn't need that many people to witness my devotion to the Lord."

"You damn near get lost in the parking lot. I know you'll never find your way inside."

She smiled at his teasing and took another gulp of coffee.

"Sargent Hanks can you make sure no one moves anything from here?" she asked, without waiting for his reply. "And we dust everything for prints." Joi angled her body in the direction of the den door. "I'm going to the car for a minute. I'll be back to complete my notes before the body is moved to the ME's." She always liked to let the uniforms clear out before she conducted a thorough exam of the crime scene. Russ knew it was his job to move them along before she got back. She spun around and looked up at Sergeant Cecil Hanks asking, "Cecil, how long before they get here?"

"The vic's ride will be here in fifteen minutes, give or take," he quipped and went back to the white squad parked outside.

"This is gonna be open and shut for ya," confirmed Hanks.

Joi gave him a contemplative look and a polite, noncommittal nod before turning her back to him. Shortly thereafter the uniforms took off and Joi and Russell had the scene to themselves.

"Russ, Cece is a good, clean cop, but he knows his ass can bunny hop to conclusions." She shook her head in disbelief.

"For sure, I'm glad he's where *he is* but I'd be sorry to be on the other end of his justice."

Joi gave Cecil credit for being a total pro, committed to solving cases rather than pushing papers around his desk. She appreciated his pit bull mentality. When he was working with you, nothing could get him off point. However, his annoying flaw was his dangerous tendency to jump to conclusions. For him everything was always just as it appeared.

Joi knew that the lack of careful examination of the crime scene and forgetting to follow all the evidence, wherever it leads, was one of the primary reasons innocent people got railroaded. Well, that and racism. She bristled over convictions gotten based on cursory information picked up from the crime scene and evaluated out of context by cops anxious to get credit for the collar. Several years ago was a prime example. The case of Travis Wells, the seventeen-year-old African American kid arrested for the death of his girlfriend Latoya Beasel, came to mind. He would have been serving a life sentence for the untimely demise of that fourteen-year-old freshman if Joi hadn't kept pursuing more evidence than what had been used to condemn the youth. There was something in the boy's father's eyes that made her dig beyond what appeared to be an 'open and shut.'

Richard Wells was a doorman at the Marriott Magnificent Mile in Chicago. He served the white, the rich and the powerful. He exemplified a demeanor of cheerful submission as a rule, but drew the line at accepting the circumstantial evidence of his only son's presumed guilt. Something about the man's fierce determination not to let his son fall victim stuck with a young Detective Sommers. She kept digging and eventually uncovered evidence that Latoya could have actually died from a brain aneurysm, which her vindictive mother had concealed from investigators. The detectives on the case had failed to look beyond the obvious. While the latter caused a ripple of criticism of the Department's investigative process, particularly as it related to cases involving minorities, it had gained her the reputation of being fair, impartial and a cop that would doggedly follow the evidence.

When the Wells case was tossed out of court, a reporter at the Chicago Defender Newspaper wrote a line that rang true. "Sometimes you don't see what you think you see, even when you're looking right at it."

Joi had received a Department commendation that boosted her promotion to detective. But in her mind, the real reward came sixteen months later in a small, white envelope left on her desk with the hand-written words "Thank You" across the front. She had opened it to read,

Dear Detective Sommers,

Travis is a sophomore at Florida A&M University. Thank you and God Bless.

Richard Wells.

She considered that note a "paid in full" stamp and kept it in the top drawer of her messy desk. It reminded her that police work wasn't rocket science and, more than anything, requires impartiality and carefully following the evidence if justice was the goal.

As Joi carefully counted her bagged samples, another item caught her eye.

"Hey Russ, remember the Cruz case?" Joi asked, enjoying light banter as they processed the scene.

"Isn't that the guy that served a dime of an eighty-year stretch for killing a kid that somebody else confessed to?"

"Riiiiiight," said Joi. "The prosecutor was itchy for a conviction. Dude thought he was a gunslinger. Always focused on getting notches on his belt. "

"Or setting his self up for politics," replied Russell, as he knelt down to flash a light under the brown leather love seat and take a look.

"Didn't the Assistant State's Attorney in the second trial resign 'cause she knew the case against Cruz was bogus?"

Russ looked up at her, eyes narrowing. "I wonder where she's working now. I'd hire her."

"Me too," laughed Joi. "That little blonde chick had balls."

Joi used a gloved hand to pick up and bag shards from a broken sandstone ceramic mug a few feet away. Maybe there were some traces of Dennis' DNA or deposits from someone very recently in his presence. The room was only twelve-by-fifteen feet and every inch could hold the key to the killer.

She bristled at the tired cliché that 'justice is blind.' Simple-minded folks might be persuaded to believe that the guilty get punished and the innocent always go free. But Joi had seen the system lock up the innocent and let the guilty walk too many times.

Justice is a skank on crack!

CHAPTER 13

Next Joi visited Ms. Asia Gibson in the split-level home to the right of the Gregg's. From her upstairs window, Joi hoped she might have gotten a look into the garden and seen something to add to the investigation.

The medium height woman had big black eyes and a blonde wig cut into a pixie style that flattered her full face. "Detective, I was at the LAX Westin Hotel in Los Angeles managing Northwestern Mutual's annual stockholders' meeting."

Joi made a conscious effort to keep her shoulders from slumping in defeat.

"But Mama was here with the kids," Asia added. She looked at Joi and smiled warmly. "Follow me Detective."

Joi obliged as Asia Gibson opened a door that led downstairs to what was probably their family room. The large open room was dimly lit by a floor to ceiling pole lamp in the far left corner.

"Muh dear, can you come upstairs a minute?"

"What you say?" a gravelly voice answered. "I'm putting a load of clothes in."

"Muh dear, can you leave the laundry for a few moments puh-leeze," Asia said exhaling in exasperation. "Someone's here from the police department about poor Mr. Gregg's murder."

A woman about 67 years old, slim, dark brown skin the color of rich coffee emerged from the basement. She had a head full of large pink foam rollers "Lawd, I heard he was kilt," the older woman said. "Why kill a nice man like Mr. Gregg? I'm sure he wouldn't a fought no robbers."

Joi peered at the woman for a moment, taking in the difference in the speech patterns from mother to daughter. Evidently the mother had made sure her daughter received a better education than she had. "Did you hear any noise that night Mrs. Gibson?" Joi asked.

"Scuse me, I'm a Crayton. Geraldine Crayton." She made a quarter turn. "She married a Gibson." The older woman pointed at her daughter with a crooked finger.

"Sorry, Mrs. Crayton," Joi said, scratching out the name on her pad. "What did you hear on the night of the murder?"

"Oh, I heard noise that night."

Joi extinguished all hope of the interview going smoothly. "Was it voices, or actual gunshots?"

"I didn't hear one dern thing from next door," said the Crayton woman. "The kids had the music blastin' in here so loud I took aspirins for my headache and I had my pastor's sermons playin' on my headphones. I couldn't listen to one mo' doggone rappin' song!"

The woman was wringing her hands nervously, as though she'd left something unsaid. She stuck her trembling hands inside her robe pockets, came up with a cigarette, and then fumbled for a clear colored Bic lighter.

"Are you sure you didn't *see* something, Mrs. Crayton?"

"Not unless you want me to make somethin' up!" Her free hand picked at the chipped red polish on the hand that held her cigarette and lighter.

Joi snapped the hard cover on her stenographer's notebook shut. "Thanks for your time ladies."

"And thank you for yours," shot back Mrs. Crayton.

Detecting an edge in the woman's voice bordering on sarcasm, Joi paused and looked back, but decided against disrespecting the smart-mouthed old broad.

Making her way back to the Gregg home, Joi went over the actions of the two women in the Gibson home. Grandmother was hiding something.

CHAPTER 14

After a sleepless night, Joi decided to head out to the Gregg's again. Russell had taken Helen to physical therapy, which gave Joi the perfect opportunity to assess things. Going in to the crime scene by herself, without an army of police swarming the area, she could avoid setting neighborhood sensibilities on edge.

When she opened the door of her apartment, a copy of the *South Holland Press* begged for her attention. The headline read: "*Prominent Businessman Murdered in Gruesome Home Invasion.*" By this time, those seven words were rolling off the lips of the citizens of South Holland. She knew for a fact that the community's rumor mill would be in full effect. Speculation and whispers of what people thought had happened would abound over coffee and pancakes at I-HOP or during mall walks at River Oaks. More than once, she had been privy to some inside news just by being in the right place when someone was spilling their guts to a friend or family member.

Now the speculation would begin. Dennis Gregg had been a church elder, a husband, a father, a mentor. He had taught fellow Christians how to walk the faith walk. Who would shoot him down like an animal in his own house?

South Holland was a close-knit community where the major increase in crime was auto theft. This grisly murder would have the citizens outraged and scared. Joi was sure that the people of South Holland were not in eminent danger. This crime, for whatever reason, was personal.

She sat in her patrol car and sucked deeply on a Virginia Slim before shorting it in the ash tray; then located a small notebook and ball point pen. After securing her handbag in the trunk Detective Sommers headed toward the Gregg home. She walked past a three-foot-tall planter overflowing with purple and white petunias and up the cobblestone walkway, only to find one uniformed officer still at the crime scene when she entered the home and proceeded to the den.

The image of that red shoe flashed in her mind, followed by the mangled body of the child they had found. Shattered innocence. Something Joi could identify with. But why would that image haunt her at this crime scene? The victim was a forty-nine-year old man with a wife and two children. His innocence was long gone before the crime had been committed. The red shoe case was one that was particularly heart-wrenching. All officers seemed to have a soft spot when children were involved. They hardened up when the victims were people they considered worthless.

Enrique Ramirez was peering out of the study window when Joi arrived. She sipped a large black coffee she'd picked up on the way and began flipping through papers on the murdered man's desk with her free hand.

"Where's the wife, Rique?" Joi asked, as she unbuttoned an additional button on her blue and white tailored pinstriped shirt. She was going to be here a while. Might as well get comfortable.

"Her doc says Mrs. Gregg's in shock," he answered, in a tenor voice that had a light accent. "The daughter just got here and took her mom up to the master bedroom. The son came in right after the daughter."

"Rique, the family hasn't been questioned yet have they?" she asked.

"No ma'am," responded, coming over to stand next to Joi at the huge mahogany desk.

"So what's your take on them?"

Rique leaned in and lowered his voice. "The mother was pretty bad off, her emotions and all," he added with a mild shrug. "Besides, they said she's real sickly. The doctor came about forty minutes ago and gave her something to calm her down. Probably Valium or something like that."

Joi grimaced. *She'll be loopy. Questioning that woman would be next to impossible.*

"The daughter was pretty broke up too," Rique said, chancing a glance upstairs. He had already told the women that Sergeant Hanks had asked his people to consider the emotional condition of the women. So nobody pressed the issue. Rique continued, "Maybe you can take their statements tomorrow?"

"Not a freakin' chance," she whispered, rolling her eyes at the Sergeant's interference. He had never been particularly sensitive to the plight of people of color. He had to have an ulterior motive for his concern. *Probably has the hots for the daughter*, Joi quietly fumed. "I need to talk to *both* of them today."

Rique gave her a knowing grin. Sergeant Cecil Hanks was unpopular with the Latino and Black cops because he made stupid remarks. He wasn't considered an overt racist, just a jerk from blue collar dysfunction that didn't know better. When he had called the Hispanic guy that mopped the bathrooms a "wetback" and no one else laughed, he looked genuinely stuck in his stupidity. He had also been overheard whispering the "N" word in snide jokes with other White officers. He wasn't the guy that would hurt a person directly. He was the guy that kept his mouth shut and went along with the ones that did.

"Let them know that I can come upstairs if they wish, but it's imperative that I take a statement from both of them today. I'll give them fifteen minutes."

Rique moved toward the staircase. "I'll go up and let 'em know. The bedroom is at the top of the stairs on the right."

❖ ❖ ❖

Officer Ramirez walked quietly up the carpeted steps to prepare the women to speak to the detective. He lightly rapped on Nancy Gregg's partially open bedroom door.

"Yes?" came the tentative response.

"Missus," he spoke his accent tinged words. "The detectives are here and they need to speak personally with you."

"Come in please," responded the younger of the two women, tenderly arranging her mother's robe to better cover her shriveled cleavage.

The officer entered, remaining at the threshold. "The lady detective, Ms. Sommers, will come. She's working downstairs … in the study, but she will need to come up.

"How soon? My mother is so tired." Kelly's face belied the annoyance in her voice.

"Yes, Missus, in about fifteen minutes."

Kelly looked over at the other woman. "Mother, you don't have to…"

Nancy Gregg nodded affirmatively.

"Alright, officer, we'll be ready." Officer Ramirez saw Kelly squeeze her mother's outstretched hand in hers as he backed out the doorway.

CHAPTER 15

Twenty minutes later, Joi took a long, slow breath as she rounded the carpeted stairs and made it to the threshold of Mrs. Gregg's bedroom door. The air was always super- charged with emotion when talking to the victim's family. Seasoned cops had no problem burying their feelings; but empathy for the victim is the fuel that drove Joi to solve the hard cases. There could be a perfect balance of both.

Exhaling, she centered herself, promising not to get sidetracked. She lightly rapped her knuckles against the wooden door.

"Come in," a feeble voice responded.

Detective Sommers pushed the door open and entered an elegantly decorated bedroom with white brocade-curtained windows overlooking the front of the home. Sunlight filtered in, creating a cozy ambiance.

"Hello," she said, directing her eyes across both women. "I'm Detective Joi Sommers."

Joi crossed the distance between them and extended her hand to the mother, who grasped it with a fragile, almost non-existent grip. Her long lashed eyes were vacant, having that faraway look that people get when they wish they were somewhere else. From the look of her dry pursed lips and the angle of her jaw, she was gritting her teeth. Then Joi perused the daughter, whose clammy grip was firm. Her eyes were wary as she sized Joi up.

Nancy Gregg's long hair was pulled into a pony-tail at the nape of her neck. The older woman stared at Joi through dark eyes that still conveyed a pride that said 'no matter what I'm going through, you will never see me crumble.'

The daughter was in her twenties and strikingly attractive, one of the hot chicks that always landed the fine men. She was petite, about 5'4", with hazel colored eyes and a perky Halle Berry type haircut. Joi surmised that on any other day of the week Kelly Gregg would be projecting a vibrant, sassy look, but today she drooped like a wilted sunflower struggling for light and water.

"I'm so sorry for your loss, ladies," Joi whispered.

In a quick move originating from her hips, Kelly lurched toward the loveseat next to her mom, and in another long dance-like stride she was at the window.

Kelly locked gazes with Joi, parted her wide mouth and said, "I hoped we wouldn't have to give a statement until tomorrow." Joi heard a tinge of exasperation in those words.

"The other officer—"

"Yes, I know," Joi cut in. "But it's been several days. I insisted on today, ladies. Details you don't even know you know could be fading."

The mother rapidly pulled four tissues from a brushed nickel holder on the corner of the bedside table.

"I know this feels harsh under the circumstances," Joi conceded. "But I really need to get your statements to move ahead with the investigation and bring whoever killed your husband," she turned to embrace Kelly with her gaze, "and your father, to justice." She paused, anchoring her comments by making direct eye contact with each woman before continuing.

"I can't stress the importance, okay?"

The widow Gregg lay very still, clutching the tissue box like a teddy bear. Unfortunately, the petite woman gave no indication that she was actually processing Joi's comments. The detective was concerned about Mrs. Gregg, but given the fact that Rique had said she was very ill, waiting was not an option. Grief could sometimes overtake a person and render them immobile. Worst yet, couples who had been married for a long time tended to leave right after the other, almost as if they were on the buddy plan.

Joi cleared her throat, causing Nancy's head to snap toward her. "You have no idea how many details get blurred in your mind. And after twenty-four, thirty-six hours, it's difficult to dig them up."

"Yes, that Latino policeman said that too," Kelly said, this time making sure she maintained eye contact with Joi.

"Good," Joi countered smoothly. "I asked Officer Ramirez to prepare you," she added, silently thanked Enrique for laying some groundwork.

Inching in a little closer, she saw that Mrs. Gregg's skin was yellow-tinged and her eyes drifted, making her appear lethargic. Something more was going on than just losing her husband. Yet, even in this dark moment, Joi admired the remnants of a once beautiful woman.

Joi pulled a small stenographer's pad from her jacket pocket, retrieved the ballpoint pen from the spiral binding, and then flipped open to a clean page. "Please bear with me. I need to make sure I have my facts straight." She looked at the daughter. "I am speaking with Mrs. Nancy Gregg, and you are Kelly Greg, correct?"

Kelly responded for the pair of grieving family members. "Yes, that's correct."

"Excuse me ma'am," she said to Mrs. Gregg. "I thought that your son was here also."

"He—he left." Kelly responded hesitantly looking at her mother for validation. The older woman gave an almost imperceptible nod.

"He … left?" Joi blinked, trying to remember if she had seen a shadow of anyone passing or making an exit from the garden. "So soon?"

The daughter shot a wary glance at her mother before adding, "He went to work. He works second shift at SBC; but he'll be in contact with us. We don't see him much anyway. My little brother's a loner."

Nancy frowned at those last two statements and gave her daughter a warning look.

Kelly became silent.

At that moment, Joi wondered if Marcus Gregg had managed to slip in and out without being seen and those two were lying.

"I need his contact information," was Joi's dispassionate response, a direct contradiction to the impatient cadence of her ballpoint pen tapping on the notepad.

"I'll get it to you when you're done speaking with us," Kelly said.

The daughter's posture was tense, almost defensive, when it had been relaxed just moments before. She had moved back to a floral straight back chair and sat with her arms folded across her chest. Joi wondered if she could get her to share information that she didn't want her mother to hear.

"Mrs. Gregg, I don't want to cause you any more pain," Joi ventured. "But can you think of any enemies your husband might have had?"

The woman blinked and a sudden flood of tears filled her eyes.

"A bad business deal, a church member that he angered? Had he had any arguments that you know of?"

The fragile woman took a moment to gather her thoughts. "Denny? Nooo, not that I know of. Detective, I'm in my room a lot. I'm on pain medication. I have cancer and the pain is excruciating. I sleep all the time." Mrs. Gregg responded with a whisper of regret, as though she was sorry that she had to admit that small weakness.

"We had breakfast together yesterday." Nancy's voice broke a little on the last word. "I wish I had been up more Friday." Her body trembled, probably from a pain too deep to voice. Tears pooled in her dark brown eyes and spilled down her pale cheeks. "I … I spent most of the day resting."

Kelly had moved over and knelt at her mother's lap. She took a tissue, using it to wipe away the steady stream of tears. Mrs. Gregg placed a trembling hand on her daughter's head.

"Detective, can't you see that my mother knows nothing!" Kelly snapped. "She's weak, can't you see that? Please leave her alone."

"Miss Gregg," Joi emphasized. "This is the most difficult, but perhaps the most important part of my job—as a detective."

Kelly Gregg's vapid eyes stared back at her—but Joi sensed that a lot was unspoken.

Concern for her mother was one thing, but the younger woman's demeanor was off-putting. Why wasn't she crying? Why did she seem to fluctuate between being a bit chatty as though she was nervous and then being guarded? Perhaps she was holding it together for her mother, or perhaps she wasn't as stricken as her mom. And that was something that Joi should look into.

"I think I have something to work with—for now," Joi conceded. "Medicated and all, maybe your mother wouldn't have heard much, but if you can get her to remember anything else, please give me a call, won't you?"

Kelly's shoulders relaxed, but only a little.

"Can I get *your* statement now?"

Kelly's back went ramrod straight again.

"Yes, yes, just a second." She turned to the sobbing woman, who was dabbing tissues at her tear-stained face. "Mommy, let me help you into bed. I'm going downstairs to talk with the detective and I'll be right back."

Mrs. Gregg gripped her daughter's hands and Kelly gave hers a gentle pat. "Momma, I won't leave. I brought some clothes and I'm going to sleep over."

Nancy smiled, her eyes suddenly filling with light.

The dutiful daughter fluffed the white satin covered pillows before helping her mother recline. Then she walked over to the windows and pulled back the heavy white brocade curtains looking out into the street in time to catch a few curiosity seekers walking slowly and peering at the Gregg home.

"*Busybodies*" Joi hissed.

"Mommy, look. It's a sunny day outside," she said, offering her mother a feeble smile. "I'll crack the window so you can breathe some fresh air." She took a few steps, then paused to look back at her mother's prone form. "The door's open; call out if you need me."

Nancy Gregg had already drifted off to sleep. The sound of her even breathing through her barely open mouth was the only audible sound for a few seconds.

Kelly turned to Joi, "All right Detective, I'm ready."

CHAPTER 16

As they descended the stairs, Joi observed as the graceful, confident young woman navigated the steps, then the hallway, leaving indentations in the thick beige carpet as she moved like a tigress carefully traversing her terrain.

Kelly Gregg led the way into an all-white living room with a second set of sliding glass doors that opened into the garden like the ones in the den. This home was the kind of dwelling that a lower middle class detective only dreamed of owning while flipping through pages in *Home Decorating* magazine. The table in the hallway that held a Dooney & Bourke handbag was real marble. Expensive Waterford Crystal twinkled in the mahogany cabinet in the entry-way. The carpet and even the walls were a stark white. Semi-gloss pigment reflected the light from the garden and another wall was covered in a white velour-like fabric that provided a soft background for two pewter framed paintings of placid country landscapes. Sunlight from the garden danced on the glass tables and illuminated the room in such a way that it seemed almost sacrilege that something so evil had occurred close to its existence.

Joi fought envy as she studied the elements of the room. "Lovely home. This must have taken a lot of—work." She fought the urge to say money. Yes, that had been the one thing Maze had never had enough of growing up. Men, now that was a different story.

"My mother particularly loves this room," Kelly said, taking a seat on one of the two white Italian leather couches. "She's put so much of herself into it."

Joi waited a moment, focusing her gaze on a bouquet of live mixed flowers which added a vibrant splash of color to the glass and pewter plant stand.

Kelly rose from the sofa, wringing her hands in a fashion that made Joi wonder what had happened in that short amount of time to make her feel so vulnerable. Maybe it was the fact that they were alone, with no buffer between questions that Kelly did not want to answer. The young woman walked past three white halogen lamps staggered at intervals around the pristine room, and carefully slid open the glass doors to the garden. She paused at the threshold.

"Detective, my mother selected and planted every flower and bush that's in this garden."

Joi stepped around the coffee table and joined the woman at the door that looked out into the garden. "She's a very talented woman, that's for sure."

Kelly continued to stare out into the garden.

"Do you know the names of all those flowers, Miss Gregg?"

"Most of them," she replied softy. "The orange and red ones climbing the trellis are roses, and there," she pointed to the left of where they were standing, "four hibiscus bushes and fading Pompoms."

Joi was unimpressed with the garden trivia. "Uh, Miss Gregg, where were you last night?"

Kelly snatched her focus from the garden and looked Joi squarely in the eyes. "Working late. I work downtown at Citibank." She paused as though wanting those few words to be enough. Joi remained silent, which tended to make people nervous … and chatty. But not Kelly Gregg.

"I'm a graphic designer. I had an important presentation due and I wasn't satisfied with it by quitting time, so I worked over."

"What time did you leave?"

"Half past eleven"

"Oh, *that late,*" Joi asked, scribbling on her tablet. "You do that often?"

"Yes, my colleagues will tell you I stay late a lot. I'm ... a perfectionist," she said, giving Joi a sheepish smile. "It's hard for me to ever let things go."

The detective nodded before scanning the room, noting that the desire for perfection seemed an inherited trait. Matching glass coffee and end tables were a final compliment to a white room that Joi thought spoke to Mrs. Gregg's need for cleanliness, order and detail.

"Who saw you?"

Kelly flinched and shifted on one leg. "I'm sure I don't know. The other designers were long gone. I didn't know I'd need an alibi," she answered, narrowing her gaze on Joi as though asking the unspoken question so many others did at this point: *Do I need an alibi?* Which was always followed by, *"Should I call my lawyer?"*

"When I finally left downtown," Kelly added, leaning on the wall, "I stopped at Subway drive-through for a salad and a diet Coke. Then I went home to bed." Suddenly the tears that Joi had expected earlier finally made their appearance as Kelly's voice wavered.

"Detective, I didn't know that anyone was ... going to ... murder my dad." She hurried across the room, flopped down wearily on the couch and buried her head in trembling hands.

Joi allowed her a moment, watching her closely as she uttered, "This is horrible. How do you even *deal* with this kind of thing!" Kelly asked, though she clearly did not expect the detective to answer. And Joi could give her enough answers that the woman would have nightmares for the rest of her life.

"My mother is sick. And my dad was just—was murdered. I've got to plan his funeral!" She looked up at Joi, her expression pleading and forlorn. "How do I *do* that Detective?"

Joi paused, allowing Kelly a few breaths before asking, "When was the last time you saw your father?" She hoped to help the distraught woman reflect on a happier memory.

Kelly blinked several times and said, "My parents had brunch at my apartment three months ago."

Joi picked up a small framed photo on the cocktail table and turned it over in her hands. She fought the urge to ask permission to smoke. "What did you serve?"

"Baked salmon with lemon sauce."

"Well at least you have that memory to hold onto."

Kelly sat silently for a moment, perhaps grateful to be talking about fish instead of planning a funeral.

"Yes right," she conceded with a small, bitter smile. "I have my *memories* to comfort me."

Joi heard the seemingly unconscious emphasis on the word memories. She reached into her jacket pocket and handed Kelly a wrinkled tissue. Remembering her promise to take it as easy as she could on the Gregg women, she realized that neither one of them was going to be much help. Maybe the son could shed some light on things.

"Miss Gregg, we are stronger than we think we are," Joi said. "You and your family will get through this. You have your friends and of course your faith," she said, having spied a well-worn leather bound King James Bible open on a low table in the hallway.

Before she realized it, she had reached over and given the woman's hand a gentle squeeze.

Kelly looked up forlornly, grasping Joi's hand as if it were a lifeline.

"Perhaps you should check on your mom," Joi suggested with a nod toward the upper level. "I have enough—for now. If you think of anything else, give me a call." Joi extracted her hand from the woman's grasp.

"Here's my business card. My cell phone is listed in case I'm not in the office."

Kelly took the card and stared blankly at it.

"I'll still need to ask you all some more questions, but I can come back." She pivoted and made her way to the door before looking over her shoulder. "Oh, and your brother, I'm going to need to get in touch with him today."

Kelly grimaced then disappeared into the hallway for a moment, returning with the dark brown with black trim Dooney & Bourke handbag. She scribbled phone and cell numbers on the back of her business card and pressed it into the palm of the waiting detective.

"I'll give him your numbers too." She breathed a visible sigh of relief. "He'll call to check on mom later today. *He always talks to mom.*" She turned, aiming to make her way up the stairs.

"Miss Gregg."

Kelly turned back to face Joi.

"Please discourage your mom from going into the study—for two reasons."

Kelly put her foot back down on the landing.

"One," said Joi, "Nobody but someone authorized by the Department should enter that room."

Kelly nodded, but then she frowned. "And?"

Joi gave her a smile. "It appears that your mother likes to keep things in order. That den," she pointed in its direction, "is my crime scene." The detective continued stating policy.

"I understand," Kelly whispered.

"When we're done here, we'll send in a company to clean. Your mother won't see any of it."

"I honestly don't see mother having that kind of energy Detective, *but you people need to remember - this is her home,*" said Kelly, walking the detective toward the front door. The detective read Kelly's defensive tone.

"It's my job to tell you Department policy, but I'll be on my way now." Even as Joi said that, the words, "*He always talked to my mother,*" begged for future exploration.

Kelly spun away from her and made it up the first three steps.

"Oh and Miss Gregg," Joi said, causing Kelly to pause with her hand on the rail. "Would you happen to know when *your brother* last spoke with your father?"

Kelly's shoulder tensed. She turned to look over her shoulder. All signs of sorrow swept from her face in the moment it took to catch a breath. "No Detective." She spoke in a voice just above a whisper, but there was no mistaking the steel underneath. "I certainly do not."

CHAPTER 17

As the sun rose, Mattie Wilson awakened dripping in sweat. The sound of Emery's snoring and the smell of stale Jack Daniels assaulted her senses, snatching her from a fretful sleep and into the new day. She looked over at her husband of twenty years. His pimply skin and scruffy beard covered the remnants of a handsome face that belied the former hunky Florida A&M University quarterback she had married a week after graduation. Emery had passed out in his clothes and shoes, lying atop the floral comforter that covered their king-sized bed. She was grateful he hadn't enough energy to start patting all over her.

As if he could perform in his drunken state.

She flipped the comforter off of her and onto him, hoping to cover his stinky mouth in the process. Mattie was glad that she only worked part-time. This morning she'd have time to take a relaxing bath before driving to the ReMax Real Estate office to a client meeting. By noon, she would shake off the fog that clogged her brain and be "fresh and bubbly" for the showing in Hazel Crest. She hoped to schmooze the perspective buyers of the recently rehabbed brick split level into a decent bid. She desperately needed the hefty commission that a sale could bring to shoulder the cost of Corey's counseling sessions.

Mattie stumbled past the wood-framed mirror anchored to her dresser and peered at the haggard dark brown face with round, thick lidded eyes that stared back at her. The image of the person responsible for changing Corey, her impish and quirky son with a ready smile, into a morose and withdrawn teen in the care of a therapist came to mind. Mattie's anger resurfaced. "Elder. Counselor," she sneered to herself. *The person troubled people sought for help was ... a demon. That's what he was. A demon, using our church for cover.* This would kill Emery if he knew, but she would see that he didn't.

Nancy, her best friend since high school, had stood by Mattie through her rocky marriage to a narcissistic, alcoholic husband. She had been there for her when their financial woes almost caused them to lose their home. Now the woman was fighting for her life and Mattie couldn't bear to be in the same room with her. She had not visited Nancy or helped with the planning of Dennis' funeral.

Even a recent call to express her condolences was laden with lies and deceit.

"Oh my God, Nancy!!! I just heard about Dennis'....murder." Inwardly, she thought, *I probably knew before you did.*

"I am so sorry for your loss." *Well not actually, but it was the right thing to say.*

"I can't imagine how you must be feeling." And that was the biggest lie of all. Of course Mattie knew that in Nancy's eyes, the sun rose and set with Dennis Gregg. And that was the main reason Mattie never shared what she knew. It would have crushed her friend. Mattie's conscience beat her up daily. Still, she was sure that Nancy Gregg had to know something.

"Mattie, can you come over?" Nancy Gregg had barely managed to whisper "I ... I just need you here. How soon can you get here?"

"Nance, I know you need me," she had whispered. "But I'm having some serious problems with Corey." When the silence on the line made

Mattie think Nancy wasn't tracking, Mattie quickly added, "Actually, he's in therapy. This could not have happened at a worse time but I have to see about my son."

"Mattie, I don't think I can go through this without you."

"I'll try to get over this evening," she lied, to give Nancy some peace. It wasn't a complete lie—she would 'try'.

"And we will all be at the funeral, I promise," Mattie said, wanting to kick herself for making that promise. She didn't want to lay eyes on Dennis Gregg again. Alive or dead. "You are in my prayers. Hug Kelly and Marc for me," was all she had managed to say before quietly disconnecting the call.

The truth, but not the whole truth. The whole truth was, *I saw your husband dead on his den floor before you did. And I am glad the bastard is dead. He deserved what he got. I only wish it would have happened sooner. Happened long before ...*

It would take a herculean effort to even attend that devil's home going. But she must do at least that for Nancy. Otherwise, Nancy would know something was very wrong. Mattie had kept the secret all this time; she might as well carry it one step further.

She was confident that the devil her friend's husband had been so faithful to for all these years would be in attendance at his funeral as Denny's soul sizzled in the fires of hell.

Mattie walked down the hall of her Georgian home and stopped for a brief look at the cherished black and white photo of Miles Davis at the Apollo Theater that hung over a long oak cabinet that held spare towels and linen for the three-bedroom, two-and-a-half bath home. She listened for a moment outside her son's room and heard nothing from behind the half opened door. She rapped her knuckles softly against the white lacquer door. "Corey, you up?"

"No," came the terse reply.

Mattie opened the door and peered inside. It was an absolute mess. Shoes and pants everywhere, atypical for her son. At the moment, he sat in front of the television, the game on pause. Quiet. Sullen. Unlike the cheerful boy he had been before. His baseball and track trophies, each with their own wall shelves, were a grateful reminder of her son's successful trajectory, before …

"Are you sure you're not up," she attempted to joke.

"Yep," was his simple reply before clicking on his video game and flooding the room with sound.

"Jokes? That's a good sign," she quipped, trying to infuse lightness into her tone. "Listen, I've got to work this afternoon, but you get out of here to school on time."

Corey was furiously making moves with the game stick. He was playing Mortal Kombat, and when she heard the phrase 'finish him,' it sent chills through her body. Corey completed the kill with deadly skill. A flash of Dennis Gregg's mangled face came to mind and she closed her eyes to regain her bearings.

"In a minute," he replied, eyes frozen on the screen, looking older than fifteen.

Her baby. Her only son. The counseling sessions had to help Corey. She didn't dare tell Emery. Not when she thought Corey was gay and certainly not now that she knew he had been molested. Emery could never focus on anyone but himself. He would find a way, like he always did, to make Corey's pain all about him. Any excuse to turn up the volume on his drinking.

No, she and Corey would deal with this together.

"Shower downstairs please," she requested. "I need the tub upstairs okay?"

"Yeah, okay," he said without making eye contact.

Mattie looked back and saw him reset the game for another session. Deciding that nagging was not the best use of her time, she kept moving down the hall towards the bathroom. She pulled back the green fabric shower curtain, turned on the tub, and poured three capfuls of Jasmine bath oil before wondering if Corey's fixation on the violent video game was helping him extinguish the anger that his therapist observed brewing within him. If it did, maybe she should pull up a chair and start playing Mortal Kombat alongside him.

She heard the computer-generated voice utter a low, chilling, guttural command. *Finish him!*

As she walked away, she envisioned the Ninja-like fighter delivering a roundhouse kick so swift and strong that blood flew from the head of the loser, knocking him dead on the mat. Yes, that was a move she approved of.

❖ ❖ ❖

As soon as he heard the bathroom door shut and the sound of his mom's bath water thundering into the sunken bathtub, Corey placed the video game stick on his bed and reached under the pillow top mattress for a small packet of razor blades. His stomach boiled with anticipation as he carefully peeled a fresh blade from the neatly wrapped paper. He carefully rolled up the sleeve of his striped cotton pajama top, inhaled deeply, and with the edge of the blade he drew a four inch line slowly across the flesh of his upper arm, releasing a thin line of dark red blood. There were five other cuts, all identical, almost tattoo-like. He stuck out his tongue and licked the trickle of blood until it subsided, and pulled his sleeve back over his cutting range. Laying back on his mattress for a few moments, a wave of temporary relief washed over him and Corey closed his eyes to savor it.

CHAPTER 18

Joi avoided the victim stretched out on the Cook County Medical Examiner's table, choosing instead to write in her stenographer's notebook. Devin Bandur was a short Irishman with dimpled cheeks, a thick head of unruly coppery hair and sparkling green eyes. He bit into a thinly sliced kosher corned beef sandwich which was smothered in mustard and topped with a kosher dill pickle that soaked its wax paper wrapping.

"How can you eat that?" she asked him, with a quick glance to the corpse, then back to the sandwich to convey her meaning.

"But me darlin', I love corned beef."

"I love beef, too," she smirked at her own joke. "But in here, Dev?"

"When you've been doing this for as long as I have, you can stomach just about anything."

Elder Dennis' mangled face grinning at her sardonically from behind its death mask with a full set of teeth may not have turned his stomach, but it turned hers.

Joi looked around the semi-sterile environment. The light grey walls were lined on one side with files of autopsied persons. Against another wall were four stainless-steel gurneys on wheels. The temperature in the room was about sixty-five degrees and Joi was glad for her long sleeved shirt and grey blazer.

"So what's his story," Devin asked between bites.

"The victim's office wasn't even robbed," she said to him. "He had a locked safe in his den that held close to ten grand."

She lifted the cover of a grey strong box and carefully reviewed the inventory of personal effects found at the crime scene and on the corpse:

an expensive Wittnauer watch still on his wrist,

a black and gold Monte Blanc pen on his desk,

an intact ATM card and credit card,

two hundred dollars in small bills in a silver and gold-tone crucifix money clip in his trouser pockets.

"Thanks, Dev," she said. "I'm going back to the office to follow up on some leads. There were a few prints at the scene, one was bloody. I'll know soon who it belongs to. Enjoy your sandwich." Then she gave him a wide grin, gesturing to the bread in his hand. "You know those poppy seeds can make your drug test turn positive."

Dev shrugged and gave her a lopsided grin as he took a bigger chomp out of a meal that was too late for lunch and too early for dinner. "Oh, I don't have to worry about that."

"I guess you didn't read that latest department memo," she said as his eyebrows drew in. "They're starting random testing next week."

He paused mid-bite and grimaced before dropping the sandwich on the wax paper. The old-timer certainly would have issues with losing a job he had held years before she arrived.

Joi turned to walk away, but took a final glance in the direction of the lifeless form on the exam table and shook her head as she whispered, "This is definitely a closed casket funeral."

CHAPTER 19

SATURDAY, AUGUST 21, 2004

Detective Sommers had deliberately postponed questioning Nancy Gregg again until after the funeral services. She doubted that she'd get more information from the widow than she had gotten from the daughter until the family had a sense of closure. Funerals were supposed to do that. But sometimes they unearthed other issues.

She dressed carefully in a tailored black skirt suit, low-heeled black Nine West pumps, and draped a string of pearls around her neck. To keep a low profile, she drove her own car and arrived a half hour before the ten o'clock funeral services for Elder Dennis Gregg were to begin.

Her phone vibrated. She looked at the screen. "Joi," she answered dispassionately.

"Where are you?" Russell asked

"I told you I'd have the Gregg funeral under surveillance this morning.

Gotta go, I'm about to walk in." She paused, stalling near the carved wood sanctuary door. "Hey Russ, did you check with ballistics to see if they got a make on the gun used to pop Elder Gregg?"

"Devin says they're stacked up. He hasn't gotten to it yet."

"Damn his lazy Irish ass," she groaned. "I'll deal with him later. He's been eating too many poppy seeds," she said, smirking.

"What?"

"Never mind," she replied, inwardly reminding herself to make sure Russ knew about the testing. "Inside joke. Gotta run!"

She entered the doors of Christ's Victory Apostolic Church, a mega church of eight thousand which boasted members of both the South Suburban and Chicago elite. The front of the elegant sanctuary had been sectioned off with thick gold tasseled ropes. The place was already a third of the way full. Somehow every last one of these people were connected to the Greggs. Any one of them could be a potential killer.

Joi opted not to sign the Book of Condolences positioned on an ornately carved wooden pedestal outside of the services. She accepted a copy of the four-page obituary from a white-gloved usher in a tight white blouse and a short maroon skirt that screamed at the seams. She was then directed by an older, more dignified usher, into the bowels of the sanctuary. The observant detective quietly scanned the house of worship, recognizing a few familiar faces. As a member of the South Holland Police Department, she could easily justify her presence as a sign of the Department's respect for a prominent Village citizen of color, but she still kept her presence on the "low" so she wouldn't stand out.

Joi often attended funerals of the victims when she was working their cases. Funerals were the ultimate stress test; an opportunity to observe family dynamics, spot the loyalties and hatreds. Everything came to light. The mistress, the outside child, the black sheep, the hidden stuff. As her grandmother used to say, weddings and funerals bring out the best and worst in folks.

Donning her Calvin Klein sunglasses, she situated herself in a center pew at the back of the Sanctuary. From her vantage point she could watch all entrances. She had a clear view of the front, where the casket lay draped under a thick blanket of yellow and white flowers, surrounded by a lush array of floral arrangements. There was an 18 x 22 oil painting of Elder Gregg with lighting attached to illuminate his once distinguished face. The portrait, anchored to a tall cast bronze easel, stood to the left of his bronze casket. The smile was majestic, omniscient even.

The portrait was the first time she had ever focused on Elder Gregg as anything more than the grotesque remnants of very foul play. According to the Obituary, *"Elder Dennis Gregg, born October 26, 1955, went home to be with the Lord, two months before his 49th birthday."*

In his portrait he looked to be about thirty-five and quite handsome. He appeared to be holding a winning hand in life, complete with a thriving computer business, a pretty wife, two kids, and from the turnout at his funeral, much respect from those who knew him. A man this handsome in his heyday would have set women's hearts aflutter in the church. *Was jealousy the motive? Was he having an affair with one of the women in the church? Several women? Did a husband of one of the church members hate him enough to whack him? Who had a beef with Elder Gregg?*

She swept a gaze at some of the women in the surrounding pews and another thought came to her: *Could I be wasting my time?* She quickly discounted that notion. Following her gut had helped her and Russ close the highest number of cases in their department.

Joi glanced at her watch. It was 9:59 a.m.

Almost on cue, at ten o'clock Nancy Gregg entered the sanctuary, assisted by a dark-skinned, scrawny woman in a dark grey suit who looked like she had seen better times on the other side of sixty. Joi had caught a glimpse of the woman in the Gregg home during one of her visits, but couldn't quite remember if she had known her name. The woman's walk, meek and bowed, made her seem more like a servant than family. She focused on Mrs. Gregg's comfort as they made their way up the center aisle.

Nancy stood at the closed casket, placing both her hands upon it as if she were drawing strength from the corpse inside. She wept while being supported by the salt-and-pepper haired woman before taking a seat on the left side of the front pew, staring directly into the portrait. This left other members of the family to adjust themselves around her on either side.

Another couple of mourners caught Joi's eye. A heavyset woman wearing a black cloche with a black Ann Klein suit kept fielding questions from the woman sitting with Nancy. *Must be Nancy's physician.* She was accompanied by a man. *Probably her husband.*

A third couple seemed to be close relatives of the deceased, judging by the female's shaky posture. She appeared almost as despondent as Mrs. Gregg. *Could she be a sibling?* She leaned heavily into a man who was easily a decade older. Buttons on his navy blue suit strained to hold the jacket together. He supported her by her elbow and looked at her like she was the icing on his cake. Married. Definitely married. Or lovers. At one point, the woman looked at her husband, dark brown eyes filled with a tangible sorrow as if she wondered how this could all be happening.

"I *bet* that's Diana," Joi overheard a woman whispering behind her. "She hasn't been *here* in over fifteen years."

Joi recognized the name from the obituary as Diana Gregg-Alman, Dennis Gregg's sister. *Fifteen years? What could keep a woman from her brother for all that time?*

"It's a shame that the only thing that brought her back was this funeral," a second woman said, her voice ripe with recrimination.

"I heard that Nancy told her that there was a lot more to offer here, but she just *had* to move to St. Louis."

"Wonder who's that man with her?" the first voice whispered.

"Looks like she finally found a fella to marry her," continued the gossips.

Joi honed in on the subject of their speculation. Diana Gregg-Alman was short and a silky milk chocolate color, like her brother. Her crinkly hair was parted straight down the center and fell just below her ears. She was thick, with wide hips partially covered by a black and white tunic. The knee length skirt revealed unattractively thick legs.

Marcus Gregg, whom she had yet to question, followed close behind.

He had a confident stride as he walked over and squeezed in beside his mother. He wrapped his arm protectively around her shoulder and she leaned on him. With his father gone, Marcus seemed to be assuming his role as the head of this family. The fact that he continued to dodge Joi's efforts to connect with him made him a little suspect in her eyes. Made her wonder about the relationship Marcus had with his father.

Joi was pissed that Marcus had not returned the six voicemails she left requesting call backs. She made a note to give it one more shot before making an unannounced visit to his job and hauling his ass away from SBC for questioning. Whether he was grieving over his daddy's death or not, she had a killer to find.

The gossiping church mavens gave a running commentary of the funeral attendees. Joi almost wished she could interview them—they seemed to know more than her fellow officers did!

"There's Mattie Wilson and her boy Corey." Joi waited a moment then inconspicuously craned her neck to see a small woman in a charcoal gray dress and matching wide brimmed hat, with a strikingly attractive teen who followed her. The boy, just under six feet, sported a dark navy suit, a white shirt and a mixed grey tie that matched his mother's outfit. His close cropped haircut accentuated a pair of ears that he would need to grow into. After they greeted Nancy and the Gregg family warmly, they sat four pews behind the family.

"Where's her husband?" the first gossip asked. "Wouldn't you think he'd show up."

"Girlfriend, Emery's probably somewhere with his lips around a Wild Irish Rose bottle."

"Ya think?"

Joi visualized their self-righteous smirks. She knew those types. Women who would smile in the face of a young girl who was the daughter of the local slut, but would not lend a hand if that same young girl reached out to them. No, they would spend their time spreading the sins of the mother to everyone who would listen.

Joi swept aside the memories of shame and low self-esteem she had suffered at the hands of narrow minded broads like the two sitting behind her. She turned toward the entryway at the front of the church just as a disheveled Kelly Gregg entered, wearing an off-white suit that swallowed her tiny frame. Definitely not normal for Miss Cosmopolitan, but that wasn't what hijacked Joi's attention. Seeing the guy Kelly clung to made Joi's heart slam into her chest.

"Goddammit, that's Chad," she whispered, spinning around to look into the self-righteous faces of the two gossips who had gasped at her blasphemy. She withered them with an intense look, then focused on the cause of her concern.

Chad Sanders took a seat next to Kelly on the family pew. For a moment, all thoughts of the murder, the victim, solving any kind of crime, flew out the window. Joi reeled in disbelief when Chad held Kelly in his arms as she wept like a wounded child.

I'll just be dammed!!! That lying piece of shit is Kelly's boyfriend? So why in the hell is he always climbing his ass into my bed?

CHAPTER 20

Rage built up in Joi and almost catapulted her from the pew. The choir entered the loft, and she sat through several spirited gospel songs only noticing a beautiful contralto rendition of *I Can Depend On God* that only served to squirt oil on an already raging fire.

Chad and Kelly? Seriously? Oh, she wanted to give that brother some pain.

Screw it and him! she swore. She would get the chance to do both, and it would be something his lying, cheating ass would never forget.

"I Can Depend on God," the choir droned on. If Joi could testify, she would shout that the only person she could depend on was herself. *Where was God when my mother's scumbag of a boyfriend Al had busted my head down to the white meat? Where was God when I was a kid in a shelter?* Perhaps some folks can depend on God, but he was deaf, dumb and blind where Joi was concerned.

When friends and family rose to give their testimonies, Joi stood to leave. Between all the singing, weeping, and seeing Chad smother-loving Little Miss Gregg, she'd had enough.

Suddenly there was a buzz in the air. Her gaze swept to the front of the sanctuary. From Joi's vantage point in the back, Nancy Gregg had collapsed atop her husband's flower-draped casket.

Mourners in the first three pews jumped into action. There was an "Oh my Lord, cover her with the blood of Jesus!" from a member while several others on the front row leapt to their feet to wrap their arms around the widow, who remained limp and almost as lifeless as the body underneath.

Joi resisted her impulse and training to take charge, deciding instead to remove her sunglasses and observe. The caregiver with Mrs. Gregg motioned everyone away except the woman she heard the gossips refer to as Dr. Crawford. Kelly, Marcus, and the fat-legged sister-in-law all came forward, circling so that others did not have a full few. Several Deacons lifted Mother Gregg and laid her gently on the maroon velvet pew.

Dr. Angela Crawford motioned to Marcus, who punched in a few numbers on his cell.

The doctor used a commanding pitch to say, "Everybody back up! She needs air."

The deacons did the doctor's bidding while she loosened the top two buttons on Nancy's black blouse. A stethoscope was retrieved from a black Gucci leather bag and pressed to the fainting woman's chest. Swiftly, the brown skinned woman moved directly into the CPR pattern, unwavering until Nancy Gregg coughed up a bit of phlegm that cleared her airways.

Meanwhile, the minister mopped his brow with a white handkerchief, then stuffed it back into his robe and gulped water from a goblet on a shelf under the clear Plexiglas podium. Clearing his throat, he spoke in a low reverent voice. "I'm calling on the Lord to work his will in a mighty way and intercede in the affairs of Mother Gregg this morning. In the name of Jeeeee-sus!" he exhorted.

Joi felt a tad sorry for the preacher and the flustered members—some who were standing, keeping their eyes on the family; others who were headed for the door. The two magpies behind her were in high gear, letting their hateful words flow between each other. This funeral, and everything about it was surreal. Joi was not new to dramatic funerals. There was one funeral where the deacon's outside son cussed the family matriarch out for omitting his name from the obituary. But the coup de grâce was the tacky north side funeral where the deceased banker's stripper girlfriend rolled up her rhinestone thong and tried to toss it in the casket, only to be headed off by the sharp witted wife, who handily beat the crap out of her in front of the open casket. This funeral, Chad's bullshit notwithstanding, was not the worst.

Joi waited until paramedics arrived. They carefully strapped Mrs. Gregg onto a stretcher and rushed her out the front door. Kelly, Chad and Marcus followed closely on their heels. Marcus was first out the door behind the EMTs. Kelly followed, clutching her mother's handbag. Chad brought up the rear. Joi didn't remember actually hissing at Chad but as he exited, he made a quarter turn and locked gazes with her for several moments. Momentarily frozen, he blocked Kelly's exit and she nudged him. He parted his lips and for a nanosecond he looked as though he wanted to explain himself. Then the Gregg wench yanked his arm. "Chad, what's wrong with you?"

"Nothing baby," he said putting his arm around Kelly and successfully turning her away from Joi's direction. "Nothing at all." He then disappeared down the church steps. She hoped he felt the hole her eyes were burning in the back of his cold black Armani suit.

With sirens blazing, the red and white ambulance sped Nancy to the hospital.

As Joi cornered the last pew, Bishop Pate announced to the mourners, "The funeral processional will continue as planned. It is our duty to conclude Elder Gregg's home going decently and in order, as well as to care for his beloved family."

Joi paused at the threshold and turned back to see exactly what he planned to do.

With outstretched hands he beckoned Diana to come forward.

"I'm asking Mrs. Diana Gregg-Alman, the sister of our departed Elder, to stand in the gap for Mrs. Nancy Gregg as we take Elder Gregg on his final ride to meet his Glorious Maker in heaven."

Diana's wide mouth gaped open but words failed her. She stared at the Reverend with a shell-shocked expression. She was a woman who was grief-stricken, but Joi deduced that the fact that she hadn't been in Illinois in fifteen years and had been suddenly thrust in the matriarch's role compounded her reaction. There was no refusing the pastor's request though, because even if he saw the look on Diana's face, he was too far gone to pull back.

That wasn't as troubling to Joi as what she saw as Mattie Wilson and her teen-aged son Corey inched out the door past her.

"I can't believe he's really dead," the teen said quietly to the woman.

Joi thought she heard her say under her breath, "Oh, yes, that devil is going straight to hell."

The detective's gut told her that there was a story behind Mattie Wilson's condemnation and the comments of the church gossips. For now, she was determined to follow the widow to the hospital and see what she could learn.

❖ ❖ ❖

Joi hurried from the church and slid behind the wheel of her blue Saturn, determined to follow Chad's white Cadillac Escalade. Again, her intuition to drive her own vehicle instead of an unmarked car with municipal plates was vindicated as she discreetly tailed the mourners to the hospital.

That damned Chad.

Joi and Chad had met at a Stepper's set. Joi was clumsy, and the highly choreographed spins and ballroom-like moves of the Southside steppers escaped her. She did her best dancing to house music, where she was free to move as the music led her. Still, she enjoyed watching the steppers do their thing.

She had met Chad sitting around the long bar at the Holiday Inn in

Matteson. They had flirted, she'd gotten drunk at the bar and he had trailed her back to her apartment to make sure she arrived safely. She had invited him in and given him more woman than he ever bargained for.

❖ ❖ ❖

Joi waited until Chad dropped Kelly and Marcus at the entrance of the University of Chicago Medical Center emergency room. He swung right. *Probably to find parking.*

Joi hurriedly gave her keys to a short Latino valet and pushed through the revolving doors of the emergency room in time to see Nancy atop a gurney, being pushed inside an elevator.

Wearing the mask of a distraught family member, Joi quickly inquired of the ER clerk in a pair of dark blue scrubs thumbing through paperwork at the desk. "Miss, my aunt was just wheeled onto the elevator. Where are they taking her?"

The woman looked down at her clipboard. Joi read upside down the words *PATIENT TRANSPORT LOG.*

"Her name?"

"Mrs. Gregg … uh, Nancy Gregg."

The clerk licked her finger and flipped a page up. "Sixth floor. Room six thirteen. Please sign in and take this pass."

As she alighted the elevator, she spied Yolanda Ross-Harris, her best friend from high school. She edged closer to the blue scrub-clad woman. After exchanging hugs and pleasantries, Joi confided her need for information on Nancy Gregg's status.

"Look girl," Yolanda whispered. "We have rules that keep us from revealing patient information." She scanned the area, making sure that even her low tone couldn't be overheard. "I could lose my job for talking to you about this patient. Haven't you ever heard of HIPAA?"

Joi leaned in to whisper, "Yeah, I know about patient privacy regulations, but this is a homicide I'm working on, Yogi." When the cautious nurse scowled, Joi added, "I promise I won't reveal my source.

I just need to know what shape the Gregg woman is really in."

Yolanda looked away for several thoughtful seconds before saying through her teeth, "You gonna owe me, heifer."

"Indeed I will!" Joi agreed, giving her a wide smile. She had more than one reason for smiling at the tall, short-haired nurse. Joi was genuinely pleased to see Yogi had made a career change, especially since the last time she had seen her, she was dangling from a stripper pole on the near north side as Miss Yo Yo. When they were kids, Yogi had fantasized about being a nurse. Joi guessed that marrying a decent guy had helped her get there.

Cautiously, Yolanda whispered to her friend, "Meet me on the second floor by the gift shop."

Ten minutes later, Yolanda motioned Joi to a small waiting area outside the gift shop.

Joi took the hint and was right on her heels. They sat next to one another, Yolanda quickly reading the medical details and Joi waiting for the cliff notes.

"Damn Joi," Yolanda said dryly. "She won't be here for long."

"Seriously?" said Joi looking down at neatly-typed medical terms that only left her in the dark.

"Her oncologist's notes say to make sure her vitals are stable and that she is pain free. Period. Pancreatic cancer is no joke," Yogi said, her tone dismal at delivering that sad news.

"Poor lady," said Joi, feeling a twinge of guilt. *Her husband was murdered in their home and now it appeared she was soon to join him.* Joi suddenly had a fleeting thought that made her wonder how she would feel if Maze was threatened with a diagnosis that could end her chaotic life. Could Joi overcome the feelings of abandonment that plagued her? For some reason, she wasn't so sure.

Yogi's final sobering comment on her way back to her post was, "I saw something in the newspaper about that family. Didn't she just bury her husband today?"

To which Joi replied, "She sure tried."

CHAPTER 21

Joi booted up her computer screen and logged onto the crime stats for South Holland. She squinted at the screen for several seconds, viewing the statistics that revealed five robberies over the weekend and three assault and batteries. The fastest rising statistic was for breaking and entering, or what cops called b&e's. The high cost of suburban living required two incomes, leaving South Holland's upscale homes easy pickings for criminals.

She crossed the room and raised the window. No matter how many flameless scented candles Joi placed in their office, the station still stank. She deeply inhaled the outside air, which smelled of a mixture of unseen flowers and trees lightly mixed with car exhaust. At least it was fresher than the pissy smell wafting up the stairs from the drunk tank, and the overwhelming smell of Pine Sol used to combat it.

Settling back into her gray ergonomic chair, she leaned back to ponder the situation. Her obvious persons of interest were Marcus, whose bloody print found at the scene put him at the top of her list of suspects. Then there was Kelly—the ice princess. The most implausible suspect of that night was the tragically ill widow.

Joi flipped open her notepad and wrote a reminder to call Dr. Angela Crawford who, besides being the woman's doctor, was a family insider. Nancy Gregg was heavily sedated. Perhaps her physician could get Joi in to question Mrs. Gregg in a lucid moment. Her gut told her that the widow was probably not the killer. It didn't make sense for a woman fighting cancer to kill the man that was the source of her livelihood and emotional support.

Well, whatever Nancy Gregg was, she damn sure wasn't a flight risk. Joi hoped that when Mrs. Gregg finally talked, she'd give her a solid lead.

The phone rang and scared the hell out of Joi. She jerked it up on the first ring.

"Hello!"

Russell was on the other end. "Heads up. The Gregg son just walked in. They're sending him up now."

"Cool, thanks," she replied, anxious to make this interview productive.

❖ ❖ ❖

Joi narrowed her gaze as Marcus Gregg entered the room wearing a scuffed brown leather jacket over his maroon SBC Communications golf shirt, black jeans and rustic brown steel-toed boots. His woolly hair was in disarray; a thick mustache framed ample lips and she was startled to find the same soft hazel eyes that reminded her of Kelly's, though smaller. She noticed a barely perceptible bruise on the left side of his face. His initial gaze was formidable but when she trained her eyes on his, his stare flickered like a candle in the breeze. Joi detected a strong mask superimposed over a fragile ego. She watched him sit up straight, suck his stomach in and take a long, slow breath.

They sat at an eight-foot wooden table that bore hundreds of scratches made by other nervous interviewees. The raggedly carved names *Bullet Romero, Gangsta Jody* and various gang symbols stared back at them from half a dozen places on the table.

Detective Sommers, sitting opposite Marcus Gregg, opened a manila folder. Laying a pack of Virginia Slims beside the folder, she asked, "Mind if I light up?"

"No, go head Detective."

If the smell of cigarette smoke was an indication of having cancer, Marcus was a walking chemo model. *Poor guy was probably dying for a cigarette,* she thought, giving way to the grin that pulled up the corners of her ruby stained lips as she lit a cigarette and sat it in the ashtray right in front of him.

"Let's start with what we know, Mr. Gregg."

"Marc, call me Marc."

"Okay." She paused. "Marc."

She thumbed through the reports from the crime scene, the forensic lab, and interviews with neighbors. When she came to the portion in the report that discussed in detail how his father's body was found, she decided to read it aloud. She wanted a rise from him.

He listened dispassionately—until she read the section of the report that said that after being shot in the back, Dennis Gregg had been turned over and shot the second time. After reading explicit descriptions about the damage that had been done to his father's head and face, the watched the head of the blue-collar guy drop, as he wiped the corner of his left eye with a grimy brown fingernail. His grief or guilt unmasked.

"Are you okay?"

He turned his head to the left at an angle that allowed her to see a small gold hoop dangling from his right earlobe.

"Um, yeah ... yeah, Detective, I think so. I hadn't heard those details—the part about the old man's—my father's brains." His voice trailed. "That part." Marcus Gregg took another deep breath and shook his lowered head in seeming disbelief.

Joi made a notation in her report. *Upon hearing details of wounds to the body, M. Gregg seems genuinely shaken.*

She watched his demeanor erode, as though he were now asking himself questions for which a guilty man would have had the answers.

"Marc, when was the last time you saw your father?"

He didn't respond. Instead he lowered his head into his right hand. Settling his jaw against his palm, he gave Joi an irritated look that showed he was groping for an answer that would be satisfactory.

"Marc … the last time you saw your father?" she pressed.

"Detective, I'll tell you again, I saw my father early in the evening on the day … uh … the night he was killed."

"What was the nature of your visit?"

"I told you that I wanted to talk to him about our relationship," he replied.

"Did you see your mother?"

"No, only my dad."

"Was she home?"

Marcus paused, rubbing the stubble on his chin. "Yes—maybe—well, I think so but I don't actually know. Usually if she's home and sees my truck, she comes down. I didn't ask."

Joi wondered why Nancy Gregg, knowing the son she seldom saw was downstairs in her home, wouldn't make her presence known. Or was he lying to protect her?

"I find it peculiar that you would come to your parents' home and not ask about your mother. Especially since she's been sickly. You wanna elaborate on that Marcus?"

Joi thought she felt him pull up, as though he were aware that he was about to lose it.

Marcus drew another deep breath and stood up abruptly.

She stood just as quickly, instinctively placing her hand on her weapon. "Hey, I'm gonna need you to ease back into your chair and answer my questions. Are we clear?

Joi was losing patience with this self-centered jerk. She was a curly hair from cussing his ass out.

"Yeaaah," he growled, low and slow like a dangerously cornered animal.

Looking directly into Joi's eyes with an *I wish I could kick your ass* look, Marcus Gregg managed a civil tone. "It was nothing. I had—something weighing on my mind. I needed to talk with him without my mom being around."

Joi's brows raised and she leaned forward. "Oh, what about? She asked and then stepped in with a quick barb.

"Did he give you that bruise on the side of your face?"

Marcus touched the dark splotch on his otherwise smooth complexion. He was stoic, glaring at her.

"Okay, let's just say it was private," she conceded. "What time was it, Marcus, when you finished your man-to-man talk?"

Joi looked at the two-way glass, anxious to get Russell's after-impressions.

"Maybe about eight. It was beginning to get dark. I didn't care because I was off that day. I left, picked up some food, grabbed a six pack, went home, ate, drank a beer and crashed."

Suddenly from outside the closed door there was commotion. Someone or something rocked the door to the room with the two way mirror, sending shockwaves against the door. She knew Russell was on the other side of the mirror witnessing her interview with Marcus. She heard Officers Cecil Hanks and Enrique Ramirez shouting, "Stop him! Grab his arms!"

Joi jumped up, loosened the flap on her gun holster and bolted for the door, leaving a startled Marcus alone at the interview table. She flung the door wide open, only to meet Russell, Hanks and Rique standing over a wild-eyed white guy with a thick mane of stringy blond hair. He was about forty, and as much space as he was taking up on the ground, he had to be nearly 6'7". If he had been green, they would have called him Hulk. He smelled like dried shit and was wearing a dingy white tee-shirt with the words *Take No Prisoners!!!* etched in blood red on the front.

"Aw hell, we got a crazy. We were moving him to the looney bin in Tinley Park when he bolted," said the agitated Officer Hanks.

"Damn, Russell, I don't know where you came from, but thanks for helping me and Cece take his big ass down. I felt like I was tackling a lineman for the Bears. He's four hundred pounds easy."

"Shit, didn't they know he needed to be medicated before we transport him?" said Cecil as Rique helped him to wrestle Hulk to his feet. 'This sucker just missed kicking me in the balls. I'd have been a gelding," smirked Hanks.

"What a loss to the females of the world," laughed Russell. He looked at Joi and they had a private chuckle. Joi and Russell recently stumbled upon the fact that Cecil was pitching for the other team.

"Excuse me," said Joi, raising her eye brows, "if you guys have the cray cray under control, I'll get back to interviewing my suspect." Without waiting for a response she said with a note of sass, "Thank you very much."

Joi returned to her interview. "Sorry for the commotion. A mentally ill prisoner got outta control. I don't want to take up much more of your time; I know you have to get to work today. This will just be a little longer, okay?"

"Yeah, I'm good for time," replied Marcus, who shifted in his seat, probably thinking about the melee in the hallway.

Joi stood and walked over to the mirror, turning so that Russell was at her back. "So let me see if I have it straight. On the night of August 13th, you *were* with your father?"

"Yes."

"You didn't see your mother?"

Marcus folded his arms across his muscular chest. "No."

"When you left your dad, what was he doing?"

"Sitting at his desk working on some papers."

"Was the parting pleasant?"

"No." She noted that his response was almost whispered. It made her raise her own voice. "Look Marcus, it's important for me to solve this case," she said after looking at him a few beats. "We don't have many homicides in South Holland. To be clearer, this is one of a handful this year, and it's on my watch. Do you get that?"

Marcus shifted under her hard glare. Joi took a deep breath and made her physique larger at the table.

"Every family has skeletons, Marcus. What are yours?"

"Detective, I don't have any skeletons in my closet," said Marcus unwrapping a candy stripped mint from his jacket pocket and popping it into his mouth.

Joi pressed, "Why did you move out of your home in high school?" Marcus glared at her from across the table, but was unresponsive.

"Mr. Gregg, I'm gonna need an answer."

"Where I lived or didn't live in high school is not your business!" replied an annoyed Marcus.

"Soo, since you and your mom got along well and it seems like you and your father had issues ..." She left it hanging for him to fill in the blank.

No response.

"Marcus, people are scared. Your father was killed in a gruesome way and you don't want to answer my questions. I want to schedule you for a polygraph test."

Marcus jerked forward. "What? A lie detector test?"

"Marcus I don't doubt your recollection of the events," Joi countered smoothly. "Let's just say I want to be able to say conclusively that I believe your statement. After all, you were, as far as we can determine, the last person to see your father alive."

"Besides his killer," Marcus interjected.

Joi's eyebrow raised again, and she almost smiled. "Yes, of course. So the test?"

"No test, dammit!" he said, his light brown eyes flashing with anger. "I didn't kill him and that's that, Detective."

"Mr. Gregg." Joi glanced outside the window, distracted by the sound of a car screeching in the distance. "Taking the test would show your support for our efforts to catch your father's killer and bring him *or her* to justice. At this point, it's a request."

Marcus leaned back in the wooden school room chair, balancing it on two legs. "Look Detective, I won't be railroaded because you people can't do your jobs. Find the old man's killer!"

"Simmer down, Mr. Gregg," she said, waving him back to the floor. "Be assured, I am *on my* job and doing it damn well. I will bring the killer to justice—no matter who it is. You got that?" She reached for her burning cigarette and took a slow drag, blowing the smoke across the table, visibly intoxicating him.

"Stay in town *and* stay available," she said, her glaring dark brown eyes meeting his. "I'll need to speak with you again. Soon."

She rose, leaving the butt burning in the ashtray. "Oh, one last thing. Did your father have any personal enemies, perhaps a disgruntled customer, business associate or even … a lover that you are aware of?" Joi let that linger in the air.

"My father and mother were happily married," said Marcus, sliding his chair from under the table. "Look, I'm outta here. You know where to reach me."

"No doubt."

CHAPTER 22

SUNDAY, MAY 16, 2004

Joi reached into the jacket of her navy blue blazer and lit up another cigarette. Taking a long pull, she turned to the window that looked out on the parking lot below. Marcus emerged from the front entrance, walked to the middle row of cars, got into a black 4x4 and pulled out of the lot like a fire had been lit under his ass.

She lit another cigarette and took a drag, savoring its mentholated coolness in her mouth.

Russell came in and sat at the chair that had to be still warm from Marcus' behind.

"What you think?" he asked, tracing the scratches on his side of the table with an overgrown fingernail.

"You heard me when I asked him about daddy having a personal enemy or former lover."

"Yeah, and he purposely chose to harp on the parents being"—Russell used his forefingers to make quotes—"happily married."

"He knows more than he's telling and based on the attitude he showed me, he could have killed his father."

She returned to her cluttered desk and reflected on her interview with Marcus Gregg. Why hadn't Marcus and his mother exchanged greetings on the evening of the murder? Even so, how did she not know he was in the home? That stuck her as whack. And what the hell would make Marcus refuse the polygraph test—that is if he had nothing to hide? She thought it had been wise on his part to admit seeing his father on that night. Especially since a bloody paw print was the calling card he smacked on the glass door to the garden. If he was stoked, she guessed he didn't remember touching the glass doors on the way in or out.

Damn! She said aloud, remembering that she hadn't asked Marcus exactly how he got into the house that night. Did he have a key to his parent's home? In some families, not hers, the kids have a door key even after they move into their own apartments. She considered leaving a message on his answering machine.

A better tactic would be to pay him a friendly visit, but not now. She had tossed and turned the past couple of nights and today she felt like a sleep-deprived zombie. She'd use the time lapse between his original answers and her next questioning session to her advantage. Hopefully catch him in a lie. She was pretty good at reading body language. The way his eyes shifted would tell all. Training and experience had taught her that liars tend to gaze off to the left. And because he hadn't done that when she asked about the last time he saw his dad, she had a hunch that despite looking guilty as hell, he might not be the killer. But dammit, he knew something. And that something could lead to the real killer. Who was Marcus Gregg protecting?

The forensic lab had specimens backed up the wazoo. She could grow a beard waiting for the analysis on all the material from the Gregg crime scene. There could have been more biologic material at the scene other than that belonging to Dennis Gregg and Marcus.

Had the killer known that the wife was loopy on pain meds and would miss the sound of her husband's brain being blown to bits? It had been over a week since the murder, and the disturbing reality was that only between thirty-to-forty percent of homicides were ever solved. Joi didn't want the killer to get too comfortable; but damn the trail was getting cold.

Joi considered herself a good dick and often took her cases to bed with her. She literally found her brain was fresher and more generative in bed after a short nap or a quickie.

The detective shorted her cigarette in an amber blown glass candy dish shaped like Africa and mentally accessed the Gregg file folder in her desk drawer, combing for answers. She couldn't bear the thought of looking into the dimming eyes of Nancy Gregg and telling her that her husband's case could be one of the 60 percent of unsolved homicides. This killer wasn't going to get away with killing a good man.

The least she could do was to give his widow that comfort before she died.

CHAPTER 23

Joi trained her focus on Kelly Gregg, who appeared to be waiting patiently in the side section of the South Holland Police Station cafeteria. She appeared poised as she brushed her short, springy brown hair away from her eyes and checked her cell phone, possibly turning off the ringer so as not to be disturbed during their interview. Chad sure had diverse tastes in women. There was absolutely no similarity between her and Kelly. Kelly was a thin waif, akin to filet of sole, and Joi was thick and juicy like prime rib. Kelly was an ice princess that expected her man to be a fixer, and Joi had been practically raised with wolves. Chad knew how to play rough and rowdy in bed but Kelly seemed to have ol' boy pussy whipped. There was no understanding men.

I bed the ones I want and keep my heart for my goddamn self. That was Joi's motto.

Once Joi's eyes met Kelly's, she detected a wounded look that she hadn't noticed before. Her suspect was uncomfortable. Joi maneuvered over to the stainless steel coffee cart and filled two beige ceramic cups with bubbling hot coffee. She placed them on a small black plastic tray and walked them over. Chalk it up to a combination of PMS and wanting Kelly and Marcus to have radically different experiences. When they compared notes, she wanted *them* to know that she had treated them differently and to wonder why.

As she reached the table and set down the Formica tray, Kelly smiled tentatively. For a moment, Joi felt a stab of jealousy kick in. This woman was beautiful without effort, whereas Joi had to apply mascara to make her thin lashes visible, have her locks re-twisted every couple of weeks and, according to her laundry count, rely on roughly fifteen pairs of Spanx in a variety of leg lengths and waist heights to hold her curvy silhouette together. It annoyed the hell out of her that some women were, as her Aunt Lorena used to say, "first-thing-in-the-morning pretty."

"Glad you could get away," Joi said, stretching herself to sound courteous. "I figured that would be more convenient than my coming to the bank."

"Yes, that would have embarrassed me."

I give less than a damn about your embarrassment, the voice whispered inside Joi's head. Quickly brushing her feelings aside, she thought fleetingly about Chad, he had hooked up with a high maintenance chick and now he was all twisted up in the game. But that wasn't her issue. She had a murder to solve.

"How's your mom?" Joi asked, offering sincere compassion, "I heard about the cancer."

Kelly appeared to bristle but Joi thought she saw her decide to be matter-of-fact. "Oh ... you did? She's alright, I guess. They'd been together a long time"

"Good marriage?"

Kelly paused for a moment, then shrugged. "I guess so. Daddy was always there for us, and they raised us in the church, which was the biggest part of my parents' life."

Joi noted a bit of attitude in the comment about church being the biggest part of their lives. Evidentially Kelly didn't necessarily like being a church girl. Well, now the women had two things in common; that and Chad.

As each woman went about the mechanics of preparing their coffee, Joi noticed that Kelly weakened hers with three hazelnut creams, no sugar.

"Kelly, when was the last time you saw your dad ... alive?" Joi asked, stirring three packets of sugar, no cream, into her own coffee. She thought she heard the tumblers in this chick's brain turning, perhaps harkening back to an unpleasant memory. Experience had taught her that good memories tended to roll off a suspect's tongue. It's the memories that you think might earn you an orange jumpsuit, with the "County" designer label, that you tend to filter.

"I had my parents over for Sunday brunch after church, a few weeks before ..."

Joi knew how the sentence ended.

"I had no contact with him after that."

Kelly shifted her body in the cafeteria's metal chair. Joi knew the feeling; there was too little padding in these seats. Kelly's gaze darted between the coffee cart and the ladies bathroom sign before she answered. "Of course I talked with my mom weekly, and since she's been sick, much more. But before daddy was ... murdered ... I hadn't seen him."

Kelly lowered her eyes in a way that Joi read as her not wanting to talk about her father's murder. But at the same time, the little birdie, or what church folks called "the still small voice", told her that there was a lot unsaid beneath Kelly Gregg's placid surface. More than the girl with the baby doll hazel eyes wanted to share.

Taking a swallow of the hot coffee, Joi paused. Holding her cup mid-air she said, "Well, Kelly *before* ... uh, this happened ... did you visit often?"

"I didn't visit them at their house a lot. Mom used to meet me downtown for lunch during the week and sometimes we shopped." Kelly's oval shaped face lit up with a smile. "My mother loves to shop."

Joi narrowed a gaze at Kelly, asking, "Any particular reason you didn't see your father much?"

Kelly blinked several times. "No, I just have more in common with my mom. You know, girl talk."

Joi smirked, mentally conjuring up the improbability of engaging in girl talk with her own mother. Frankly, there was a lot about her mom that she preferred not to know.

"Kelly, do you know of a reason why anyone would want to harm your father?" She sat close and stared directly into Kelly's eyes. "And before you answer," she pointed her coffee stirrer in the woman's direction, "I need you to give this some real thought."

She loved to ask that question. Most people, even if it was just in anger, have an answer ready, even if they're not ready to divulge it. She loved to watch people squirm, deciding whether to respond to the question truthfully or counter with another question.

"Why would you ask me that?" Kelly challenged, taking a sip of her coffee and replacing it on the table.

"Kelly, not all murders start out as a murder. Sometimes things spiral out of control and turn into murder." Joi leaned forward, taking another sip of the strong coffee. "Know what I mean?"

"Are you saying that murder can be an accident?"

"Look, this is not your first time around the block. You're a smart woman, even when you try to hide it. If you have an answer, I want it." Joi was annoyed at herself for pulling off the cloak of vulnerability the girl tried to operate out of, but daylight was burning.

"This is a murder case, Miss Gregg, and someone had a reason for wanting your daddy dead."

She let those words float mid-air for several beats.

"Again, I'm asking, do you know of anyone who had a grievance with your father, anyone he had argued with lately?"

"No," came the terse response. "Maybe it was a robbery. My father was a counselor for our church. He got along with everybody. Any disagreement would have been minor, not something someone would kill him over, *Detective*."

Joi kept her focus on the woman, inwardly thinking, "Oooh, the bitch has a bite!"

"Miss Gregg, one of the things I'm concerned about is the fact that your father was *not robbed*. He had a few hundred dollars in his wallet, a bankcard and a stack of credit cards. His very expensive watch was still on his wrist. Somehow, Miss Gregg, I suspect that whoever killed your father knew him." she locked gazes with her. "Perhaps even loved him."

"Loved him? That is absurd! How could someone *love* my father and kill him in cold blood?"

Joi gave her a patronizing smile. "Oh yeah, love is often complicated. Love can easily turn to hate. My gut says someone who loved your father killed him. But as a matter of law, we'll just need to follow where the evidence will unquestionably lead us. Then we'll know who killed your father."

Kelly's shoulders slumped as if taking a blow. "I get your point Detective."

Joi made a mental note to dig a little further into Kelly Gregg's history. And while she was at it, Chad Sanders' background too.

CHAPTER 24

The little girl's tiny frame is dented from the weight atop her. She struggles to breathe, freeing her pinned arm from the prickling of a thousand tiny needles. As her pink pajama bottoms are removed, in her mind she escapes the warm pain spreading throughout her loins and quietly slips away from the weight and the wetness.

Pink satin ribbons choke their braids. Their thick bangs tangle with the cold wind. Small girls are outside in November without a coat, but they are not cold. She holds Polly's hand as they glide laughing like fools down the long corridor of silver. Whooosssh! She braces herself for the landing. Plop! They lay in the damp sand staring into the face of the sun. It is brilliant: a sizzling yellow, orange and red. Polly embraces her, kissing both her cheeks. Nestled in each other's arms they sleep.

She cracks her eyelids just as the Monster breathes fear and fire on her. It grunts, slumps over on its side and is still. Then as silently as it had come, it stands and tucks her under the pink chenille spread that covers her bunk. The door cracks and the stream of light that permitted the Monster entry sweeps it out again. Her bed is wet and slimy as she and Polly slip down to the hardwood floor and hold each other. Polly keeps her safe on the floor, away from the poisonous bedding. On the upper bunk, a little boy sleeps.

❖ ❖ ❖

Kelly Gregg awakened sweat soaked and emotionally limp. That nightmare never left. Like a car's engine at a stop light, the darkness idled in the background of her life, resurfacing to painfully remind her of her brokenness.

She swaddled herself inside the soft pink comforter reflecting on her last attempt to get her parents to tell the truth. Her truth. Trish Snowden her therapist has said that as a family, if they could admit to the truth, they could possibly work through it.

Kelly had certainly set the stage; a spotless apartment, a delicious meal and elegant table setting that her mother would approve of. The lyrics of a popular gospel song rang true. "After you've done all you can, you just stand."

Much had changed in the months since the May brunch disaster. It had been exactly two o'clock p.m. when she had hugged and kissed Polly, her well-worn rag doll, and replaced her carefully on the satin pillow.

Her hands had trembled as she had opened the door to greet her parents. Time stopped. She had inhaled and exhaled deeply, listening to the muffled sounds of her parents' shoes as they exited the elevator and strolled innocently down the carpeted hallway towards her apartment. She smoothed her rust-colored wrap skirt and matching tee-shirt. Barefoot as usual, her feet, with their expertly groomed tangerine colored toenails, gripped the floor.

Chad was her anchor. She had given him permission to be her witness. She visualized him sitting on the couch were he would be her reference point. If she ever doubted she was doing the right thing, she could close her eyes and feel his warmth. She felt ready when her parents reached her apartment door.

Trish's words echoed again. "If they can admit to the truth, then you can face the truth together."

CHAPTER 25

Kelly peered out of the window at the parking lot below. Residents exited the mixed income high-rise and entered the driveway in search of their cars on foot. There was no movement from the elm trees that graced the perimeter of the building. It was warm for May. She looked forward to warm summer days when she could run along the lake. Today would be a new beginning.

The gentle knocking on her door signaled that her parents had gotten the elevator to the eleventh floor quickly. She took a deep cleansing breath, and smoothed her hair.

Kelly opened the door of her apartment and hugged her mother, reveling in the spicy, woodsy scent of her signature Donna Karan perfume. Her father, as usual, smelled of Old Spice Cologne, a scent that always turned her stomach.

"Hi, Mom, Dad," she said, infusing cheerfulness into her tone. "How was the service?"

Nancy pushed up the sleeves on her baby blue knit suit, revealing a lovely pearl charm bracelet that matched the single strand of pearls that accented the neckline of her dress. Her hand lingered on her neckline. "You know, Reverend Richards preached for Bishop this Sunday," she said. "I think Bishop Pate's planning to retire one of these days and preparing the young man to take over.

"The boy is *real* good," said her father stepping into the living room, removing his suit jacket and laying it across the back of an empty chair. "He's young, but he has an anointing on him. He can really preach the Word. Saints know when the Holy Spirit lights a fire under him we are going to have *church!"*

"This morning he tore it up," cosigned her breathless mother.

Did just the walk down the hallway cause her to pant?"

"Umm, I'm glad you both enjoyed service," Kelly said, feigning interest while filling a carafe with cold water from the fridge.

"Kelly, won't you at least visit one Sunday?"

"I will Dad, soon," she lied, avoiding direct eye contact. "Listen, if you want to wash your hands first." She motioned toward the bathroom. "Everything's ready."

Nancy gestured towards the beautiful table setting and the array of tempting serving platters arranged on the credenza. "This is so elegant Kelly." She smiled. "I am really impressed."

"That's the plan." Kelly smiled nervously, but she noticed that her mother's steps were slower, almost cautious as though each one was measured. Or painful. Painful is what came to mind. She would ask her mother about it the next time they were alone.

"You two keep on talking," Dennis Gregg's gruff voice intoned as he swept a gaze over the breakfast spread. "My hands are already clean and I'm going to get to work here."

"You go right ahead, Dear," Nancy said with a chuckle. "*I'm* going to wash my hands."

When Nancy returned to join her husband, he was still deliberating over the appetizing buffet arranged on the credenza that ordinarily held Kelly's precious collection of giraffes. Today they grazed in silent vigil on the straw mat under the credenza. Growing up "a Gregg" made it taboo to serve guests on paper or Styrofoam dishes. Even when the family picnicked, Nancy Gregg packed a colorful set of melamine dishes and managed to scrape and rinse them before leaving the picnic grounds.

Kelly took pains not to detract from her delectable brunch with a sloppy table setting. The lemon yellow, crisply starched and carefully ironed linen tablecloth was a perfect background for complementary place settings.

The buffet was set with three perfectly grilled salmon steaks, hash brown potatoes, fried corn with tomatoes, red and green bell peppers, an a salad of razor-thin cucumber slices, kidney beans and cilantro in honey and lemon marinade. A basket of hot buttered corn muffins and Lipton iced tea completed the spread.

Kelly's mother smiled proudly as she moved gracefully, but still cautiously, toward the table—as if it required some effort. "Dear, this is impressive. Everything looks so appetizing. I feel like I could eat a bear!"

"Then you'll be a *woman of substance* for sure," he said. The look passing between them signaled Kelly that maybe her mom was on another diet. "Everything does look great, Baby. You took your homemaking skills from your mother for sure."

"Thank you, Daddy. Will you bless the food?"

The family bowed their heads reverently while Elder Dennis Gregg blessed the food with an elaborate blessing worthy of a minister. For all of fifteen minutes, the room was filled with an eerie, superficial calm as the Gregg family savored the food and bantered about the not-so-special things that bound them together.

Kelly fueled the lie that she was contented with her job as a graphic designer at Citibank, then asked her father, "How's the business coming? Mom told me you hired two more guys."

"Business is pretty good now. I replaced the software developer I lost to Aigner Consulting last month, and the nut I fired for switching the manufacturer's parts for generic ones and pocketing the money. If it would've been, as you kids say, 'back in the day,' I'd have beat his ass and fired him, but I didn't want him suing me so I just dumped his thieving ass."

Nancy placed a fluttering hand over her heart. "Dennis, for Christ sakes, we just left."

"Excuse my language."

Kelly shrugged. "Well, you handled it the way you had to, I suppose."

Nancy prattled on about organizing the benefit gala committee for the local chapter of the United Negro College Fund and her dismay over the sheer volume of calls needed to get commitments for valuable and unique donations for their Silent Auction.

"Sweetie, I can't tell you how many incredible young people receive funding through UNCF donations."

The brunch crawled along a slow and predictable path as Kelly's gut boiled.

"Seen Marcus lately, Kelly?" Dennis asked.

"Oh, I talked to him last week, Daddy. He's fine. He was just back from Santa Fe buying silver with Milagros."

"Milagros? Who the heck is—?"

"That's his girlfriend," Nancy explained, then fell silent when Dennis gave her a pointed look. He never liked any reminder that Marcus kept in touch with his mother but still had nothing to say to Dennis himself.

"He's painting again," Kelly said, trying to bring the mood back to a lighter point. "In fact *that's* his," she said, pointing a tangerine lacquered nail toward the sunny landscape depicting a woman sitting on a bench in a Chinese garden with a crown of butterflies circling her head.

Nancy rose from the table and ran her fingers over the framed canvas. "It's magnificent. Not one of those awful grim pictures he usually paints. And I don't feel that typical Spanish influence here. The details on the flowers in the garden are absolutely exquisite!"

"I know!" exclaimed Kelly, brushing back stray hairs across her forehead. "He is still seeing Milagros, Mother, so he does have an affinity for Spain."

"That girl is Mexican, not from Spain. And I don't know why ..."

"Never mind, Mother." Kelly wasn't ready to stomach another comment about Marcus choosing outside of his race. She pulled the discussion back to art. "He gave me this lovely garden scene. I bought the only other bright painting he had in his studio as a wedding gift for my friend, Lisette."

Her father did not rise, nor did he acknowledge the painting in any way. A smiling Nancy soon returned to her seat across from her husband.

"Mother, Marc *said* that *you* would notice the detail on the flowers. He's so gifted," she gushed, glancing over at her father, who made no comment.

Kelly wished, on all she held sacred, that she could simply savor the meal and relish spending time with her parents. The weight of her real mission was oppressive. A painful lump rose in her throat, threatening to choke her. Her temples pounded. She pushed back her bangs and felt moisture oozing around her hairline. Desperately, she searched her special corner and was relieved when an imaginary Chad egged her on from his seat of reverence.

'Now Kelly', she heard him shout. 'Tell them now!'

"Mother, and Dad," she blurted. "I asked you over ... wanted to talk to you both because I've been seeing someone ... a doctor. Actually, I've been seeing a therapist because I'm having problems."

Dennis Gregg slowed his eating and glanced up at her. Kelly noticed his face absorbing her words like a sponge, then becoming a stony mask. She tensed.

"What kind of problems?" said her mother, furrows of concern rippling across her forehead.

Her father continued eating, chewing slowly, deliberately, as though waiting for a clap of thunder. Kelly watched his jaw tense then tighten. Kelly sat in silence, too conflicted to get to the heart of what she needed to say because there was no easy lead-in. She glanced again at Chad, who shouted again, *'Now Kelly!'*

Her words burst out as she simultaneously pointed an accusing finger. "Daddy, I have suffered so much because of what you did ... and I ... I just need to know why, why did you do that to me? I was your baby girl!"

The rest of Kelly's words lodged tightly in her throat. Her eyes flooded with tears. "You molested me. You hurt me. Your own flesh and blood."

Her father's eyes seared hers as he instantly pushed back from his plate.

Before he could utter a word, her crimson-faced mother yelled, "How *could* you say something awful like that to your father? He would never do such a thing."

Kelly, choking on her disclosure, moved her lips but no sound escaped. Suddenly she thrust her body to a standing position with enough force to mercifully release her vocal chords.

"Enough!" Kelly snapped. "Don't take up for him, Mother! I'm talking to daddy now." She narrowed her focus on the man across from her, his anger evident in the throbbing vein of his temple. "Daddy, *why? I-am-your-daughter!* I knew it *would never end* unless I went away, would it have, Daddy?" she rambled. "I went far away to college, even though that was never my plan. I wanted to stay here, to study at the Art Institute. *That* was my dream, the Art Institute. Not being all dressed up in heels and fancy clothes at Spelman College."

She brushed a hand across her face to remove another barrage of tears. "I was so alone at Spelman College. All these years, you had Mother. I had no one! Even in high school, I had no one because of *YOU!!"*

Kelly was trembling now as tears streamed down her cheeks and lapped under her chin. For a heartbeat, she imagined her father's eyes softening; that he would own up to what he had done; that it would all be out in the open so she could begin to heal.

But when Dennis Gregg opened his mouth to speak, his lip curled like the predator he was. Inwardly, she begin to shrink. Even with the presence of her mother across the table, Kelly was transported back to those times. She was a little girl alone with the Monster again. She frantically searched for Chad, only now her mother was blocking her view.

"Shut up, girl!" he snarled. "You just had to bring something up to spoil everything. Couldn't even have us to supper without dredging up the past. The past is gone. Let it die, Kelly! What I did, I did."

"What?" Kelly shouted, shaking her hand at him. "You crazy man."

"I've humbled myself to my Maker," he shot back. "I don't have to explain anything to you!!! You are my daughter. Stay in a child's place. I took good care of you. You never wanted for anything, did you? You should be glad you never got messed up by those good-for-nothings that tried to come around. I protected you!" he said, shaking a thick finger at Kelly.

Dennis Gregg jerked himself to his feet and escaped into the bathroom, slamming the door.

"Protected me!!!!" Kelly looked over at her mother, then to the apartment's floor-to-ceiling windows, wishing with all her heart that she could fly.

"Mother! Did you hear what your husband said? He hurt *me* and that's his comment, *he saved me from boys my age ...* he *protected me!"*

Nancy Gregg looked straight through Kelly, then opened her mouth to speak, her voice shaking with emotion. "Why did you bring all that old stuff up? Why can't you just let the past be done and gone?" Nancy walked toward the window. As if in an afterthought, she shouted in desperation, "You have a good life now. Chad's a fine man. Think about your future, girl! We struggled to keep this family together."

Finally she said in a tone that was pitiable, "Kelly, regardless to what you think of us, some people envy us."

Kelly was too stunned to reply.

Nancy turned her back on the lake view and walked back toward the buffet.

She began to weep, wiping her tears with a white embroidered handkerchief retrieved from her dress pocket. "Your friends always admired our home and the advantages we gave you and Marcus, Kel—"

At that moment, to Kelly Gregg, her mother, the woman she had trusted to protect her, now resembled a disembodied soul, not a flesh and blood woman, not a loving mother.

"No, Mother," Kelly said slowly, pinning a gaze on the woman who was fingering her pearls as though they were rosary beads. *"You are crazy*!!! No amount of pancakes, strawberry preserves, and link sausages made up for the fact that my Daddy raped me and raped me over and over again and again."

Nancy closed her eyes to shut out the truth that was being crammed down her throat.

"He poisoned me with his sickness and you have the nerve to stand here acting like I'm out of order for insisting that we face this! Face what happened to ME!" Kelly screamed, pointing to her chest. "Are *you* ashamed?

"Please stop, Kelly," said Nancy putting a finger to her lips—a childish gesture if Kelly had ever seen one.

But before her mother could speak again, Kelly found the strength to say, "Oh hell no. No, don't you dare try to shush me, Mother. I'll scream it! I don't *care* who knows it because you can't hide it anymore!"

Dennis Gregg emerged from the bathroom, having apparently washed his hands of the goings on.

Kelly spun around and found herself standing in her father's face, her legs akimbo and hands on her slim hips. "You are a sick person!" she said. "You are the reason that I can't even be a real woman with the man I love. You took that away from me and she helped you."

Suddenly calmness washed over Kelly as she turned and trained her gaze on her tormenter. Tears burned in her eyes as they brimmed over her lids and spilled down. "Maybe you and Mother can forget, but I don't have the luxury of forgetting, I live with this … this mess!" For an instant she thought she saw a light flickering in her father's eyes. Then they clouded over as her mother shrieked "And you think we don't?!! Is that what you think, Kelly??!"

"I think you married a monster and just stood by and let him rape me. That makes you a monster, too."

Nancy raised her right hand to strike Kelly and suddenly aborted the effort mid-air.

Dennis Gregg made a beeline for the door. Tethered by an invisible cord, Nancy Gregg moved in lockstep with her husband.

Kelly stealthily crossed the living room, and clutched the neck of her largest giraffe, a heavy ceramic figure about eighteen inches tall, forcefully throwing it towards the door a split second after it closed. The pottery fragments shattered across the room. The collision left a nick in the paint of the tan metal door. She reached for and hurled the treasured giraffes one after the other until their broken remains lay scattered beneath the scarred door.

Flinging herself onto the couch, right in the position that her spiritual Chad once held, she curled into a fetal position, clutching Polly, the beloved rag doll in her arms.

If it's the last thing I ever do in my life, my father will look me in my face and apologize. No matter what it takes.

CHAPTER 26

Pulling into a parking space at the South Holland police station wasn't something Marcus wanted to make a habit of. He hadn't been officially named a person of interest—at least not yet. But this was the second time he was being interviewed and he was starting to feel that he was being considered a suspect.

The fact that he and the old man had fought bitterly the night his father was murdered was never far from his mind. The irony of him stepping to the old man in Corey's defense was also not lost on him. Maybe helping Corey *was* his destiny.

Marcus struggled to control his demeanor. The cops didn't always seem to care that the right person was prosecuted, just that somebody was, and he sure as hell didn't want to be a scapegoat.

Shit, I could be locked up for keeps!

His head pounded as he realized that he desperately needed to get a lawyer if today's 'routine conversation' didn't completely exonerate him as a person of interest.

Marcus wondered if that chick, detective Sommers, had new evidence.

There had to be a damn good reason for her to call him to come less than twenty-four hours since she had questioned him.

Detective Joi Sommers entered the small, dank smelling room with a manila folder and a small black notebook in hand. She pulled out one of the mis-matched wooden chairs and plopped herself down harder than he thought was appropriate for a woman.

His heart thumped wildly inside his chest as he pulled a cigarette from the smashed package in the breast pocket of his jacket and struck the match.

"How was work?"

"Well, when it rains, like last night," he said, with a look out the window at the overcast sky, "we're scrambling to reconnect downed phone lines before the morning when customers wake up upset over outages." He rubbed one boot-clad foot across the other. "My feet are killin' me from standing on the rungs of my ladder. I'm beat and I may get paged to go right back to work in a few hours. But you didn't call to talk about my problems."

Joi's lips curved into a smile. "Look, I'll make this quick so you can go get some sleep."

"Appreciate it," Marcus replied, careful to keep his attitude in check.

"Tell me again about the last time you saw your father alive, Marcus."

Russell entered the room with a small tray that held three cups of coffee, stirrers and a paper cup with packets of sugar and powdered non-dairy creamer. He set a cup first before Joi and then Marcus, taking the last cup for himself.

"This is my partner," she said with a nod toward the statuesque, athletically built man sitting beside her. "Detective Russell Wilkerson."

Marcus nodded.

"I went to see my father because we've been out of touch for quite some time. He was controlling and I'm a grown ass man. I kept my distance."

Russell looked him square in the face, tilting his head to the right and said, "Let's get at the truth, buddy".

"No special reason," he said, shrugging. "Well he does—did—a lot of counseling with the church folks. I thought with Friday being the end of the week, he wouldn't be so busy."

"Was he?"

"Nope, he was alone in his study."

Joi rose and crossed the room, nonchalantly looking out the window and into the parking lot below. "And?"

"And we talked."

She remained silent.

"My father has …" Marcus closed his eyes for a moment and when he opened them, he continued with, "He had this incredible way of glossing over the most important things to people. Nothing was resolved but at least I tried," he whispered. "At least I tried."

Russell stated, "Bet he made you damn mad."

Marcus hesitated a brief second as he shifted his gaze to Joi. He replied off-handedly, "As usual."

"And what did you do when he got you pissed off?" Shot Joi abruptly.

"Detective, we both lost our tempers."

"You don't say," Joi pressed.

"Yeah, but I didn't kill him!" he shouted, finally losing grip of his tenuous self-control. "I wanted to, at least in that moment, but I just picked myself up and left."

Joi and Russell shared a knowing glance before looking back at Marcus. "So there was a struggle?"

"We scrapped, yes."

"Who knew? Did your mother know about the altercation?

"I doubt it," he said in a low tone. "I remember yelling hello to her when I came in. She never answered. If she knew I was home, she would've come down."

Russell toyed with the coffee stirrer in his cup, raised his heavy brows and looked directly at Marcus. "So, Marcus, you and your father had a fight and your father is murdered the same night."

"I know this looks bad, Detective," Marcus countered shakily. "That's why I didn't say that we argued the first time you had me come in. All I can do now is tell you the truth. I could've tried to continue to lie, or run away," said Marcus, exasperated. "Clearly, I didn't like my father. He was a controlling bastard. But I did not kill him. *Understand. I did not kill him!*"

"Then I'm going to ask you again, do you know of anyone else that would want your dad dead?"

"No! Like I keep sayin', the man was all up in his church," he spat.

Joi gave him a half-smile and cut her eyes. "And churchgoers don't kill?"

Marcus shot back an angry look, clinching the fingers of his right hand.

"Okay, Mr. Gregg," Russell said roughly. "You go on home now. We have your um …" He looked at Joi before adding, "revised statement. Don't leave town."

"Oh, and Mr. Gregg, if I were you, I'd hire a lawyer," Joi advised.

Marcus looked at her vacuously and exited, leaving the door ajar behind him.

Russell looked at her. "Joi, did you notice the ring?"

"Sure did. I bet the missing stone is the one I dug out of what was left of his daddy's cheek."

CHAPTER 27

Joi drove from South Holland to the Cook County Medical Examiner's Office. Thursdays were slow. Devin Bandur, the hot Irish pathologist, was usually willing to take time to talk with her about her cases. She opened the door to the lab and as usual was grossed out. She pushed open the heavy grey metal door only to have Devin spin around to display thick speckles of blood peppering the front of his white coat He looked more like a butcher than a medical professional.

"Hey Devin, do you ever change your coat? Or should I call ahead to let you know that company is coming?" She smiled sarcastically.

"Me darlin', the bloodstains on me coat are like paint on an artist's smock, part of the creative process."

"Uh huh. Dev, I'm on a mission. Ya got a minute?"

"Anythin' for you, me darlin'," he said, thickening his Irish brogue as his eyes devoured the length of Joi's curvy brown legs exposed by her steel grey skirt suit.

"You know I got a make on your bullet this morning," he said, rifling through a small stack on his desk and holding up a small plastic zip-locked baggy with two spent bullets inside. "They come from a 38 Glock automatic. The first bullet entered and lodged in the back of the head, a few centimeters above the neck."

"Oh, yeah!" Joi took the clear plastic evidence bag containing the bullets removed from Dennis Gregg's head and held them up to the light.

Devin sighed. "You know, what beats me is why the perp flipped the victim over like a pancake and fired again at point blank range. Now that's pissed off."

With a beige cotton sheet, he covered a body that was cut open from the neck to just above the belly button. "Got a feeling you'll be able to find who owns this gun pretty easily."

"Yeah, looks like this is going to hit pretty close to home."

"Did ya ever find out about that stone you found embedded in the victim's jaw?"

"Actually, I didn't want to overplay my hand, but we interviewed the son a second time and I noticed a stone missing from the ring he was wearing today." Joi looked around the room to the shelves loaded with jars of tissue samples suspended in containment fluid. Jars containing body parts involved in some kind of testing. She would rather face dead bodies every day than live in the world that saw people only as their dismembered parts. "He probably hasn't even noticed it's out."

"I s'pose," he replied.

"Right now, he's looking pretty good as a person of interest." Having an ID on the murder weapon was good, but Joi knew she needed the murder weapon in hand to tie a bow around this investigation. She wanted the shooter.

"Ya think?" the pathologist joked. He looked pensive before asking, "Hey Detective, you busy tonight? How about havin' a cocktail with me a little later?"

"Sorry, I'm seeing someone."

"I hope he's married," replied Devin spitefully.

"He is," came Joi's flippant response. She hadn't ever dated a white guy, but she was a sucker for Devin's dimples.

"I've got next. Me darlin'."

Joi kept walking, shaking her head as she exited. She closed the door quietly, pausing in the hallway to savor the silly look on Devin's face.

She rifled through her oversized leather handbag, trying to get to her cell phone. Coming up empty almost a minute later, she wished she had chosen a smaller purse. When she finally retrieved her cell, she speed dialed her partner.

"Russ, Devin says a 38 Glock was the murder weapon in the Gregg case. Send some officers over to the Gregg's with a metal detector. They need to go back over everything in that garden."

"I'll do my best," said Russell. "Rimmer is gonna be pissed off that we didn't—"

"Screw Rimmer. Our case, our rules."

"Like I said, I'll do my best. If I have a problem I'll let you know," responded Russell crisply.

As if to sell her urgent request for the combing of the Gregg backyard, she added, "I'm convinced that the killer ditched the weapon in the backyard. Especially have them go back over that hill of dirt for metal. I'm gonna take care of a few things while I'm downtown but I'll be back in a couple of hours."

She looked down at her feet, wishing she had not worn three-inch stilettos this morning and dreading the long walk from the Medical Examiner's office to the Michigan Avenue underground parking structure.

CHAPTER 28

Joi had dispatched crime scene technicians to carefully comb through the Gregg's lush backyard, armed with rakes, shovels and a metal detector. Anxious to get the report on what they had found, she postponed a call to check on her mother—a call she didn't really want to make anyway.

Christo Brouwer, a short beefy white detective she had asked to accompany the evidence technician to the Gregg yard, entered the office loosening his gray striped tie around his sweaty red neck.

"We didn't find a fuckin' thing in the backyard, Joi," he said dryly.

"Nothing?"

"Correction, we found a rusted combination gym lock, a broken rake head that had gotten buried over, but no goddamn gun. You can color this afternoon a fuckin' waste a time," smirked the potty mouthed Christo, showing a picket fence of coffee-stained teeth. "The killer must a taken it with him," he concluded.

"Or her … couldda been a woman," Joi remarked pointedly. A knot wedged in her stomach. She hated wasting time and she hated the glaring look Brouwer was showering her with.

So where is the goddamn gun? Joi shot Russell a pissed off look that she hoped signaled that they needed to be more aggressive with this case. Russell leaned back on his chair so that it balanced on two legs. His feet were propped up on the radiator and he unwrapped his regular afternoon snack, a Kit Kat candy bar. Pulling apart and inhaling two of the four chocolate covered wafers, he lowered his loafer-clad feet and spun his chair around, reaching for the black desk phone.

Russell spoke in between bites, "Look Joi, I'm pretty certain that if we search the son's home we're gonna find *something*. He swears that when he left, the old man was alive and yet, the diamond from his ring somehow got embedded in the old man's mug, they argued bitterly, his bloody fingerprints were on the glass sliding door, and his DNA all over the vic's body. All *that* says he's our killer."

Joi walked over to a large well-mounted dry erase white board where she listed her clues. She had printed the names, Marcus Gregg, Kelly Gregg, Chad Sanders and Nancy Gregg in that order. Picking up the green marker she drew a line through Nancy Gregg, but didn't erase her off the board. Turning to face Russell, who was savoring the last of his chocolate treat, she said,

"This will be our third time interviewing Marcus Gregg. He makes the most sense and unless the evidence or my intuition tells me something different, I'd say we will soon be arresting him for the cold blooded murder of Elder Dennis Gregg."

CHAPTER 29

Marcus awakened from a fitful sleep. His shoulders ached like hell from hauling his two-hundred-pound utility ladder on and off his SBC service vehicle. Despite the fact that he worked with a climbing belt and spent the better part of his day lashed to a telephone pole, Marcus never entrusted his full 185-pound frame to his harness. *No equipment is one hundred percent fool-proof.*

His biceps felt raw from hanging from twenty-eight feet and looking at a tangle of wires to detect what more often than not was one singed wire needing repair. After his ten-hour shift and a gaggle of onion-smothered White Castle burgers drowned with a thick vanilla shake, Marcus tumbled into his king sized sleigh-bed. He felt like he had been ridden hard and put away wet. When he finally exhaled the smoke curls from his last Newport it was three a.m.

Seconds later he was entangled in a nightmare, racing away from a demonic force that haunted his sleep. For years he had squashed his pain and now THAT muthafucka had resurfaced. Pissed at being robbed of the possibility of sound sleep, Marcus swung his legs across the bed's side. He stood shakily and grabbed a pair of soft black fleece sweats dangling from the handlebars of his ten speed bike. Stepping angrily inside them, he pulled a Chicago Bulls jersey bearing Luol Deng's number 9 over his wooly, black hair.

Shit.

After jamming his feet in his unlaced black Timberlands, he snatched up his black and grey gym bag, locked the front door and descended the eight steps to the front of his home two at a time. Seconds later, sliding behind the wheel of his 4x4, Marcus sped north on Parnell toward 103rd and west to I-57 at 99th. Eighteen minutes later he exited at 47th and headed for Bally's Fitness on 47th and Kimbark.

Initially he and Kelly had worked out together on the buddy plan, but because of his schedule, he rarely saw her in the gym. He worked swing shift and varied his gym times, but he preferred getting in at five a.m. If he missed more than a couple of days, his body craved a brutal, uninterrupted workout. He wanted to punish his muscles until his inner anguish surrendered to his outer pain. Maybe then he could sleep soundly.

❖ ❖ ❖

Marcus' mind transcended his drive to the gym as he remembered his fateful Walmart encounter with his mother's dearest friend. He rarely ever saw Ms. Mattie anymore. She'd been best friends with his mom for years. Nancy Gregg was the one person Ms. Mattie confided in about living with her boozing husband Emery. Running into her at Wal-Mart was a coincidence. They almost collided by the shaving cream. Marcus had just picked up a can of his favorite glycerin based shave cream, his beard was wiry and when he shaved in the shower, used a new razor and properly softened his beard and skin he managed to minimize the appearance of the dreaded razor bumps.

"Marcus, I thought that was you."

"Hey Ms. Mattie. How are you?"

"I'm well, and you?"

"I'm good. Just outta shaving cream."

Mattie sorted through several small electric shavers dangling from hooks.

"I can't figure out which to get Corey, *he* thinks he needs to shave but he really doesn't have much hair, just some fuzz under his chin," said Mattie, smiling and stroking her squarish chin with her thumb and fore finger in illustration.

"How is Corey?"

"He's just fine, growing up so fast."

"You might just want to get him some of this cream," he pointed, "but I'd go with a small electric shaver like this one," said Marcus, plucking one from the rack and handing it to Mattie.

"He's with your father you know?"

"Huh, with … *my* father?" Marcus whipped around, to face Mattie.

"Yes, Elder Gregg took him camping. Says camping will make a man out of him. They go sometimes twice a month …"

The rest of the conversation was a blur. It was happening again, only this time it wasn't him. It was happening to Corey. Marcus hadn't ended the conversation, he'd simply walked away, leaving Ms. Mattie standing in the aisle with the razors and shaving cream.

His face burned and he broke into a sweat. He wanted to wring his father's fuckin' neck. To twist and twist it in his hands until his neck snapped and to squeeze the warm skin until it turned cold and lifeless in his hands. For years he had carefully constructed a fortress around his pain, and in one instant, the unsuspecting Mattie had flung the door wide fuckin' open!

❖ ❖ ❖

Marcus pulled on a pair of thick padded red and black boxing gloves and slammed a combination of his right and left fists into the weight bag. Each flurry of blows jarred his forearms. Sweat poured down his chest, to his abs, soaking the band of his trunks.

His father had pretended to be 'healed." That muthafucka was active again!

❖ ❖ ❖

When he had first taken refuge at Scott's during their sophomore year of high school, Marcus would slip in once the parents turned in for the night, then he'd hide in his friend's bedroom, quietly sneaking out before dawn. One Monday morning as Marcus slowly opened the heavy wooden door, deftly turning the inside tumbler, Scott's father stepped into the hallway and surprised him attempting to carry out his predawn departure.

"Marc," he'd said. "When you come in from school this afternoon, your trunk will be in the spare bedroom. That's where you'll bunk from now on."

Marc's mouth was wide open when he heard, "See you at dinner." He never cared about the details of the arrangement, but his grades improved and he wasn't half-hungry all the time.

Ben Weathersby was a short, burly man of about one hundred sixty pounds. He parted his thick afro on the side in a futile attempt to tame it. His forehead was wide and creased and his bulging eyes were framed by thick coke bottle glasses. There was a slight limp in his gait. He told Marcus he battled arthritis from decades of working in the cold.

Ben Weathersby wasn't a big talker, he was a watcher. Something told him that Scott's dad knew more about him and his family than he let on.

To demonstrate his gratitude for the refuge with Scott's family, Marcus was polite and respectful, performing the few household chores he was given and enjoying his friendship with Scott. Before he knew it, he and Scott were in their senior year.

Scott Weathersby was planning to attend college at SIU. Marcus worried about his life as an adult. He vowed never to live under his father's roof again, but he didn't actually have a plan. The military or a men's shelter if need be but fate intervened in a most unexpected way.

One afternoon, Scott's dad picked them both up at school in his service vehicle. When he pulled up to the family's three bedroom colonial, both boys jumped out and he said, "Marcus, get back in the car. Take a ride with me."

The boy's suspicions were aroused. "Where?"

"In the car, boy. You'll see soon enough," Mr. Weathersby had responded sharply. As the car rolled out, he threw his hand over the steering wheel, looked over at Marcus and said, "Scott's going away to college this fall. With you just barely graduating, I figure you're gonna need a job to take care of yourself. If you can climb the pole, I can get you hired at SBC."

Marcus sat quietly as Scott's dad had pulled into an alley and parked alongside a telephone pole. He pulled out two blue and white hard hats and after twenty minutes of safety precautions he pulled the ladder off his truck and leaned it against the pole.

"You can do this, Marcus," said Scott's father firmly.

"What? Man, how do you know that? That pole is high," said Marcus, looking up the knotted wooden pole from where he hung twelve inches off the ground with spikes placed a foot apart. He felt his bowels loosen.

"Twenty-eight feet."

"I never said I wanted to be a telephone guy."

"Marcus, I see you drawing all the time and the pictures are good, but I can't see that putting food in your belly or a roof over your head. This will, but if you don't want—"

"Lemme try."

"It's up to you. Do you want to do something for yourself or let 'certain' people see you fail?"

Reflecting on the way he said those words gave Marcus the gumption he needed to scale the pole. With Ben's quiet insistence he mastered the pole, realizing that if he did exactly as he was told, taking one foot at a time, he could slowly get to the top.

Then came the day of the SBC field test. The trainer had given Marcus and four other guys their equipment and instructions. Marcus had strapped on the safety harness, attached the gaffs to his boots and scaled the pole like a pro—at least, he looked like a pro to someone that didn't know that he was so terrified he almost shit his pants. He knew he was in when two of the guys in his class had walked off during training.

His confident appearance on the climb made Marcus a standout. He started work as a full-time SBC line-technician two weeks after high school graduation.

He had quickly earned respect from the older techs because he was always on time and paid attention to details. He took every assignment, no matter how tough, without complaint and rose to top pay in four years. Mr. Weathersby had given him the best graduation gift ever—a lifeline.

CHAPTER 30

Kelly Gregg snuggled against her boyfriend as he navigated his white Escalade onto Lake Shore Drive. It had drained her to get dressed and downstairs for their double date with Lisette and Bryan. She would have much preferred escaping the sweltering humidity curled up on her couch gazing out at the lake. Perhaps an evening with friends would help her forget the police traipsing all over her parents' home.

Even the normally calming scenes of evening runners and bikers along the drive didn't ease her apprehensions about Detective Joi Sommers. How should she take her? One minute she seemed kind and sympathetic, and then came at her all hard and aggressive. She'd need to remember to be on guard from here on out.

"Chad, I'm afraid I'm not going to be such good company."

Chad momentarily took his eyes off the winding drive, trained his gaze on her and asked, "You sure you still want to go?"

"Probably not, but Lisette has called me three times to confirm. If we didn't go, there would be no peace."

He adjusted the knob on the air conditioning.

"I guessed as much, and it's probably good to get away from everything—not that you can forget." His voice trailed and he switched topics. "So how's your mom?"

"She's taking daddy's murder really hard. And she also seems oddly ashamed."

"Why would she be ashamed?"

Kelly didn't respond immediately. Instead she looked out the window and beyond. She felt a sudden chill and pulled the bright yellow shawl around her shoulders, "Mother has *always* been concerned with our image. She made a remark yesterday, that it doesn't look nice for me not to be living at the house now."

Kelly thought back to the brunch at her home and the havoc that had shattered her giraffe collection. Her mother never could face the ugly truth.

"Is that really unreasonable?" he asked in measured tones. "I mean, given that she's not used to being alone."

Kelly was silent, weighing her mother's side of things. "My father was an Elder and his church takes care of their own. She already has a live-in companion and the deacons are constantly in and out. I drop in almost daily and call her from work."

"Sounds like you are doing all you can."

"But not all she wants," Kelly said with a vigorous shake of her head. "I just can't live there. Period!" Her voice rose and she fought to recover her composure. The thought of sleeping in that place, being there longer than necessary, made her physically ill. That's why she had insisted on hosting the brunch for her parents at her apartment back in May.

"Ease up on yourself, Babe," said Chad. You have a right to privacy. You're grieving, too." He reached his hand across the seat to engulf hers with a stabilizing squeeze.

They rode in silence for a bit longer, exiting the Drive at the Museum of Science and Industry and taking Hayes Drive.

"The detective assigned to daddy's murder is a woman."

"Seriously?" Chad said, with a lift of his eyebrow. "I guess I never thought of females as homicide detectives. Seems like they're a better fit in juvenile work or sex crimes. Women and dead bodies don't mix."

Kelly shot him a glance and responded defensively, "How did you come to that conclusion?"

"Babe, I didn't mean to—"

"She's actually very thorough, but the way she asks questions about Marc and me crosses the line. She needs to be looking for our father's murderer instead of hounding the family!"

"I agree. What's her deal?"

"I'm fed up with police!" she snapped. "It's time for them to get what they need and stop pawing around my parents' home." She lowered her voice to a mocking masculine pitch, "Or as they say, 'the crime scene'."

Chad smiled, edging the truck into a right turn. "At least you can joke about it. That's a good sign. Speaking of Marcus, how is he?"

"Stubborn," she said, remembering the last conversation they were able to have. "He has refused to call the detective back. He said they need to do their, and I'm quoting, 'damn job and leave him the hell alone'."

"You need to talk to him," Chad said, giving her a sideways glance. "That's not gonna be a good strategy. The more he evades her, the more she'll think he has something to hide."

"I know. She's so annoying, though," Kelly said, shuddering as she remembered how uncomfortable her interview with the detective had been.

"Understood, but try to get him not to piss her off."

Kelly didn't respond. All day long she felt as though she was about to implode; but at the moment she was glad she was sitting next to Chad, inhaling the rich scent of his woodsy cologne. He was always impeccably dressed, even when he threw on something casual. His creased jeans and starched and slim tailored sparkling white shirt seemed like the effortless choice of a man who instinctively made good decisions. In her current state of upheaval, being with Chad made her feel protected and safe.

He slid in Nancy Wilson's *RSVP* CD and relaxed as they cruised past the Museum of Science and Industry and wound through Jackson Park.

Chad grinned at her and said, "Smooth ride, smooth music, smooth woman. A brother has it all."

Kelly gave him the first real smile she'd been able to manage all evening as she squeezed his hand. The silky sounds of the jazz legend echoed through the truck.

"The title of this is RSVP. What's that about?"

"RSVP means Rare Songs, Very Personal. You like it?"

"Um hum," she purred. "Really nice." Then a stab of grief pierced her heart, making her feel a tad bit guilty that she was enjoying herself while her mother was in bed a medicated zombie. But there were so many hard days ahead and there would be few moments where she could snatch some respite to make sense of it all. "I love that the songs are simple and uncomplicated," Kelly said. "Right now, I need slow and uncomplicated."

Chad responded by pulling her to him, so that her head lay on his shoulder. Silence carried them the rest of the way to the theatre.

❖ ❖ ❖

The valet at eta Creative Arts Foundation took their keys and the couple hurried to meet Lisette and Bryan inside the crowded lobby. Lisette was a girl of medium height with her long, dark brown hair swept into a chignon at the nape of her neck. Unlike Kelly, Lisette was wide-hipped and her short pink and green floral dress strained to contain her curves. Her husband Bryan, was a former college football lineman that still kept up the grueling exercise regimen that produced a ripped chest, flat belly and cut and defined arms. He was thick- necked and broad shouldered.

He wore a black tee shirt tucked neatly into tan linen slacks.

Kelly could barely utter hello before being wrapped in the comfort of Lisette's arms. "Girl, I'm sooo sorry for your loss," purred the long-lashed Lisette.

"I'll be okay," she said with a small sigh. "Just as soon as I can get past Daddy's funeral." She looked away, and then back at Chad. "Babe, this my bestie Lisette and her husband, Bryan." She paused just long enough to control the trembling of her voice and exhaled, "They're like family."

"Glad to meet you both," said Chad, smiling but peering at Kelly for a moment. Evidently he had heard the very thing she had tried to hide. "Thanks for the invitation," he said to Lisette. "She needed to get away for a while," he said looking down at Kelly, who latched onto his arm a bit tighter.

"Kelly, I'm sorry I wasn't able to get to see your mom sooner," said Lisette. "Let her know I'll be over before the weeks out."

Just as Kelly nodded, the theater lights flickered, signaling that the play was about to begin. The group moved forward along the industrial grade brownish-gray tweed carpet, finding their way through the throngs of people. They entered the modest theater with surprisingly comfortable red velvet seats—the majority of them filling up quickly. *Their Eyes Were Watching God*, adapted from the book by Zora Neale Hurston, was playing to a sold-out crowd.

The playbill said the drama, set in the 1920s, was "The story of a woman's timeless struggle to finally find Mr. Right and an opportunity to love and live fully." A classic, and Lisette knew the book was one of Kelly's favorites.

The play unfolded slowly, but Kelly felt anchored beside Chad, sliding her small hand inside his. She leaned her head onto his shoulder and absorbed his strength. Kelly's mind wandered and she began to ponder her parents' marriage. Her mother and father valued their vow to cleave to one another, but she had never seen that spark between them that would make a woman stay with a man for decades. Kelly needed more than the appearance of closeness in a marriage. She wanted connection— the spark. Without that spark, what was the point? She'd never need a man for a meal ticket or to validate her worth. Looking at Chad, she smiled inwardly because he provided the spark.

Surprisingly, in the middle of the play's second act, Kelly had neatly compartmentalized her feelings about her father and his murder and suddenly found herself completely enthralled in the plight of the characters in the play. All thoughts of Detective Sommers and Marcus slipped into the back of her mind and she actually began to enjoy the scenes unfolding before her.

❖ ❖ ❖

When the play ended to roaring applause, Chad joined the majority of the audience in a standing ovation. He whispered to Kelly, "Baby, I didn't think I was gonna like this play, but I'm surprised."

"I'm glad Lisette thought this would be good for us," she answered, looking up at him with a smile. "Thanks for coming along. I knew this was a stretch for you."

She looked at him timidly, with a smile forming on her lips. "Did you want to stay for the discussion?"

"Sure, we can do that."

Kelly peered over at their companions, "Bry? Are y'all staying for the discussion?"

Their heads bobbed and the men took their seats again as about half of the theater-goers left, while those remaining waited for the actors to arrange a few stools on the stage for the discussion.

Kelly gave Chad a peck on the cheek and said, "We'll be back in a few, girl time," as the women excused themselves to the powder room.

"We know how that goes, right Bryan?" Chad teased.

Bryan nodded. "Every man has been kicked to the curb for chick talk."

"Whatever," Lisette shot back, with a playfully dismissive wave of her dark brown hand. "Bry's a Bears fan like you. I'm sure y'all will figure something out."

She put a little dip in her hip and did a shimmy that caused Bryan's head to shake.

Chad looked at Bryan, and said, "Your wife is 'special' in a good way, bruh. She was just what Kelly needed tonight."

"I know my baby is a crazy handful," the former linebacker smiled.

As the women walked away laughing, designer handbags in tow,

Kelly said, "Thanks for pushing me into coming. It's good to get out and laugh."

Lisette's look turned serious. "Girl are you okay? I was reading the South Suburban papers and going 'Whaaaaat!'"

"I'm hanging by a thread," Kelly replied, grabbing a wad of brown paper toweling and wiping the sink's marble-like ledge before setting her designer bag down. Opening the zippered compartment, she retrieved a lip gloss and retouched her lips.

Good you have Chad in your life. He seems to be a sweetie," said Lisette, running a comb through her shoulder length tresses.

"He's that and more," said Kelly

"*And* he's been around a minute. I mean girl you know you have tended to move on quickly in the past."

"Hush you, I gotta pee," said Kelly, entering a stall.

"Chad's got a nice butt too," Lisette commented, her voice echoing off the bathroom walls. "Not as good as Bry's but—!"

"Girl quit!" Kelly laughed.

❖ ❖ ❖

After the theater discussion, the couples met in Hyde Park for pizza, wine and easy conversation at the Medici.

In the company of her friends, Kelly momentarily vanquished the string of events that had churned her life. The evening went as smoothly as Nancy Wilson's contralto voice. Rare Songs. Very Personal.

Yet she knew in her heart that this was but a short respite from the trouble that lay head.

CHAPTER 31

As Kelly and Chad drove the final ten blocks back to her apartment, the atmosphere was alive with the harmonious sounds of nocturnal birds, crickets and katydids. An occasional breeze ruffled through the trees, bringing relief from what had been a hot and humid day.

Chad drove casually, left hand slung over the leather-covered steering wheel, body leaning towards Kelly. He could tell from the smile she gave when his free hand grasped hers that she relished the stability of his touch.

The silence between them was more potent than conversation.

As he pulled through the gate and navigated the entrance to her Hyde Park high rise, Chad unbuckled his seatbelt, preparing to walk around to help her from the car.

She halted his movements with her hand and asked, "Want to stop up for a while?"

Chad's eyebrows raised; but he quickly covered his surprise with, "Sure, I'd like that."

They had not made love since before her father's murder and he took the fact that she was inviting him inside her apartment as her signal that she was ready to have sex again. Tonight, Chad was prepared to make it all better.

Moments later, he followed Kelly past the building's short, balding security guard and onto the elevator up to her eleventh floor apartment.

The small living room was refreshingly cooler than the muggy August evening and they sat on the orange ultra-suede couch while the television replayed the latest episode of *90210*.

"So you really enjoyed the play or were you just saying that for my benefit?" she teased, focusing the remote at the screen and turning the volume down.

"I wasn't into it at first," Chad admitted. "But I really enjoyed it. I was surprised that I actually got into the storyline. The acting was surprisingly good."

"Surprising? You mean because it's at a community theater on the South Side and not downtown?" she challenged.

"You got me," he said, chuckling—probably more at her delivery than her insinuating that he was bougie. "I guess I was being a little bit of an ass. Plays always seem a little high-brow for me. But I seriously dug this play tonight. How's that?"

"I'll take it!" she teased.

"Matter of fact, the Janie character reminded me of you a little."

"Oh she did? How so?"

Chad was silent a moment. All signs of his previous smile disappeared. "She seemed to be trying to find her own way. Her mother chose her first husband but after that, she was searching to define herself, until she finally found the love and the life she wanted."

Kelly became quiet for several seconds before responding. "Yes, that sounds about right."

"Our women have been forced into some hard choices, "said Chad.

Kelly was silent.

She settled back into the curve of his right arm and they sat there on the sofa looking out at the horizon where blue-black sky meets dark blue water. The restless sound of the fusions splashed against the rocks in the distance.

He was almost content to sit quietly, holding her in his arms. Beneath what appeared to be a self-assured demeanor, he was still bruised after a failed teenage marriage. Chad purposely kept his relationships with chicks either transactional or casual. *No strings.* But this wisp of a woman was like water, seeping into his off-limits places. He looked at the top of her head nestled on his chest and felt himself become hard with desire.

"Hey you," he whispered, reaching over and pulling her face closer. His lips parted barely a few centimeters, but enough to release his tongue, enveloping her in a tender kiss. They spontaneously and tenderly undressed, and when they were naked, she lay on top of him on the sofa. Chad fought the urge to plunge into her depths. She kissed him tentatively at first. Her tongue pranced tenderly along his lips, played inside of his mouth and sent tiny electric shots that made him crazy.

Almost frightened to touch her, he placed his hands on her buttocks and pressed her across his manhood. She became wetter and wetter each time his penis moved past the opening of her vagina. He stuck his tongue down her throat as if it was his penis going inside of her and she sucked his tongue. He remembered a saying he'd heard somewhere: as above, so below. He found himself inside the warmth of Kelly's vagina and she moved her hips as he lay still, until he could no longer hold the posture and he realized that he was engaging both her gateways.

As above so below.

CHAPTER 32

Diana Gregg-Alman settled into her husband's Toyota 4-Runner, which sped onto I-80 west and then to I-55. She needed to put some distance between Chicago and all of the painful memories that came with it.

She looked out at the rolling, flat southern Illinois terrain and was grateful that Tommie had come with her. She couldn't have handled the funeral without him. Her plan had been to leave directly after the funeral, even as the pallbearers had escorted the casket, and to completely forgo the burial. She had been mortified that the pastor had called upon her to speak words over her brother at the burial. Fighting her conflicted feelings of betrayal, loss and recrimination, she struggled to do justice to the life his fellow church members and neighbors had experienced with him.

Diana had been completely overwhelmed when Nancy passed out, leaving her the only close relative at the gravesite. And the questions that bombarded her from nosy people who remember that she had been absent from the family's life for fifteen years made matters worse.

After her brother's burial, Diana had used her husband's job as an excuse to make a fast getaway. Tommie's part-time job as a security guard wasn't as demanding as she let on. It was his play money. But there was simply no reason to stay in Illinois one minute longer than necessary.

"Di, you been awfully quiet. Wanna talk?"

Diana shifted her gaze to her husband of seven years. "Not really but I guess I can't keep the genie in the bottle forever."

"Nope, that's a bad idea."

Kelly's angular face floated into view. Her niece had looked like a lost waif at the funeral. The off-white Carol Cole suit was literally falling off her frail shoulders. Diana realized that the warm hug they had shared had meant more to her than she realized. It transported her back to their warm summers together and made her ashamed that she had let her niece down so miserably.

"I just feel so guilty that I didn't stay longer," Diana said more to herself than to her husband. "But I just couldn't face her."

"Your sister-in-law or your niece?"

"My sister-in-law," Diana answered. "The last time we really had a conversation, I demanded that Kelly come live with me. Nancy told me everything was alright. It wasn't."

"Why would she want her daughter to live with you?"

Diana became suddenly silent, thinking back over her last phone call to Nancy, so many years ago.

"Di, did you hear me?"

Diana snatched her gaze away from the thick cornfields rushing past her window. "I'm sorry, what did you say?"

"Why would you want Kelly to live with you?"

"Stop asking me questions, will you?" she said. "I still don't feel like talking!"

"I always did love a mean woman," Tommie quipped, good-naturedly catering to his grieving wife's wishes.

She feigned a smile. "That is not what you got! It's just a long, sad story and I'm too drained emotionally. I'm gonna take a nap."

Diana closed her eyes to shut out her husband's curiosity, but the one thing she couldn't manage to shut out was her guilt. Tommie only wanted to help, but he didn't need to know about things that could not be undone. She regretted that her distaste for conflict had allowed Nancy to prevail in their last argument. Kelly might have had a totally different life if Diana had simply called the police. Something that her own parents should have done when they learned the extent of Dennis' injuries those many years ago. Instead, they allowed shame and concern about what others would think to cause them to sweep the incident under the rug. She had faulted them all these years about not doing anything when they knew the truth. Now she understood her parents' actions more than she ever wanted to. She had allowed herself to become them.

She 'played possum' for what seemed like a quarter of an hour, feeling the cool air blowing into the metallic blue car's sunroof and listening to her husband's road music. Tommie would drive anywhere as long as he had a cooler of Coca-Cola in his back seat and his dusties playing.

Diana couldn't remember when she fell asleep, but she awakened to her husband's road anthem, Kool and the Gang's "Summer Magic". She reluctantly opened her eyes, aware that the rider in the front seat should actually help keep the driver alert, instead of giving in to her need to sweep away memories that were better left in the corner of her mind.

With Chicago a distant memory, she finally unwound and the day's events slammed into her.

I just buried my baby brother.

Her eyes were dry and there was only streaked makeup to belie the fact that she had cried until no more tears remained.

Nothing could have prepared her for getting that phone call from her beloved niece telling her Dennis had been murdered in his study.

Who slips into a man's home on a quiet Friday evening and kills him, and in such a horrific manner?

As the flat countryside, rich with the warm colors of summer rolled past her window, she unpacked long suppressed memories of never-ending Sunday services that framed her childhood as the daughter of a preacher man. So many of her formative years were spent in her father's small storefront apostolic church.

She smiled the minute she recalled the luscious Sunday dinners cooked up by the good sisters of the church, served at long plastic-covered tables in the basement of the small but up-and-coming church. She thought of how they never had to wait in line for Sunday supper because the members of the church treated PK's—pastor's kids—like royalty, no matter how impish they were. Just thinking about those times covered her like a cozy handmade quilt.

As kids, they complained to one another about the length of Sunday services, but knew better than to let those complaints reach the ears of Daddy Gregg, the stern, no-nonsense shepherd of the Holy Ghost filled congregation. Back in those days kids were to be seen, and not heard. Dennis would sneak all kinds of sweets, from Now and Laters, to Boston Baked Beans, to Hostess Suzy Q's into Sunday school and secretly share the sugary treats with her while they passed silly notes to one another.

As children, Dennis and Diana Gregg led an idyllic life inside the warmth and safety of their church. That is, until one life-altering morning in the park when a depraved soul had turned her baby brother into a hyper-vigilant introvert, and shattered the bond between Dennis and Daddy Gregg forever.

The brother that she had known and loved had died in 1967; it had just taken thirty-seven years to bury him.

Diana reached up to wipe away the single tear that burned a salty trail down her face. She might have been all cried out from her brother's death, but she would never stop shedding tears for his lost innocence.

CHAPTER 33

The morning after her mother was released from the hospital, Kelly called Citibank and added three vacation days to the three bereavement days employees were entitled to. She filled a tote bag with three pairs of designer jeans, a few casual tops and essential toiletries, and was out the door, aiming to share a few precious days with her mother.

As she searched her refrigerator and tossed items that would not survive her return, she put in a call to Chad. He picked up on the first ring and she said, "I'm glad I caught you before you left for work."

"You need something, baby?" came his half-awake response.

"No, I just wanted to let you know that I'm going to be at mother's for a few days. I need to set her up with a private duty nurse."

"Understood. Actually, I kinda thought you might be moving back home."

"That's not *my* home," she snapped. "Not anymore. I told you I could never live there again." She was ashamed at the noticeable rise in her voice.

Chad was silent on the other end, probably because he wasn't used to her sounding this way.

"But I do want my mother to be well taken care of and I'll be seeing her almost every day." She paused, relieved there was no judgment from Chad or any questions on whether she was alright or not. She was never alright when she had to go to that house. Too many memories swirled around her for it to ever be a pleasant experience. However, Kelly was forced to overcome her aversion to take care of the woman who had taken care of her.

"I may not be reachable for the next few days. I need some time to process everything that's happened."

Chad was silent for a moment.

"Call me if you need anything, Babe. Even, if it's just to talk, you hear?"

Kelly was touched by his sincerity. "Sure, but I'm okay, seriously," she lied smoothly, but inside her a still soft voice whispered, *"There is nothing he can do to help me anyway."*

❖ ❖ ❖

Kelly slept in the downstairs bedroom near the kitchen but made frequent trips upstairs during the night to check on her mother. Nancy Gregg had redecorated and transformed Kelly's childhood bedroom into a bright sewing room while Kelly was away at Spelman. She would never have slept upstairs again,u anyway.

Kelly was content to spend time cooking her mother's favorite meals and coaxing her to eat. She recreated the fork-tender salmon with lemon sauce that had gone uneaten when she had prepared it in May for the ill-fated brunch at her apartment.

The hospital had helped Kelly tap into the registry and hire a private duty nurse to take care of her mom. But the church sent Sister Ollie, a longtime member of Christ's Victory Apostolic Church, to be her mother's live-in companion.

The day Ms. Ollie arrived to take care of Kelly's mother, she exited the Ride Right livery cab service with all the authority of a five star general. She unloaded her own suitcase from the trunk, then tipped and dismissed the driver. Kelly had met her at the front door and showed her to her first-floor room, which had an adjoining shower. Ollie Ralston was a tiny piece of leather at 100 pounds. Her piercing thick-lidded eyes gave her a reptilian appearance. She arrived wearing a maroon coat dress with double-breasted gold-toned buttons. She carried a black cardigan and wore a pair of closed-toe, low-heeled, run-over pumps. Her hair was whipped into a salt-and-pepper curly frenzy that Kelly found out later that evening required ten or fifteen of the pink foam rollers packed in the oversized handbag that doubled as an overnight case.

"Ms. Ollie, we can't thank you enough for moving in here to help mother," the well-bred daughter had the presence of mind to say.

The old woman rested her handbag on the bedside chair and deposited a small suitcase nearby.

"Mama Gregg mean a lot to me," she said. "I usta be a street girl. She found me unconscious behin' da chuch, an' it were jus' Gawd. She were comin' outta bible study. When I come to in the hospital, the chuch let me stay in the basement and she come to me."

"I never knew that," said Kelly, thinking, *another secret carefully hidden by mother*.

"Yo mama got me a place to live and tole her friends I could clean real good if they tell me what to do." She beamed a warm smile. "I couldn't clean worth diddly squat, but yo mama, she showed me what to do. Miss Kelly you gon' see how good I cleans now," said Ollie, whose small body seemed to levitate when she spoke about Nancy Gregg.

"My mother is a kind woman."

"Miss Kelly, she way betta than good. She fulla Gawd."

Kelly stammered, suddenly caught between two opinions of her mother. One of a rescuer of an abused hooker, and another of a woman looking away from the abuse of her own child. She steadied herself with a cleansing breath. "I'm confident you're going to take the best care of my mother." She managed a smile as Ollie laid her cardigan on the beige chenille bedspread and placed her shoes by the nightstand.

Ollie turned out to be the proverbial "dog with one master." Anybody who got in the way of what was best for Nancy Gregg, caught holy hell.

❖ ❖ ❖

Kelly spent most of her mother's waking hours on the bed next to her, thumbing through old family photographs which had been meticulously stored in scrapbooks over the years. The matriarch had carefully preserved the faded photos of their earliest church affairs and copies of programs in which Kelly and Marcus had speaking parts. Turning the cardboard pages of the albums, Kelly passed her the occasional stray photo that had slipped from its cardboard mounting.

Kelly lowered to her knees and dug a little deeper into the Lane cedar chest, uncovering an especially-thick, paisley cloth-covered album labeled Our Adventures. The spiral-bound volume chronicled seven magical summers spent with Auntie Diana. Upon opening it, Kelly was instantly transported back to her middle school and high school summers. A feeling of joy and peace claimed her.

"Mother, look!" Kelly exclaimed, coming to her mother's side. She stroked a hand across the cherished album. "I didn't realize you still had this!"

"Of course I kept it," Nancy whispered, reaching over to grasp her daughter's hand and giving her a weak smile. "Young lady, you dreamed all year of summers with Diana. She took you on some great trips."

"Auntie Di always loved to experience so many different things. I guess that's why she was a school teacher in the first place," Kelly said, replacing the current photo album on Nancy's lap with the first journal Kelly had ever kept the year she left home for Spelman.

Nancy turned a page in the thick album, their gazes sweeping across pictures of Kelly that showed her hairstyle changing from two stiffly-ribboned pigtails on either side of her head, to a sleek pageboy with cut and flattened bangs, then transitioning to a casual flip with a side part and finally morphing into her first really short haircut the summer before she left for Spelman.

"She certainly taught you a lot," her mother remarked. "I'm sure that's partly why you breezed through college."

Kelly looked away, unable to voice her deepest thoughts. Diana Gregg-Alman had been so much more than her favorite aunt and tutor. That brown-skinned woman with the thick untamable curly hair had been her summer safe harbor.

"I was sooo happy to see Auntie Di at daddy's funeral," Kelly said, remembering the perfumed warmth of her aunt's embrace in the church lobby. "But I'll never forgive her for leaving right after the burial." Her spirits took a nosedive at what she had considered a total brush-off. Tears formed in Kelly's eyes. "I just knew she was going to be here when we got back from the hospital. You have tons of room here and I just didn't get it."

Nancy Gregg sighed. "Sweetie," she said, eyes focused on the photos in the album. "Didn't she say something about Uncle Tommie needing to get back to work. He was the one that drove, you know."

Kelly was quiet. There were so many questions swirling around in her head. The main one was why wouldn't her aunt want to stay? Didn't she still love her?

Nancy's gaze swept over Kelly's face, but before Kelly could form a question her mother added, "Over the past few years she didn't have much to say to us. She was just coming to pay her respects."

Kelly wiped away a traitorous tear and tried to focus on the pictorial array spread on the bedspread.

Nancy squeezed her daughter's hand again. "It was *you* that Diana was especially fond of. She loved spending the summers with her niece. You were always her pick."

Kelly wasn't mollified by those words. "If she really loved me, she should have spent more time with you and me after the funeral. I don't understand what she was thinking."

Nancy sunk a little deeper under her sheets. "Her husband had to work, Kelly."

"That man is basically retired, for Christ's sake! Auntie's not hurting for money. She could have flown back to St. Louis."

Nancy released a long, slow breath that sounded raspy. Realizing that she was upsetting her mother, Kelly feigned a smile and picked up the album once again. Sliding a colorful photo from under the plastic that held it prisoner, she stared into a photo of her with the majestic Grand Canyon as her backdrop. The photo triggered a vivid memory of the day. The sun was setting and she was wearing a blue sleeveless short set. Her thick hair was gathered up into one bulky ponytail, minus the ribbon.

"Mother, look at my hair!" she laughed softly, holding the photo so that her mother could see.

"Diana was good at a lot of things, Baby. Clearly taming that wiry hair of yours was not one of them. But she had you looking nice otherwise," Nancy said, scrutinizing the blue outfit with sparkling white socks and white tennis shoes. "Did she make you say 'cheese', because I see almost ev-e-ry tooth in your mouth."

"She did!"

The women laughed and Kelly was happy to see her mother's face come to life for even just those few moments.

Kelly and her aunt had visited the Grand Canyon for seven days, taking multiple day trips from their lodgings and exploring surrounding towns before Diana had taken that final photo on their way back to the hotel to check out. That trip to the Grand Canyon surfaced in her mind as if it was only yesterday. She was grateful that her happiness and the closeness she had with her aunt had been recorded.

So why did Diana leave so quickly? Especially when mother was so ill? And when Kelly needed her so badly?

Kelly stroked a finger across that photo once again, remembering how they had shared that rickety king-size bed at the Mesa Motel. Kelly had felt safe curled up like a furry kitten against her aunt. No matter how many trips Kelly made to the bathroom all night, she'd fall immediately back into a sound sleep and always awakened to find her arms clutching Diana, as if for dear life.

Kelly remembered longing to tell her aunt that summer about the nightmares, but she was afraid to disturb the peace she so richly needed and enjoyed. Her silence ensured that she always had her summers to look forward to. Evidently, those summers were all Auntie Diana had to give.

CHAPTER 34

AUGUST 30, 2004

Kelly returned to work a week after the funeral. She hadn't realized how difficult it would be. People constantly stopped her in the hallway to express their sympathy. She read the genuine empathy in their eyes, yet she felt the added pain of insincerity each time she lied and said she missed her father. She missed Dennis Gregg as much as she missed having her tooth pulled.

Upon reaching her cubicle, she hung her sweater on a hook and rested a bulging rust-colored Prada handbag on her desk. Her sense of smell was aroused by the perfumed fragrance emanating from a large bouquet of colorful flowers on her worktable. The card was signed by her co-workers. Hector, her manager, and his wife had attended her father's funeral on behalf of the staff. She was sure he had told them her mother had passed out at the funeral. Hopefully, no one would be classless enough to mention it.

When Chad had called her early this morning to wish her a happy day, she almost came unglued.

"Chad, I'm so exhausted and worried about Mother," she had said. "Ollie called, scared because her mother's refusing to eat. When I got over there, she was weak and dehydrated. So we rushed her back to the University of Chicago Hospital last night." Kelly took a deep, reflective breath, glancing over at the white calla lilies in the bouquet. "Oh God," she gushed, "I'm just not ready—for her to leave me."

"Listen to me, Sweetheart," he said in a reassuring voice. "You're doing the best you can and so is your mom. The rest is up to God."

Yeah Right! Where was God when she was a helpless little girl?

She somehow managed to politely respond, "Chad, I know *you* are a praying person. Please pray for my mother. I don't know what I'm going to do without her."

What she didn't add was, "Please pray for me too, because what I'm feeling right now can't do me any good."

❖ ❖ ❖

Kelly sat in her cubicle, a cup of cream-laden coffee in her hand. She pulled out the sketches and work requests from her portfolio, then opened a handwritten note attached to the most recent version of a presentation.

Kelly, I have returned the CD with Reagan's *PowerPoint presentation. I like it. The color is nice ... pretty even ... though I am not sure that it will be appropriate for the Board of Directors meeting. Please revise.*

The note was dated Friday, August 13, the day her father had been murdered. Kelly slipped the CD into her disk drive and pulled up the file. "Bitch," she rasped under her breath when she saw the abundance of red deletions and strikeouts on the page. *Why didn't she just tell me to delete the whole presentation and start over!*

Kelly had been assisting Grace Li in creating the PowerPoint presentation for Walter Reagan, the bank president who was meeting with the bank's trustees. She hated working with Grace! Kelly felt that her own esthetic concepts were unique and Grace stifled her creativity by insisting that the presentation be laid out in that regimented corporate look. Mixing their visions could combine the best aspects of both, but Grace *always* played it safe. Kelly felt that Grace tended to overvalue tradition, but it was damn near—no it was completely—impossible to get that woman to think outside the box. Kelly, on the other hand, felt that she lived outside the box.

"Good Morning," chirped a voice with a light Korean accent.

"Oh. Grace," Kelly turned, wondering how long the woman had been standing outside her cubicle.

"Should you not be at home with your mom?" Grace asked. "How is she? How are *you* doing?"

"I'm doing," sighed Kelly. "Thanks for asking." Under Grace's pointed gaze, she quickly added, "My mother was like a little child when I left her in the hospital last night. I'm so afraid that with Dad gone, she'll just wither away. He was her whole world. I just don't know. Mom is completely devastated. She had to be—"

Kelly exhaled, mentally kicking herself for almost going overboard and sharing personal information with a woman who was so irritating.

"I am so sorry," Grace said in a tone that sounded as if she had genuine empathy for her coworker. "I understand, Kelly." She gave Kelly's shoulder a gentle pat. "You just take it easy. I do not have much on my plate today, so I'm happy to help you."

"No thanks," Kelly responded, still miffed at Grace's rebuff of her PowerPoint design. "I need to work hard. I can't forget what has happened, not really, but when I'm focused on my screen I'm at peace."

Kelly noted that Grace was nodding. She used this as an opening to say, "Can we talk about Reagan's presentation?"

Grace's gaze shifted from Kelly's face to the document she had on the desk. "Sure."

"Well, I looked at your comments and while I agree with *some* things, I disagree with other parts of your edit."

"Oooookay," said Grace, drawing out her words as though needing time to come up with new ones.

"Look, I'm dying to produce something innovative, something exciting and still crisp," said Kelly, folding her arms across her chest as she stood, practically towering over her tiny Asian colleague.

"I know, Kelly," said Grace in a patient tone. "You do beautiful work. The numbered text boxes look very elegant, as I noted on your mock up," she said, gesturing to the 23-inch monitor. "My main concern is that your colors are a little too aggressive," she said squeezing her thumb and forefinger together. "Corporate formatting is subtle. That is a fact and you will have to accept that 'burden' on your designs. George wants me to turn the design work for the monthly Board of Directors meeting over to you. I need to be sure that you understand. This is not ad agency work. It just is not."

Kelly leaned against her desk. "Okay Grace, but I've *got* to break out of this conservative box."

Grace lowered her eyes a few inches and quietly said, "One of these days, but not with *this* presentation." She sauntered toward her cubicle on the opposite end of the floor.

Kelly sat and spun around in her chair. She looked at the file on the screen and wondered why the president's executive assistant didn't just whip this stuff out herself. The answer was obvious—either laziness or lack of creative skills. She rocked back on the high-backed chair, closed her eyes and envisioned the freedom she'd taste when she was free of all that held her back. Free to open the *Kelly T Design Group*. "Tee" had been her grandmother's pet name for her. She quickly sketched a 'T' on her desk pad with large angelic wings sprouting from each branch of the consonant. There were wings waiting for her beyond Citibank and she was determined to fly by her own rules.

❖ ❖ ❖

Five o'clock couldn't come fast enough. Kelly didn't drive to work every day but the thought of riding the train had made her sick to her stomach this morning. Her office was mere minutes from Lake Shore Drive and today she didn't want to gamble on whose path she might cross on public transportation.

Cruising along and occasionally focusing on the view of Lake Michigan's sparkling waters at high tide, Grace's condescending bullshit came to mind.

"Boring bitch!" Kelly spewed aloud.

Seconds later, as she pulled under the 47th Street viaduct and into the left lane, a thick gray tomcat strutted arrogantly in front of her Toyota Camry. It didn't even attempt to get out of her way.

A sudden impulse overtook Kelly's mind. She pressed the car's accelerator and barreled down on the helpless feral cat. The feline hissed and leapt out of the way.

A temporary wave of serenity washed over Kelly as she glanced through the rear view mirror, as the cat sprinted away.

Damn you ... next time you see me coming, cat, get out of my way!

CHAPTER 35

LABOR DAY MONDAY, SEPTEMBER 6, 2004

As Joi pulled up on the Gregg's tree-lined block, she took one last pull from her cigarette, exhaled and shorted it. Seconds after slamming the car door, she took a deep breath and was immersed in the unmistakable aroma of charcoal briquettes and hickory smoke. It was scarcely half-past eleven and the grills were fired up for Labor Day. She could imagine the anticipation of families she presumed were in the various backyards and on patios, lined up around the grills like NASCAR drivers revving their engines at the starting line and waiting for the green flag. Her stomach growled loudly in protest that she wasn't one of the ones about to load their paper plate.

Several homes proudly displayed the American flag. Full of neat bungalows, ranch-style homes and neatly manicured lawns, the neighborhood was still a mixture of Whites and a light sprinkling of upwardly mobile African-American families. This cozy village reminded her by feel, if not economic status, of Kenwood Oakland, the Southside community where she was from. *Good place to raise kids.*

Three children whirled neon hula hoops around the waists of crisp short outfits that were holiday-new. Growing up, if relatives were coming over, her mother would dress her in new clothes. On more adventurous days during the summer, her mother would fasten her thick braids in loops over her ears, giving her the appearance of a whimsical bunny rabbit.

Joi scaled three concrete stairs and pressed the Gregg's bell, releasing the rich sound of an expensive chime. The door barely cracked open, and a woman she recognized from the funeral as Sister Ollie peered out at her.

"Yeesss?" Sister Ollie's voice sounded more like the growl of a pit-bull than a middle-aged woman.

"Detective Sommers," Joi responded.

"Can I see yo' I.D., officer?"

"Yes ma'am," said the detective, pointing to the detective's shield clipped to the waistband of her beige slim-cut slacks.

"You mind?" asked Ollie, inferring that Joi unclip the badge and move it closer.

Joi gazed directly into the eyes of the woman, who returned her stare. Several ticks of time passed. Since antagonizing Ollie was not going to accomplish what she wanted, Joi unclipped the badge and raised it to eye level.

Ms. Ollie only widened the crack after carefully matching the detective's face to the Department photo ID card.

"Thank you, officer."

"Ma'am, it's detective," Joi corrected.

"Oh, thank you, *detective*," said the woman, pursing her lips. "No offense meant."

"None taken," said Joi, relaxing into her professional role.

"You here to see Mother Gregg, right?"

"No ma'am, I'm not. I'll just need a few minutes in the den and living room. I'm still gathering information."

"Can I get you anythang?" Ms. Ollie offered in a much nicer tone than the one she used when answering the door. "Coffee? Water?"

"No, but thanks for asking, Ms. Ollie."

"Mother Gregg wouldn't have it any other way," responded the dutiful attendant.

"Please give her my greetings."

The salt-and-pepper haired woman nodded. "She's sleepin' now but I will when she wake up."

Ms. Ollie shuffled toward the stairs and gave one last lingering look at Joi before making the climb to the second floor.

Most of Joi's investigative work had taken place in Dennis Gregg's study, but this afternoon Joi decided she needed to get a better feel for the home in general.

Walking into the comfortable living room, she sank into the Gregg's white leather sectional sofa.

Joi closed her eyes, rehashing the case in her mind. Dennis Gregg's blood had left massive burgundy stains on the beige carpet where he had fallen. Once she closed her examination of the crime scene, she'd ordered a sanitation crew to clean up and rip out the stained carpet. Although the room had been expertly cleaned by the company, Joi could feel the spirit of violence still hovering in the room. Her investigation had turned up partial prints of almost everyone in the family and several others on the entry and garden doors. Russell would follow up to determine if any of those other prints belonged to anyone recently with Elder Gregg for counseling. Marcus' print was blood tinged, making him rise as a primary suspect. She looked forward to cracking him during his interview.

It would be great to have events happen just as they appeared for a change, but she had no illusions. While Dennis Gregg had been a businessman, a counselor, and a church elder, her gut told her that there were more questions to be asked. Whittling down the field of suspects would call for the real heavy lifting. Marcus Gregg firmly stood out in her mind. Only someone with something to hide dodged the police with such diligence.

She tried to reconstruct the events of the night of the killing.

What was the killer thinking when they shot the victim from the back and then stuck around to shoot one more time for good measure? Did they know that Nancy Gregg was upstairs, sedated? Did they think that no one else was in the house? Or was this a hit man using a silencer. In that case, the killer would not have been concerned about noise. Especially since it was thundering that night.

A hit? She didn't find any mob or gang ties in the victim's background, so she could safely rule that out.

Alone. In the house. The perfect opportunity.

Joi regretted that she had not vigorously questioned Widow Gregg sooner. She couldn't shake this odd feeling that Nancy Gregg was also keeping something close to the chest. The Gregg woman was the polar opposite of Maze, Joi's narcissistic mother. Mrs. Gregg seemed, at least on the surface, to exude sensitivity and kindness. Her daughter seemed to love her. Even in her distress, when she had come to question the women the day after the murder, Nancy Gregg had asked her daughter to make coffee and bring a coffee urn, bowls of real cream and sugar and ceramic cups into the study for the officers. Joi remembered thinking, *she must be an extraordinary human being to be concerned about civility at a time like this.*

But on the other hand, she could be a Black Widow Spider. Perhaps she *had* actually killed her mate. There were thousands of cases where the person least suspected had done the deed. As much as Joi wanted to believe that Nancy Gregg could not, and would not, have done such a horrible thing, she also had to keep everyone in the crosshairs.

Joi bit her bottom lip in steely resolve. She ran her index finger around the rim of her Dunkin Donuts cup to dislodge a bit of sugar. It was only a matter of time before she caught the murdering son-of-a-bitch. Son, mother, daughter, and that strange sister who practically ran from her brother's funeral were on her list. But then again, Joi also had to look into Dennis Gregg's business and church affairs.

There might be a whole other range of suspects that could surface.

CHAPTER 36

LABOR DAY AFTERNOON

Joi could only wish for a childhood where she could play with other children. Instead, she'd had to play parent to her mother. Every time her mother left the house on the weekends, Joi was worried she wouldn't come home. It made her unable to trust; made her a person who struggled to control the situations and the people in her life.

As she walked the concrete path leading to a ranch-style home just to the left of the Gregg's residence, she turned around her theory that the Armand family should have heard any commotion at the Gregg's that fateful Friday night. Detective Sommes retrieved a ballpoint pen and black stenographer's notebook from the depths of her brown leather Coach handbag. Using the doorknocker, a red and black replica of a black butler, she rapped out her presence at their front door.

The woman who answered was rail-thin and had her long cornrows gathered into a pony tail. She wore skin tight jeans and a blue cropped top. She was appropriately suspicious and demanded to see Joi's badge.

After presenting her badge and confirming that she was at the home of Stacy and Gregory Armand, and that she was speaking with Stacy, she reiterated that there had been a homicide and she was questioning neighbors in the event they saw or heard anything on the evening of Friday, August 13th.

"May I come inside, Mrs. Armand?"

She sighed and looked around a living area that she seemed to be in the midst of cleaning. "Yeah, O.K. for just a minute, this isn't a good time, I have a lot to do. I'm having company shortly and I—."

"—I understand, I'll be brief." Joi stepped inside and followed the woman a few steps inside the home. Armand sat looking a little exasperated on a hallway loveseat, Joi continued standing and went to the heart of her investigation.

"Mrs. Armand is your husband home?"

"I wish," snapped Stacy Armand, grabbing the end of her pony tail between her thumb and forefinger.

"Pardon me?"

"He's a consultant for Accenture, travels way too much for me, but it pays for this house." Stacy Armand gestured around the expanse of the entry hall and Joi could see from the high ceilings, winding staircase and ridiculously thick carpet on the floors that the traveling gig was worth it.

Joi had heard of Accenture. People there got paid a big buck. She made a note to check the Mrs. Armand's statement, but was temporarily satisfied.

"Where is your bedroom?" Joi inquired.

The woman gave a wary look. She rolled her eyes and answered cautiously. "We sleep right upstairs."

"Facing the back of the property?"

"Yes," came her clipped response.

For a minute, Joi felt hopeful. From that upstairs window, she might have gotten a look into the garden, seen the killer escape into the darkness.

"Sorry Ms., Uh Officer," Mrs. Armand stammered. "I don't know where you're going with this but we were in River Oaks at the movie Friday night, and then we went to Denny's to eat. We didn't get back 'til after 10:30 that night."

"We?" Joi asked with a lift of her eyebrows.

"Me and my girls. I think you passed them on your way in."

Joi remembered the invitation to hula hoop and smiled. "Yes. Cute kids."

Talk of the children seemed to make Mrs. Armand less guarded. A few more seemingly unimportant questions might put the woman at ease.

"What did you see?" asked Joi.

"*Anchor Man-The Legend of Ron Burgundy.*" Will Ferrell was hilarious in that role." She caught herself. "But I won't spoil it for you. Good movie. Probably not Academy Award good, but funnyy."

"Hmm." Joi grimaced at the fact that her lead had not panned out. She also knew that neighbors often dismissed clues that they didn't realize they had or that they consider unimportant. Joi decided to give her some time to reflect. Perhaps it was simply a matter of giving a potential source of information an impetus and some time to dig deeper.

Joi reached into her jacket pocket "Mrs. Armand, here's my card. I want to be able to close this case for the victim's family. We don't get a lot of homicides here in South Holland. If anything comes to mind, even something small, please give me a call."

"Um hum," grunted Stacy Armand almost snatching the card and stuffing it into her back pocket.

Joi gave her grin and looked around the disaster zone, "I'll let you get back to your cleaning."

As Joi walked away the door slammed. A few steps closer and the door knob would have hit her in the back. While she was on the block, she decided to return to the Gibson household and talk to Ms. Geraldine Crayton, again.

❖ ❖ ❖

Fifteen minutes later

Geri Crayton carefully closed and locked the door behind Detective Sommers. She peered through the peephole just in time to see that girl detective turn and do a double take back at the house. She'd asked questions about the evening of August 13. The night poor Mr. Gregg had met his Maker. Asia, her daughter, had been in Los Angeles. Geraldine had been home supervising her grandkids.

The elderly woman sighed as she descended the ten steps to the garden apartment. She sat at the circular table and poured herself a fourth cup of black coffee. Ordinarily she wouldn't be drinking coffee this late in the afternoon. Caffeine and the Newport cigarette plucked from the pocket of her blue plaid robe would have to stabilize her for now.

She leaned against the high back of the wrought iron dinette chair and took a deep pull from the cigarette, exhaling the thick smoke through her nostrils. She hoped that girl detective believed her lie about not hearing anything because she was wearing earphones to shut out the kid's music. She didn't need to get involved. She had her own demons to deal with.

"Did my duty calling that noise in to the police," she muttered.

"My grandkids, with their noisy selves, actually seem to like having me here!" she said, taking a sip of the hot coffee.

She was not going to spoil that.

Geraldine had watched enough boob tube to know that defense attorneys scrutinize the lives of the witnesses for the prosecution. She wouldn't risk her daughter finding out she had been drunk the night of August 13.

She could slap her own face. After staying clean and sober for twenty-four months, she had craved the taste of scotch. And not the cheap stuff, either. She could close her eyes and feel the sweet thickness on her tongue and the burn of the savory liquid sliding down her throat. She had known that Asia would be gone and she would be alone with Jasmine, Li'l Marshall and that loud damn music. Friday afternoon, when she had made her snack run to the grocery store, she didn't avoid the liquor department.

Taking another sip of coffee, she remembered that the riveting sound of the thunder and lightning had drawn her to the window. With the trees bowing in the wind and the rain pounding the sidewalk, it could have been thunder she heard—but she didn't believe that. She had grown up on the Southside of Chicago and knew what the blast from a hand gun sounded like. That night, she was certain that a gunshot had exploded from the Gregg home. Then she heard it again.

Shortly after, she'd seen a man leave. She'd seen the small built woman with wet hair in a tank top came running out the back gate. She'd seen it. That's what happened and that's what she tried to tell the cop when she called the station. But he kept asking her to "speak up ma'am, speak clearly."

She was speaking clearly, dammit! At least she thought so at the time. But after downing four glasses of that damning brown liquor ... now she wasn't so sure.

Skip you, she thought. I don't have to say a damn thing!

Geraldine Crayton picked up the phone and dialed her sponsor. "Adele...this is—"

"— I know who it is," her sponsor of three years responded. "Gerry, how the hell ya been?"

Geraldine focused on the framed photo of Reverend Martin Luther King Jr. on the wall over the small credenza holding her good china. That and the pink floral couch and matching arm chair in the room made her surroundings the coziest they had been for a long time. "I'm good ... and not so good."

"You know that's bullshit don't ya?"

"Yes, I do," Geraldine replied with a weary sigh.

"Wanna talk about it?" replied the no-nonsense voice on the other end.

"I slipped."

"Did ya slip Gerry or did ya fall?" Adele asked.

Geraldine shifted in her seat. "What damn difference does that make?"

"If you slipped, it was a one-time thing. You picked yourself up and stopped."

Geraldine felt an instant of relief at having the difference pointed out. "Then I slipped. I'm so ashamed and it's complicated."

"Complicated?

"Adele, something happened while I slipped."

"Was it a man again?"

"I wish it was that simple," Geraldine answered, unperturbed by her sponsor's reference to the time she slipped, got drunk and was so disgusted with herself that she went to a women's shelter until Asia found her and promised her another chance. Just remembering that night and fighting her constant craving for alcohol sank Geraldine's spirits lower. The bottle of JB Scotch was burning a hole in the hidden compartment of the credenza, behind the silver-rimmed porcelain dinnerware.

"Should I come over?" Adele asked in the softest tone that Geraldine had heard from the woman.

"No, the grandkids will be home in a while. I'd rather you come pick me up this evening. I'll tell Asia that I'm going to a movie with you. Adele, I only missed three meetings and look at what happened."

"Four. You missed four meetings, Gerry." The caller paused, as though realizing that kicking someone while they are down wasn't helpful. "I'll grab you at six this evening." Before she disconnected the call she said, "Gerry, pour out the leftovers."

Geraldine closed her eyes, praying for the strength to do just that.

CHAPTER 37

After leaving Ms. Geri Crayton, Joi considered her options. She was confident that officers had thoroughly checked behind the houses of all the neighbors. Yet they hadn't turned up anything that the killer had left behind. She had hoped she'd be able to talk with Dianna Gregg-Alman, since the gossips had provided enough information to pique her interest. There was some family drama that might provide a motive.

She was disappointed that the victim's sister had driven straight back to St. Louis right after the funeral. Given the fact that her sister-in-law had collapsed at the funeral and been hospitalized, Joi wondered what the big rush back to St. Louis had been about. Why wasn't a family member stationed at the house helping Mrs. Gregg, rather than Miss Ollie? The Gregg family was a lot less ideal than it looked.

Joi resolved to have Russell start fact-checking alibis after he got back from lunch with Helen. She hoped his wife was having a good day.

MS was a bitch. Some days Helen could barely move. Dealing with the chronic disease had taken its toll on Joi's partner and had clearly thrust both detectives into a place they shouldn't be—covering for him on days when his commitment to be there for his ailing wife outweighed his duty to protect and serve.

Returning to the Gregg home, she was admitted by the stoic Ollie who allowed her into the den. She exited through the den as she assumed the killer had. Her three inch heels sunk into the garden's mulched pathways, and a few wood chips found themselves under her instep, making the walk uncomfortable. She took another cursory look around the Gregg's garden then hurried back into the home through the sliding glass door she had left cracked. The detective removed a blue glove from her purse, snapped it on, and lightly touched the edge of the glass doors to reenter the study where Dennis was killed. Kicking off her shoes at the garden entrance, she tossed a few wood chips back into the garden.

Something urged her to walk back outside to the rear of the garden. She paused when a mountainous compost heap drew her attention.

Brouwer's crew said they hadn't 'found a fucking thing,' she thought, cringing as she recalled his gritty voice. Combing through that compost was tedious, she hoped they'd been thorough, and yet ... she hoped they had been thorough. So much for her theory that the gun was stashed there.

Joi looked up when a shadow drew her attention. Miss Ollie stared straight at her. The pensive look on the woman's face was enough to make Joi realize that Miss Ollie had been carefully watching her. Weird.

"I'm about to leave," Joi said. "You want to close the door?"

"Yes ma'am," was the woman's passive aggressive reply.

Miss Ollie closed the door and the tumblers on several locks fell into place on the other side of the front door. Maybe the nosey broad had overheard her call to the station and that was her way of saying 'good riddance, Detective.'

Joi started to knock again, just for the hell of it, but she needed to sink her teeth into Marcus Gregg again. Ms. Ollie be damned.

She lit a Virginia Slims menthol and re-twisted a thick lock of brownish bronze hair, tucking it back behind her ear before sliding under the steering wheel of her Saturn and accelerating out of the driveway of the Gregg home.

CHAPTER 38

SEPTEMBER 10, 2004

Marcus turned into the police station parking lot a full half hour before his eleven thirty appointment. He had worked a couple of hours extra on his last shift to cover a guy who was running late. It was three a.m. when he knocked off. By the time he showered, scarfed down a few White Castle burgers, onion rings, and a Coke and finally laid down to take a nap, it was 4:45 a.m. Afraid that he'd oversleep Marcus hauled a comforter off his bed and crashed on the sofa. When the alarm clock startled him awake at ten o'clock, he popped up like toast, showered to revive himself, and headed out.

He pulled into an open space midway the parking lot, near enough to see the front entrance from his car. His truck was behind a row of empty white squad cars and a police wagon that looked like it had seen its best days. He turned off the truck's ignition and began to daydream. Before he realized it, he nodded off to sleep. He dreamt that he was hand-cuffed inside a paddy wagon, crushed against other male prisoners and shackled around the ankles.

Marcus imagined bloody pools on the floor from suspects tortured into confessing to crimes they had not committed. He felt his power draining away through the soles of his feet.

The image of his father stretched out on the floor in his den flickered and pushed away the image of the casket which was his final resting place.

The sound of a car horn awakened him from his sleep. His heart was racing and he attempted to calm himself by lighting up a cigarette. He sat composing himself and wishing this whole ordeal was over. The dashboard clock read eleven twenty. Taking a final puff from his cigarette, he stubbed it out in the ashtray. He took a deep swig from the coffee he'd picked up *en route,* hoping that the combination of caffeine and nicotine would quell the nerves. He needed to be alert and steady, even after completing a fourteen-hour shift. The detectives *had* to believe that he had not murdered his father. Dennis had seen to it that he knew how to shoot, but he had never even owned a gun.

He knew that their father had died from gunshot wounds, not from the ass-kicking he had delivered. He needed to convince the cops that the old man was moving on the floor when he had left the scene.

"I actually *wanted* to kill him that night," Marcus admitted to himself. "I left to *keep* from killing him."

Marcus felt ashamed, remembering his last visit and the way they had spent the final moments of his father's life.

❖ ❖ ❖

His father hadn't even expected him. Why would he? They hadn't been alone, in the same room, for years. Marcus had been sickened at the thought of confronting his father, even after downing three courage-boosting Rolling Rock beers and circling the block twice before pulling into the driveway. The knot in his solar plexus caused him to want to double over. Could he even reach the old man?

He replayed Kelly's nagging and probing questions about his distance from his father. Even though she was older, Marcus felt he was stronger. Maybe Kelly's sessions with her shrink would get at the root of her emotional paralysis; he had known the root of his angst for a long, long time.

Once inside, his father's quick motions pointed to an easy chair. "Sit down, Son."

The word "son" sent hot spasms through Marcus' body. He approached the chair and plopped his 5' 7" frame down harder than he intended, but he was relieved to get the weight off his feet. There was nothing he could do about the knot in his stomach but bear it. Gripping the sides of the chair stabilized him.

Dennis' gaze permeated his flesh. Marcus fought for composure.

"How've you been," Marcus asked, trying to ease into a conversation that had no easy entry.

"O.K.

"Business is a little slow but I've used the time to counsel some of the Brothers at the church, you know. How 'bout you, Marcus?"

"Good. The job's going well. I moved to a bigger place in West Pullman."

"West Pullman?" asked Dennis, his voice rising.

"Yeah, West Pullman. I have a real sharp place, good neighbors. It's a nice block," Marcus defended. "Mostly settled people like you and Mom, at 107th and Parnell. I'm renting with an option to buy," he said nervously. "I enjoy the space and the solitude."

Marcus gazed beyond the patio window to the garden. "Man, Mom still has her way with plants."

"Your choice," said his father, ignoring his son's hasty digression to gardening.

Marcus sat motionless and then in a sudden outburst blurted, "Dad, look! I need some closure here. I need to understand. The last time I tried to talk to you about this, you got mad. Don't you see, this is MY LIFE I'm trying to live here and I'm so fuckin' confused and … mad, dad. I'm mad at you. How could you have—"

"Oh, here we go again!" Dennis Gregg said, walking towards the study door as if he was going to leave. He spun and moved towards Marcus.

"*Again!*" Marcus felt awash with bewilderment. "What are you talkin' about? Me and you haven't ever—"

"Let me tell you something boy, I'll never address THAT subject with you or your sister again. Not today, not ever. I was healed of my affliction by the grace of Almighty God and if He doesn't judge me, who do you think you are?"

Marcus sat straight-backed, fighting to control the rage that swelled inside him.

The elder man flailed his arms. "Do what you need to do for yourself—pray, get counseling—but leave me out of it. And leave your poor mother out of it too!"

"HEALED! Healed? You're a goddamned "healed" liar! If I thought you were healed for one second—but no, you are not fooling anyone, nigga. I KNOW about Miss Mattie's son! I saw her at Wal-Mart and she told me that you have taken Corey camping. She said his dad was drinking again. I'll bet you told her he needed some guidance. Bullshit! That's how it started with me. You are NOT healed. I know what you are up to and you are NOT going to get away with it. Not this time!"

Dennis' eyes flashed fire and he began moving around the large desk towards Marcus.

"Shut up, Marc!" spat the elder man raising his hand as if to strike. But Marcus was beyond his reach. "You don't KNOW a DAMN thing! Get out! You can't come in here lying on my name. Why are you so concerned about Mattie anyway? If she had her way, I'd be lying in bed with her!"

Marcus' thoughts raced. Lowering his voice to just above a whisper, he asked, "What have you and my mother been doing all these years? IF I even thought you were healed, I would be so happy for you. I could try to forget the way you fucked up our lives, all of us. But you aren't healed. You just found fresh meat!"

Dennis' nostrils fanned. He lurched toward Marcus and, with a lightning swing, delivered a sucker punch to his son's brow, sending him reeling backwards into his chair. A small bloody gash opened over his left eye. Marcus struggled. He felt woozy as he climbed to his feet. He lunged across the table at his father, grabbing him by the throat.

"Son-of-a bitch, you took me camping, didn't ya? Fishing, hunting, all those bonding experiences … sick faggot!"

Mid-sentence came a crash of the shorter man's fist on the side of his son's jaw, sending pain spiraling through Marcus' face. Reflexively Marcus returned the blow, striking his father in the neck and knocking him to the floor. As he repeatedly struck with his knuckles across the fallen man's skull, pain radiated though his muscular arm.

Dennis struggled to his feet, only to be slugged again with all the suppressed pain and humiliation that had plagued Marcus Gregg all of his adult life. Dennis fell again. This time he lay still. Searing anger so blinded Marcus that he was certain that if he stayed in the room another moment he would take the heavy paperweight replica of Africa from his father's desk and gladly bash his head. He knew why he stayed away from his family. People thought he was the family black sheep but it was easier to stay away than to live the lie.

Rotten son of a bitch! What had begun as a confrontation to spare Corey had resulted in even more pain and violence.

Suddenly Marcus was suffocating, but he had the presence of mind to remember that he had called out a greeting to his mother on the way in. He needed to escape before she came downstairs. Desperately he reached for the sliding glass door, glanced at his reflection, and fled shakily through the garden, into the night.

❖ ❖ ❖

"Even now this bastard is in control!" Marcus seethed as he sat in the truck. The violence between them, once it erupted, seemed to frighten both men. The moment reminded him a little of a bid whist game. Once a card is on the table it must be played.

Marcus was puzzled. He knew Kelly had good reason to hate their father, but in his wildest dreams he couldn't fathom his beautiful sister, with her feline grace and charming manners, ever harming a single living thing. He remembered Kelly's hysterical phone call scarcely a month before. She'd begged him to drive over to kill a baby mouse stuck in a glue trap under her kitchen sink. Kelly had been shaken when Marcus had told her about a black cop recently killed in Roseland, a few blocks over from his house, when he got hemmed up during a drug bust.

No way was Kelly a killer. And it for damn sure wasn't him. Knowing his father's secret, it wasn't a stretch that Elder Gregg had probably been offed by one of his victims.

Marcus made a conscious decision in the front seat of his car, outside the police station, not to share the real reason for the fight. The old man was dead. He wouldn't be harming anyone ever again. His mother was sick. He'd be damned if she died a minute sooner because someone unearthed that shit.

Marcus silently rehearsed his story, taking an additional sip of caffeine courage. *Yes officer, I was in the house that night. Yes, we did argue, men do disagree you know. My father and I did not have the best relationship. No officer, I definitely did not murder my father!*

He would feel more convincing if he didn't have a nasty scab still over his left eyebrow where the old man had cuffed him. Still, he would have to be careful not to get railroaded by police.

I'm not the one, he resolved. His mind turned again to the hundreds of thousands of Black men on death row with slimmer alibis than he had. Realizing the gravity of his situation, he whispered, *I've got to make them believe me.*

It wasn't as if he had a lot of voices in the community that could speak up for him. He was the loner, the "nonconformist" his father had accused him of being. He didn't attend his family's church. In fact, he had not set foot in church after he left home in high school.

Their mother was skilled at guilting Kelly into attending church "Friend and Family Days," but Marcus was steadfast in his scorn for congregational worship. He agreed with Karl Marx that "religion is the opium of the people."

And his father had used the cloak of the church as a cover. Marcus walked into the building with an aura of gloom about him. He knew on the one hand that he had not killed his father, but that he didn't have the best alibi and that there was evidence of his having been in his father's office and having fought with him.

He walked past the front desk

A gruff voice called, "Hey, where ya goin buddy."

"My bad, I'm here for Detective Sommers."

"You're sposed to stop here first buddy, but go on up, you obviously know the way." He lifted the phone and Marcus assumed he was notifying them upstairs.

Marcus found his way to Joi's office and stood in the doorway. She instantly looked up and waved him over to her desk motioning him to take a seat in the black chair that faced her desk. Its rolling casters told him it had once been under a desk and now served as a 'guest' chair.

"Good morning, Mr. Gregg. I appreciate your coming in."

Marcus, irritated at his third trip in responded, "Did I have any other choice?"

"Not a wise one, Mr. Gregg, but you'd be surprised … anyway, as you know we are still examining leads and eliminating suspects." Joi rolled her chair closer to her desk and toyed with the tangled spiral cord dangling the phone receiver.

"So I take it I'm still under suspicion?" asked Marcus.

"Well, let's say you haven't been eliminated but others are under consideration."

"Like?"

Reaching for a yellow stenographer's pad and her pen she chose to respond to Marcus' question with a question of her own.

"Marcus, do you know Chad Sanders?"

"I wouldn't say I *know* him, but my sister Kelly is dating him, he was at Dad's funeral—"

"—Has he ever been physically violent with her?"

Marcus stretched his tired neck backward to release the mounting tension. Then looking down his nose at her he replied, "I'm sure he hasn't."

"How could you possibly know that?" she countered.

"Because I know Kelly," he said slowly, wanting to make sure he was clearly understood.

Joi nodded her head, and took a deep breath. "Got it." Then she reached into her bottom desk drawer and arose with a small floral case in her hand.

"Excuse me, I'll be back in a moment," she walked quickly into the hallway, he could only guess she was headed to the bathroom.

Marcus rolled discreetly back and forth with the chair. He was tired, annoyed and afraid that his life was about to change for the worse. There was nothing to read, and he didn't dare look over the notepad with two others seated at their desks.

Damn near ten minutes passed before the Detective returned. He wondered whether she purposely kept him waiting or if she really needed a potty break.

She pulled the floral case from her jacket pocket and hastily threw it into the bottom desk drawer.

"I apologize for your wait, I just have one or two more questions."

Marcus nodded, resigned to the inevitable.

"Would you consider your sister persuasive?" Joi asked, looking Marcus straight in the eyes.

"What?" Marcus frowned, squinting across the desk at Joi.

"I'm asking you," she paused, "if your sister had a problem with someone, would she ask a big brother *or* a boyfriend to help her solve it?"

"I wish you'd get to the point—I know you are already trying to pin the murder on me and I have told you that I-did-not-kill my father."

"How close are they?" Joi pressed.

"They who? Detective?" he responded, his voice raising a bit from the knowledge that she was trying to lead him somewhere he didn't want to go.

"Marcus, do you think that your sister's boyfriend could have something to do with your father's death. It's my job to explore all the possible—

"Detective, I hear you, but if you think I'm going to throw a man I barely know under the bus, you're wrong."

"Marcus, give everything we have discussed some thought and if you think of any relationships worth exploring, no matter how small, you have my card."

"Yes, I do," he said shifting anxiously in his seat, "and if that's all you've got, I'm dog tired."

"We're done here, catch up on your rest."

As he rose to leave she added a menacing, "Stay close."

CHAPTER 39

OCTOBER 2, 2004

Kelly opened the medicine cabinet's white enamel door. Reaching her mauve-manicured nails past a box of tampons and cotton swabs, she retrieved a pink and white cardboard box she had stashed.

She'd associated her nausea and the alien feelings in her body with the trauma surrounding her father's murder, but now her period, usually regular as clockwork, was three weeks late.

Kelly pulled up her soft green nightgown, straddled the toilet seat and released a stream of first-thing-in-the-morning pee onto the pregnancy indicator stick. Taking a deep breath, she waited.

The thought of motherhood terrified her, yet she sensed Chad had the seeds of being a loving father. Inhaling deeply, she looked at the stick. She smiled a deeply satisfying smile.

The results were crystal clear.

❖ ❖ ❖

Kelly and Chad planned to meet for lunch at the Promontory Point, provided he could get away from his office early. She dressed slowly, feeling a mixture of fear and a twisted kind of happiness. It was as if destiny was guiding her instead of the terrible facts that lurked in the dark places of her mind.

As Kelly walked along the lake's shoreline toward Promontory Point at 55th Street, for the first time, she was oblivious to the morning mist over the lake.

The Point was her spot when she needed to think. The young woman walked closer to the water, finally sitting amidst a cluster of boulders at the water's edge. Her eyes scanned the water, head resting on dainty fists as she struggled to come to grips with recent events. Kelly flicked away a spider crawling up her shorts. When she reflected upon the fact that her father—the origin of so much pain for her, for their family—was dead, she felt numb. Death—no, murder—was not the logical resolution of hatred, not for most people.

Her cell phone vibrated in her tote bag. She retrieved it and was warmly embraced by the cozy resonance of Chad's voice.

"Hey, babe, where are you? Weren't we going to the Point this afternoon? I'm standing in your lobby."

"I'm way ahead of you today," she whispered softly. "I'm already at the Point. Hurry up, slow poke."

Chad groaned his frustration. "You asked me to pick up at eleven a.m. right?"

"I just needed to do some soul-searching first. You know me and my water."

"Oh. Okay I'm on my way. Did you bring everything you needed?"

"Pretty much," the depressed Kelly responded. "On second thought, bring sunscreen."

"Sure. I'll be there in ten or fifteen minutes."

Kelly disconnected the call and sat with her arms wrapped around her knees as she watched two little girls playing with an older man.

"Probably their dad," she said aloud. He was tossing a blue, orange and yellow beach ball to the girls, whose braids flopped like puppy dog tails as they ran alternately catching and throwing the ball back to their father and each other. *That's the way it's supposed to be.*

She cautiously glanced around the area, slipped a black plastic bag from the tote, unknotted the end and let the heavy, shiny, silver object inside slip effortlessly into the depths of the murky water.

CHAPTER 40

Joi had a rough few days. She and Russell had another open case. This time they knew the thug they were looking for. Still, pressuring the members of his crew to give him up was time consuming.

The jaw breaker was that at two a.m., when she finally drifted off to sleep, she got a call from Maze.

"Hel-lo?" she responded sleepily. She listened to the voice on the other end for a couple of seconds before answering, "Aw Maze, what now?"

She could hear the alcoholic slur in her mother's voice.

"Mutha fucka hit me, that's what!"

She sat up, quickly gauging whether she needed to be ready to kick ass or if this was another recovery mission. "He still there?"

"Hellll naw, he know betta," stammered Maze with unfounded confidence.

"Indeed," sighed Joi, feeling like a rat on a very familiar and fucked up treadmill.

"Stay put. I'm coming." Joi shook her locks as a wake-up and disconnected the call.

She entered her walk-in closet, pulled on a pair of grey sweat pants and a matching hoodie, stuck her feet into a pair of loafers and clipped the holstered gun to the thick waistband of the sweat pants. Seconds later, she had armed her burglar alarm and bounded down the steps. No time to wait for the building's elevator. Maze had been on the wrong side of a man's fist. Again.

On the drive from her small apartment, she wondered if Maze Sommers would ever get tired of hooking up with low-life men. It seemed she got reassurance of her worth by flitting from one unworthy dog to another.

As her Saturn pulled up to Tina's Lounge at 79th and Racine, she pondered the fate of the woman who still felt that stretch marks from her pregnancy with her only child had forever marred her beauty. Having to constantly rescue and relocate Maze was driving Joi nuts. But no matter what she had to do, she would never allow her mother to move in with her. It was one thing to respond to her mother's drama as a dutiful daughter. It was another thing to invite the drama to her house to stay.

She picked up her cell from the seat of the car and dialed. After two rings she heard her mother's slurred speech on the line.

"I'm outside, Mama. You need me to come in or you alright to walk to the car?"

While waiting for her mother to say her goodbyes to the regulars that frequented Tina's, Joi reflected on how she had come to leave home at a time when most girls her age were contemplating getting a date to the Junior Prom.

As she watched her mother's 5'2" frame staggering towards her Saturn, she was embarrassed at how she looked. A cheap straw-colored wig was styled in a low ponytail that trailed ridiculously down her back. The striped orange and blue tank top had a stain, probably from an overturned cocktail, and one of her brown bareback sandals had a broken heel, causing Maze to walk with a dip. Detective Sommers couldn't help comparing her mess of a mom to Nancy Gregg. Mrs. Gregg was terminally ill, bereaved, and yet still managed to maintain her dignity.

"Heeeyy, Baby Girl," Maze said, stumbling over a large flattened plastic Mountain Dew soda bottle that littered the sidewalk. "I know I can always count on you to be here fo' yo' mama."

"Yeah sure," Joi said dryly. "Get in Mama, I'll take you home."

"I cainn eben pick a gooood man to savemylife Suggaa,. They alwaysthesame man wit a newww face. No mattaa—alwayyysss the saamme," her voice trailed. As she began to sob quietly, Joi fought the urge to hold her mother as she had done so many times before. Instead she said, "Ma, there's some cigarettes in the glove compartment." She gestured to the cup holder, "And there's a lighter right there. Grab yourself a smoke."

Driving past the commercial strip that was just settling down after a night of partying and carousing, she was thankful that her mother's current boyfriend, who was barely a few years older than Joi, wasn't a live-in.

As the street scenes streamed past her window, Joi remembered Al, the live-in step daddy that forced her from her home. The son-of-a-bitch had slapped her for stepping in when he tried to beat on her mother. Before Joi could regain her balance, his hands were around her throat, squeezing. She scratched at his hands, but his grip was like a steel vise and she felt her eyes bulging in their sockets. No air was getting to her lungs. Things started to go dark. When she came to, she was laying on the floor and he was kicking her.

Al shouted in fake falsetto, mimicking her mother. "Little Miss Special Joi." She could feel his toenails as his big-ass bare feet continued to kick grooves in her side. "This is a lesson for you. You gonna be cured of messin' in this man's business with your mama. Ya hear me! Next time we handlin' our business, you stay the hell out!"

After his final kick, he bent down close enough for her to smell the beer on his breath. She could barely see his ass through her tears and the snot that had pooled on the side of her face. Then Al picked up his Budweiser like hadn't a damn thing happened.

Joi had collected what was left of her spirit and stumbled into the bathroom to take the last shower she would ever take under her mother's roof.

It hurt Joi that whenever Maze referenced Joi's early departure from home she said that Joi had 'run away' never that she had "been run away" from her home by Maze's abusive lover.

❖ ❖ ❖

Luckily, this time Joi wouldn't need to tap into her shelter contacts to find temporary housing until she could find another permanent spot for Maze. She exited the Dan Ryan Expressway at 87th and headed east. In short order, she pulled up to her mother's apartment over Uncle Joe's Jerk Chicken. She then instructed her mother to lock and bolt the door and not allow anyone in—at least not that night.

"Call me if that creep shows up here." Joi took a shallow breath to avoid deeply inhaling the smell of flat beer that was part of Maze's body chemistry. She avoided her mother's eyes to hide her disappointment.

"He bedda not, my poooooleeese ocifer daughter'll have his ass," Maze slurred half under her breath.

"Ma, you might want to make yourself some coffee."

With those final words of wisdom, Joi swung right and hung a U-turn, heading back home. Hopefully she could shut her brain down and fall asleep before dawn.

CHAPTER 41

THURSDAY, OCTOBER 7, 2004

Joi inhaled deeply at the front door of the station. The early morning clean air from outside was overpowered by the stale air inside caused by poor ventilation and the active drunk tank. The stench of homelessness and hoes smacked her in the face. It irked Joi that no matter what cologne she applied to her pulse points, the precinct "eau de rank humanity" overpowered it. She sighed as she climbed the steps to her office, meeting Officer Brice Dolen midway.

"Brice."

"Hey, Joi. I left something on your desk that'll interest you."

"Oh?" she responded, still exhausted from the night's rescue mission. "What you got, Brice?"

"Ballistics report from your murder case. That joker got whacked with his own piece. Don't they say *home is where the heart is?*"

"Ya think?"

They exchanged knowing glances.

Joi hurried to her desk, nodding greetings at her colleagues along the way.

She lifted the manila folder Brice left. There it was in black and white. The gun used to kill Elder Dennis Gregg was one he had purchased in Round Lake, Illinois at Brankin's Gun Shop, January 29, 1995. Paid for in cash. Also purchased at that time were two boxes of ammo for the same gun. Why had Dennis Gregg felt he needed a weapon?

She snagged a plum Danish from the assortment one of the detectives had opened up on the grey file cabinet in their office, put it in a paper towel, then poured herself a cup of coffee.

She reviewed the ballistics report that Brice had left on her desk. Dennis Gregg had been killed with his own gun. Was it an accident that the killer came across it? Or had they known exactly where it was?

Later today they'd be interviewing Chad Sanders, to see what, if anything he knew about the Gregg case. Her last conversation with Marcus Gregg had been a waste of time. He didn't give her any additional information and her period coming down in the middle of the conversation was not helpful at all.

A lump formed in her throat. As much as she had tried to keep her life simple, it was now complicated as hell.

Chad stood out in a crowd of men when they had first met at a club on the North side. He was total eye candy, but she was never really into Chad. Who could be? To her he was just a full-of-himself pretty boy, and she had been drunk and lonely. Nearly a month had passed since Chad had been in her bed. Before that, she had slept with him maybe seven or eight times.

Truth was, nobody really 'got it done' for her like Russell. She was ashamed of what she felt for Russell. It was supposed to be just sex. Perhaps her feelings deepened because they worked together, but at the end of the day, she knew that he loved Helen. She needed to keep her feelings for Detective Wilkerson tightly under wraps.

The fact that Chad was a murder suspect's boyfriend and Joi's, every now and then, 'bed boo' made her life feel like an ugly, twisted tree trunk.

❖ ❖ ❖

Joi looked over the rim of her cup, taking a long sip as Chad Sanders entered the South Holland Police Station wearing a heather grey suit, light blue shirt and solid grey tie. He always looked like cash money, not that she spent much time looking at him in clothes. In fact, she usually saw him in jeans and a sweater or tee shirt—something he could get out of quickly. This morning her gaze ran the length and breadth of his tall muscular body, and she had to admit that among his more "earthy" talents, he wore the hell out of a suit.

"Russ, uh, can you wait outside for a few minutes. I want to get started and have you join."

"No problem, Joi."

"I'm going to take him in room 3."

Her partner gave her a look and said, "Sure, I'll let you get started. I'll be watching from the behind the two-way glass." She interpreted that to mean, "Who is this chump and did you just haul me down here for revenge?"

Joi couldn't help but think, *He's got his goddamned nerve.* Her relationship with Chad wasn't Russell's business.

"*De-tec-tive* Sommers?" Chad said dryly as he looked behind him before taking a seat in the dingy room.

Smirking, yet a bit self-conscious, Joi responded casually, "Yeah. I told you I was in law enforcement. Did you think I was a prison guard?"

"Honestly I didn't give it that much thought," he replied.

Joi hated that her personal and professional life were colliding. Tension between them was palpable.

"Well, there's nothing personal about this, Mr. Sanders. I'm going to do what the citizens of South Holland pay me to do. Ask you some routine questions," said Joi beginning to let the irony of the situation get under her skin. "I expect you will answer truthfully and to the best of your knowledge, and then you can get on with your day." She gave her head a sista-girl bobble-head roll.

Then she lifted an eyebrow. "That alright?"

He nodded, tightening his jaw.

She crossed the room and opened the door wider than necessary. "Detective Wilkerson, will you join us please?"

Russell came in and got right down to business. He was masterful, knowing how to get suspects to reveal information when they thought that they had not. He mentally rolled up his sleeves when he was about to go to work on a suspect's psyche. When he stood up, putting one brown loafer on the wooden chair Chad sat in and leaning over him casually, Chad began to shrink in his seat. Joi saw that he didn't know what to expect from the dark-eyed detective who could have passed for a salesman were it not for the cold gritty look in his eyes.

"Mr. Sanders, where did you meet Kelly Gregg?" said Russell abruptly. "How long have you been dating?" asked Russell.

"About six or seven—yea, about seven months," responded Chad. He looked suddenly afraid that he could possibly be a serious person of interest.

"Intimate?" said Russell, now seated across from Chad and deliberately burying his head in a manila filing folder that contained case notes. He stopped as if he found something new and interesting. Joi knew he had not. It was just part of his ruse.

"Meaning *what*, Detective?"

"Let me put it this way," said Russell, pausing. "Have you and Kelly Gregg had sex? Have you done her? Is that clear enough?"

"I don't need to tell you our business."

"Our business, eh? Sounds like you *have* done her."

Chad sat, looking stupid, as if an eighteen wheeler was rolling over him and he didn't know why.

"What do you know about her relationship with her father?" came the next abrasive inquiry.

"Not a lot."

Russell seemed to smell a lie.

Joi was painfully aware that he was obviously smitten with Kelly. *Whipped* was a more accurate term. This woman was such a princess he probably only got laid once a month—which is probably why he found himself at her bedside eating Harold's Chicken, tossing back a beer, and straining those beautiful biceps and buttock muscles to satisfy her lust.

Joi was glad that Russell stepped in to ask the question that would have stuck in the back of her throat.

"Mr. Sanders, would you say that you are in a serious relationship with Ms. Kelly Gregg?"

"I would," he responded, looking directly at Russell and deliberately avoiding Joi's eyes. "Where is this going? My relationship with Kelly is personal. Aren't you investigating her father's murder?"

Russell pulled a pack of gum from his pocket, took a piece out, unwrapped it and pushed the pack over to Chad. Chad cocked his head and stared at Russell, waving off the gum. "Look, Mr. Sanders, I don't want to waste your time so let's get to it. Did you know Dennis Gregg?"

Chad paused, gave a long look at Joi, then to the detective and back to Joi. A small smirk relaxed the tension in the corners of his lips.

"No, not really. I have *met* him."

"What was your impression of him?" asked Russell.

"What? I didn't really *know him*," Chad replied smoothly. "I'm dating his daughter. I'm not paid to like or dislike her daddy."

"I get that. Please answer the question. What was your impression of Dennis Gregg?"

"Look, dude," Chad snapped, then corrected himself. "Officer, I didn't get a *vibe* from him. He was a short man who kept trying to make himself bigger, like he had a complex about it. Seemed to like to be large-and-in-charge. I felt like his wife was intentionally walking two steps behind. Maybe that was just my perception but I really don't give a damn."

"I didn't mean to piss you off, Mr. Sanders. I'm just trying to get at some truth here."

"And that's what I just gave you, bro."

Russell fell back and Joi took over. Sharp-ass Chad was in sales. He made a living manipulating situations to his advantage. *Not this time my brother.*

"Uh-hum." Joi cleared her throat. "Mr. Sanders," she said, causing Chad's attention to snap to her. "Would you know of anyone in the Gregg household, anyone in that family that had a reason to want Dennis Gregg dead?"

"I read in the paper that it was a robbery," said a mildly defensive Chad. "I don't live in the area and neither does Kelly." He paused momentarily, squinting at her in a way that was a very transparent attempt to connect with her personally before saying, "Detective, Kelly has had a real rough go of it lately. She's had some personal struggles and then to top it off, her father was murdered."

Joi stared openly at Chad and almost smiled at his subtle attempt to rein her in. Now that Chad had declared his love for Kelly, his protective juices had begun to flow. He actually thought he had the right to request that she take it easy on Kelly because, "she has had a hard time of it lately." Tough titty!

His concern for Kelly cut Joi in a way she hadn't anticipated. She found it oddly painful to be the one unearthing Chad's feelings for Kelly. She realized, dammit, that she was jealous. Could she be hiding her feelings for Chad, even from herself? Inhaling deeply, she realized that despite their sexual intimacy, she had never let Chad or any man into her own personal struggles. *Who the hell does Chad think I am?*

"Mr. Sanders, what exactly is Kelly "going through?" she said, unable to keep the sarcasm from her voice.

"I'm not sure," he said, flinching at her tone. "But I know she's ugh, getting help."

Joi fought another sarcastic response that sought to leap from the back of her tongue—which was more like 'give me a break'. She inhaled and exhaled slowly. "What kind of help is she getting?"

"I believe she's seeing a therapist."

As soon as he mentioned the therapist, Joi looked up from her note pad just in time to see him grit his teeth.

Sooo Ms. Kelly Gregg is a nutcase.

Chad quickly added, "I don't really know exactly why, but *my point* is that she is seeking *and* getting help."

Liar. He very likely knew exactly why the ice princess was seeing a shrink and had enough sense to realize that it was something that might be incriminating.

Joi scribbled on her yellow note pad, '*talk to the Gregg chick's shrink.*'

The interview continued for another twenty minutes, probing Chad's connection to the family; whether he knew other family members; what motive could he have possibly had for wanting the old man dead or killing him for Kelly. The elephant in the room was the on-again, off-again sex they had shared, that despite his rock hard microphone, was now going to be a thing of the past.

After Chad left, Joi sat quietly at her desk, rehashing the painful forty-five minute interview and writing up her notes.

"Old friend?" said her partner, placing his hand firmly on her shoulder.

"Yeah." Joi responded, feeling somehow smaller.

"It happens," he said smoothly, before walking away. It wasn't the comment, but Russ' delivery that left Joi's face stinging. If she had been a lighter shade of brown, her cheeks would have been crimson.

Russell, like all dicks, figured out things that didn't need to be spelled out.

Joi picked up the phone and stabbed ten digits. She was quickly connected to what was becoming a familiar voice. "Hello, Miss Gregg? This is Detective Sommers. How are you?" Only after Kelly's response that dealt with her mother's health did Joi have a little twinge of guilt. "Your mother was hospitalized for dehydration?—so sorry. Give her my best." Joi took a long slow breath, and the image of Chad flashed into view, which swept aside all guilt about questioning a grieving Kelly. "I know that this is a hard time for you but I need to get some additional information."

"What kind of information?" came the dry reply.

"I need the name of your therapist." After several silent seconds, Joi said, "Miss. Gregg? Kelly?"

"Yes, Detective," she responded, her irritation apparent. "Why is that anyone's business?"

Pleased that she had ruffled the young woman's feathers, Joi continued,

"Well, ordinarily the fact that you are seeing a doctor of any kind is not police business. However in this case, I'm sure you—"

"Doctor Patricia Snowden. I don't have her number with me but she's on 53rd and Hyde Park. She's in the phone book."

"Thanks much, Ms. Gregg. Again give my best to—" Before the click on the other end signaled an abrupt disconnection, Joi overheard the polished little miss snarl, "Bitch!"

CHAPTER 42

MONDAY, OCTOBER 11, 2004

As Joi drove east on 93rd Street, sweat trickled from her armpit down the side of her tan tee-shirt. *It's hot as hell already, and it's only six-forty five in the morning,* she thought as she waited for the air conditioning to kick in. As she backed into an open spot in Parking Lot A, she remembered how much she hated being in hospitals. As a homicide dick, she occasionally found herself in hospitals interviewing eye witnesses or escorting a grief-stricken family member to identify the body of a loved one.

Today her business was personal.

On this muggy October morning, she walked under Advocate Trinity Hospital's purple and white awning, and found herself coping with the sights and smells of that unnerving antiseptic environment.

A sleepy looking Latino security guard at the front desk failed to acknowledge her presence. Joi waited a few moments, then cleared her throat and whispered, "Good Morning. I'm here to see a patient. Ms. Maze Sommers. She would have come through the ER last night."

The dark-haired man looked at a log on the counter and shifted through several sheets of paper before saying with a Spanish accent, "Yes, Meez Sommers is here." He gave her a clip-on visitor's badge. "She's en room 214." He pointed to his right. "Go down this co-rid-dor and you'll see the elevators on the left."

As Joi moved through the hallways, the mounted photographs of the hospital board members and staff drew her attention. She felt comforted by a diverse array of dignified faces staring back at her from the drab beige walls of the southeast side community hospital. But the hollow echoes of the steps of hospital personnel made the walls of her stomach constrict.

As she entered the semi-private room, she was glad that her mother had the bed nearest the door. She hated schlepping through someone else's trouble to get to the source of her own. Her mother sat, watching a rerun of *The Jerry Springer Show. Doesn't the woman have enough drama in her life?*

She was glad that her sneakers masked the sound of her footsteps. Her mother didn't hear her enter or see her only child wince at the first sight of her. At fifty-three, Maze Sommers was a tight little knot of a woman. Smooth almond skin stretched tightly over her angular canvas. When asked about her high cheekbones, Maze claimed to be descended from American Indian and African-American stock. But then so did a lot of Black folks that didn't want to admit to having a proud ancestry diluted by white slave masters.

Joi took a deep breath and exhaled before speaking.

"What happened this time, Mama?" she sighed, weary of this dance. Just five days earlier she had retrieved Maze from Tina's bar. She was suddenly overwhelmed by the conflict that raged inside her. The cop wanted to conduct the questioning. The daughter was sickened to her stomach and ached to hold her mother, but she didn't. She couldn't. Maze sported a second shiner to go along with the one she had received at the bar. Now she had a pair. The damage was so intense that the white of her left eye was completely red with broken capillaries. A foul joke she overheard some asshole cops saying when she worked in the city came to mind: *"Hey, what does it mean when a hooker gets two shiners?"*

"I don't know, tell me."

"Means her pimp had to tell her twice!"

Maze's voice penetrated Joi's fog. "Oh hi, Love, I didn't … I didn't hear you come in," stammered the woman

Joi paused, trying to get her bearings. "What … what happened to you, Maze?"

"That no-good asshole hit me for nothing, Joi."

Maze's lame response assured Joi that she was alright—at least mentally.

Joi took a quick look to the right at the empty second bed. At least their conversation could be private. The window was cracked and fresh air seeped into the room. Even propped up on four pillows, Maze looked frail. Joi took a deep breath and allowed herself to embrace the perverse mixture of relief and anger that fought inside her chest.

"Seriously Ma, you got real poor taste in companions." She wanted to say more, but it wouldn't help. Never had.

Annoyed by the strains of "Jerry! Jerry! Jerry!" that filled the sea-green hospital room, she took the remote control from the bedside tray and powered the television off.

Maze glanced at Joi, but remained silent.

The damaged eye looked ready to burst and spray blood onto the bed.

Joi scanned her mother's face. A raised scar the size of a dime on the right side of Maze's forehead caught her attention. A physical reminder of Al, the boyfriend that had forced the teen-aged Joi's premature emancipation. Her mother had wept for days when that bastard died of prostate cancer.

Joi on the other hand had thanked God for letting him languish in pain. In her mind justice, though delayed, had been served. His hateful ass lived forty-seven years too long.

Whenever she was forced to think of Al, which was basically every time she looked at Maze, she mentally referenced the tiny raised ridge on the left side of her hairline that was covered by thick locks of hair. Al's kick had opened a gash that required five stitches and a hospital stay.

"Let's talk," Joi said.

"Nothing to talk about," Maze said, turning the television back on and flicking through the channels on the controller. "I'm in here for a day, two max. I'll be fine soon."

"Ma, you were drunk or high on something last night and you got your ass beat again." Speaking now with raw emotion, she added, "Have you seen how you look? When will it end? When I find you laying in an alley dead!"

"But Joi, baby it wasn't like you think. And the drugs here are pretty good. I'm feelin' no pain."

For the first time in a long time, Joi placed her hand in her mother's hair. Maze's hair was fine, unlike Joi's coarse dread-locks. The thick row of baby hair across her forehead softened the angles of her face. Her eyes were almond shaped, with thick lashes, puppy-dog eyes that magnetized men to her until her dark pouty lips spewed some nonsense that had somehow earned her a chipped front tooth.

"Ma-ah, what's *wrong* with you? Why can't you just have a few drinks and call it a night?" she whispered. "Why does it have to end with you getting beat down by some no good jerk? Why?"

Joi's voice cracked as she lost the battle of self-control. She'd heard that prisoners thrown in solitary for extended periods often deliberately did something to get themselves beaten. They needed some type of human contact to stimulate their will to survive. Maybe Maze fed off the exchange of physical and emotional energy invested in the kicking of her ass. Was her mother taking her loveless life to the bars and picking fights to feed her survival?

"Look, l'il' girl," Maze said, steely gaze narrowing at Joi. "That's not a question to ask me—ask them!" came the feisty response. Joi looked past the woman that she had rescued so many times before. The reason for her mother's downward spiral was hard to grasp. Did she ache so deeply to be loved that she'd made up her mind that any level of contact with a man was better than being alone?

There was nobody that Maze wouldn't stand up to, which also accounted for why the petite woman got knocked down so much. She had a potty mouth and when she was drunk and decided to harass a man, she could verbally cut off a guy's balls. Unfortunately, his comeback was often a fat lip or, in this case, two black eyes.

She glanced over at her mother's pitiful raccoon like mask and thought, "Something's gotta give or some asshole is gonna kill Maze."

Joi watched her mother fumble around the bed for the remote. She was painful to look at, even from the side view. The young detective kept trying to distance her emotions from her mother, but it never seemed to work. Maze was bad news.

She cocked her head, which felt like a fifty pound weight, half looking at her mother and half escaping beyond the tiny hospital room. She gazed through the gauzy curtains, longing for a less complicated world before exhaling the words she had dreaded.

"Mama, let's get you packed up," she whispered. "I want you to come stay with me for a while."

CHAPTER 43

Joi's morning had been emotionally draining but Maze was settled and she could move on with her investigation. Dr. Trish Snowden, Kelly's shrink, had an office located in the Hyde Park Bank Building. Joi relished the drive into the city from South Holland. Near the University of Chicago campus, Hyde Park felt almost like a college town, reminding her a bit of the University of Ann Arbor where she had gotten her bachelor's degree.

The therapist's dilemma was that she was booked solid, but that was not going to stop Joi from getting the interview she needed. Rather than trying to muscle Snowden into canceling several patients and driving to the south suburbs to answer questions, the detective agreed to meet the therapist at her office during a short break in her full schedule.

Time away from the office—and Russell's probing gaze—would do her some good. Smooth jazz from WNUA radio helped her tune out the crackling voice of the police dispatcher.

When she reached her destination, she rode the elevator up to the 8th floor, presented her business card and whispered her name to the receptionist. The woman smiled as though she was expected and immediately took Joi and her card to an interior office.

"Miss Sommers, I'm going to take this in to Dr. Snowden. She's in a session." She lowered her voice to just above a whisper, "You'll definitely be next, Detective."

"Alright, thanks." Joi looked down at the slim silver watchband on her wrist. "Right now, I'm okay for time."

Dr. Snowden hadn't lied about being overbooked. The L-shaped waiting room was thickly carpeted and looked more like an upscale living room than a psychiatrist's office. It appeared that Snowden's patients came in all flavors. Across from Joi sat an angry looking teenager with a woman—probably his mother. A pregnant woman was sitting alone with her face buried in a *Parenting* magazine. There was a well-dressed young woman of about thirty wearing a stunning tailored suit with chocolate brown designer shoes that had a bright red bottom. Detective Sommers thought, *Snowden must be good.* The olive-green suit and Nine West pumps Joi wore made her feel like she blended right in. She picked up the August issue of *Essence* Magazine.

"Ms. Sommers." The receptionist called her name without her title. *Perfect.* Joi followed her into the therapist's office.

"Detective Sommers," Dr. Patricia Snowden said, extending her hand.

"Good afternoon, doctor," Joi said, noting that the grasp she met was self-assured and damp.

The tawny-skinned woman motioned for Joi to take a seat in the comfortable black leather chair opposite her desk.

"I see you have patients waiting." Joi looked around at the huge mahogany desk and butter-soft leather chairs. "I appreciate your seeing me." She removed a yellow pad and a black and silver pen from her oversized bag.

"You're quite welcome Detective. Now how can I help?" Snowden's tone was professional and clipped.

"Dr. Snowden, I know that Kelly Gregg is a patient here. Have you treated her for long?"

"Miss Gregg has been my patient for all of about eight months."

Joi allowed herself to sink into the soft leather. "Does she see you often?"

"I could check, but off the top of my head, I'd say that I've seen her ten or so times."

Dr. Snowden rose. "Tea?"

"Excuse me?"

"Detective, would you care to join me for a cup of tea?" Trish Snowden strode in her perfectly tailored toffee-brown suit over to a small wooden tea cart, and with a flourish of expertly manicured hands, offered an assortment of designer teas.

"I never drink coffee, can't stand what it does to my breath. Care to join me?"

"Oh, no … no thanks. I prefer my coffee you know … "high test", but you go ahead."

Joi stopped writing and asked, "On medication?"

"I beg your pardon," responded Dr. Snowden, pouring water from a delicate sterling tea pot and dipping an Earl Grey tea bag into the steaming water.

"Have you prescribed medication for Kelly Gregg?"

Trish took a sip of tea, swallowed, and said, "No, she's not on any medication."

"Does she *need* medication?"

"Detective, if she needed medication I would have written her a script."

Sensing that she was not going to get anywhere if she pissed Snowden off, Joi quickly took a softer tone.

"Doctor Snowden, why is Kelly Gregg seeing you?"

Setting her china cup onto its matching saucer, Trish Snowden replied, "Detective, that's privileged information. You know I can't reveal that to you."

That didn't come as a surprise. Joi knew that she would have to be clever to gather information within the purview of the doctor-patient privilege.

"Doc, I do understand your situation, however, this is a murder investigation. If we go to trial I can subpoena your records and you can be forced to testify. A man lost his life and my job is to find out who killed him. I'm just doing my job."

"And this is not my first time around the block, Detective." Snowden stood, signaling that she was done. "Do what you have to do."

"Meaning what?" Joi glared at Trish, who stood defiantly between her and the door of the office.

Joi closed her yellow tablet and stood with her legs akimbo. "Let me ask you this, *Doctor*," she said with a menacing emphasis on the woman's title. "In your medical opinion, is Kelly Gregg a dangerous person?"

"Detective, it is my professional opinion that Kelly Gregg is neither a danger to herself nor to anyone else."

Dr. Snowden continued. "Millions of people are in therapy—movie stars, athletes, even dockworkers. Therapy simply means that one is seeking professional help for one's problems. It doesn't automatically mean that you are a dangerous person."

Joi's gaze narrowed on the doctor. Something in the doctor's tone hinted her conviction that her patient was harmless.

"Thanks for your cooperation Doctor. If I need you, I'll find you," said the detective, in an attempt to rock the doctor. She pivoted and without uttering another word abruptly walked toward the office door.

"Detective Sommers."

Joi turned to face the smiling Trish.

"Please take my card." She extended her card. "I have several law enforcement officers as patients. Yours is a very stressful job. It might do you good to talk to someone like me."

"You are right about that, doc," Joi said, noticing that Dr. Snowden was looking down at her shaking hands.

Joi took the card, returned the smile and exited the office. She wasn't out of earshot when she heard the rattled woman say, "Anya, please give me ten minutes before you send in my next patient."

CHAPTER 44

TUESDAY, OCTOBER, 11, 2004

Nancy Gregg slowly opened her eyes and glanced around her cheerful hospital room. Ms. Ollie had done her best. She had folded a thick bottle-green blanket atop the stark-white hospital blanket, and refreshed the flowers in the vase that sat on the window ledge beside several family photos.

She looked to her right and her gaze landed on an 8x10 silver and gold rimmed frame holding a smiling photo of her and her husband during happier times. The photo made Nancy feel that Dennis was still with her, so much so that sometimes she talked to it.

Nancy heard familiar footsteps outside her cheerful hospital room.

Right on time, she thought, gathering her courage for Kelly's entrance. *I have to ... have to tell her today.*

Kelly entered the spotless hospital room and smiled as she inhaled the scented roses. She lightly kissed her mother on the cheek.

Nancy drew a heavy breath. She was unworthy of the devotion the beautiful young woman at her bedside gave her. She was tormented about where to start, but the brunch was as good a place as any—given the way it had ended.

They exchanged pleasantries and Kelly sat gracefully in a small green leatherette bedside chair. She looked furtively at Nancy.

"Mother?"

Nancy was not entirely lucid. "Kelly, you remember the brunch you arranged with your father and me?"

"Mother, let's not talk about this now, wait until you get better."

"Listen to me," Nancy said in a soft whisper. "I'm not going to get better."

Kelly gave her mother's hand a gentle pat. "Of course you are, Mother. Don't talk—"

"—I *know* better. I need you to understand something."

"Mother, I understand more than you know," Kelly replied. "I don't think it's a good idea to talk about something so serious right now."

"Kelly." Nancy raised up in her bed to almost a sitting position, "I want—no, I *need* to get this out."

"Fine, Mother," said Kelly.

Nancy fought to control her own anxiety. She remembered the ill-fated, but carefully-staged Sunday brunch, and she knew Kelly did too.

Kelly eased back fully in the chair.

"I remember inviting you over to my apartment and that you and Daddy refused to talk to me. You left. Remember?"

It was obvious that Kelly's anger was bubbling like a shaken up soda. "Kelly, I believed you. I always knew. I just couldn't face it." Nancy wept. "I'm so ashamed for the way that your father ..." Her frail body shook as she continued, "I couldn't admit it that afternoon in your apartment. Couldn't bear to face the humiliation." Looking directly into her daughter's eyes, she gasped, "Do you know that your father and I never even talked about it? All those years. It was a shock, you saying those things that day, baby. But everything you said to us was true."

Kelly stood abruptly, towering over the older woman's shriveled figure. "Mothers protect their children! Don't you understand that?" She paused, swallowing hard. "You loved Daddy more. You didn't save me. You never, even tried!"

Eyes riveted on her daughter, Nancy swallowed painfully. She knew she earned this treatment.

"He *stole* my innocence!" Kelly snarled. "Made me ashamed, afraid to trust. Every day I remember. Ev-er-y-day!!!" Tears poured down her cheeks. "Was I such a bad little girl? Was that why you allowed him to hurt me?"

Nancy watched her daughter collapse into the chair like a rag doll, looking like she had been transported back to that time.

"No! No-Darling. You were adorable," said Nancy, raising her left arm, totally unconscious of the IVs still attached. Her eyes glazed over. "Baby, you had the sweetest little smile. Whenever someone gave you any little gift, you said 'thank you' in such a touching way. I always loved clamping pretty barrettes on the ends of your pony tails. No, it was your father's sickness, not you children, Kelly."

Nancy watched painfully as her only daughter sat, head in soggy palms as if she were shutting out her mother's words.

"Sweetheart, try to understand. Our marriage was everything. I made a vow ... a sacred vow. And I kept that vow—for better or for worse. Your father was a good man." She placed a hand on her chest. "In his heart he was good. His weaknesses ... just seemed to overcome him, no matter how hard he tried."

"Mama, he hurt me!" Kelly snapped. "He hurt me for a long, long time. I grew up feeling like a dirty little girl." Her saucer-like eyes overflowed with tears that spilled down her face.

Nancy's eyes closed. She fought to draw strength from an empty well.

"Kelly." She glanced over at the photo of her and her departed mate and exhaled the words, "I know he loved you both."

Kelly wiped her face and looked directly at her mother.

"He loved *us both*, Mother?"

At that moment, Kelly realized that her mother was admitting more than she ever imagined.

CHAPTER 45

Joi realized it had been exactly ten days since she had collected Maze from Trinity Hospital. She had to admit that they were actually getting along pretty well, or at least they gave one another their space.

Detective Sommers pulled into the driveway of her apartment building, glad that the day's shift was over. She felt like an empty shell, hungry for something or someone to pour into her. Her deepest desire was to shed her clothes at the front door, slip into a pair of soft pajamas, and grab a brewski. Then she'd channel surf or doze off while reading a few chapters of a steamy novel.

She turned her key in the door and called out, "Ma, I'm here," immediately pulling off her grey blazer and tossing it onto the hook on the closet door.

Moving toward the guest bedroom, she planned to stick her head in the door before retiring to her own room. She'd fallen into the habit of sitting with her mother to talk about her day. Typically it was one set of bad news after the next, but occasionally she had something positive to share.

Every day, it was becoming harder to stay connected to the reason she had become a homicide cop in the first place. Today had been a series of knocking on doors and prying information from the unwilling. Well, except Ms. Geraldine. Joi had a feeling that maybe grandma's conscience world make her come forward with something about the night of the Gregg murder.

As she pushed open the door and peered inside, she immediately saw that the queen-sized bed was made up. That was unusual, but it wasn't cause for alarm. Then the folded paper laying on the bed caught her attention. Her heart sunk as she opened the note.

Joi love, I need to do me. Thanks and keep safe. Maze.

P.S I got the 50 bucks you left for groceries. I hope you don't mind.

Joi sank onto the guest room queen-sized bed and was flooded with a strange combination of regret and relief. For years she had fought the idea of having her mother live with her, but now she had to admit that it was comforting to have her to come home to at the end of her shift. Better than waiting for a call in the wee hours of the morning from someone who only wanted to have sex with her.

She glanced around the bedroom and noticed that the small boom box that normally sat on a wrought iron stool near the window was also gone. She figured Maze must have hooked up with an old boyfriend. Grocery money and something to play music on was her initial contribution.

So be it.

CHAPTER 46

Kelly looked at her mother, her loveliness smothered by illness. For one fleeting moment she saw the mirage of the beautiful woman she had grown up in awe of. The woman possessed of thick dark brown mane drawn into a bun at the nape of her neck. In signature sheath dresses and matching pumps, the mother she knew played bridge with the Village's elite, volunteered at the church and collected silent auction prizes for their annual gala. Nancy Gregg, on the surface, seemed perfect. So did their nuclear family. Yet beneath the surface of perfection...

Now after hearing her mother's confession, she looked at the stained pink night gown and wispy, fine hair as if she were seeing the woman for the very first time.

Nancy seemed lost in her own thoughts as she spoke. "I know what your father did was so very, very, wrong. I just wanted to hold our family together. Kelly *every* family has problems. I just wanted to keep us together, *as a family*, and deal with our troubles and not break down ..." Her voice trailed. "This medicine makes me so sleepy, but I ... want you to know ..."

"Mother, you never made him stop," Kelly said through her teeth. "He was your husband! But *you* were supposed to be my protector. You gave birth to me. All I ever wanted was to know that you loved me."

She covered her eyes letting the weight of the rest of her mother's confession settle in. "And Marcus too! Oh God, I feel sick ... sick."

Nancy reached over with trembling hands and slowly lifted a small green plastic cup and haltingly drank a swallow. While attempting to replace it, she lost her grip, sending the half- empty cup tumbling to the floor. Kelly grabbed a wad of tissues from the dispenser and soaked up the water, replacing the cup to its place. She gave Nancy an exasperated sigh and walked to the open window.

"I have had this dream, *the same dream* a thousand times." Kelly sighed, pulling the cord that fully opened the curtains to daylight. "In my dream, I'm a little girl and a monster comes into my room. He's big, with huge hands that he uses to cover my eyes. The monster crawls into my bed and lays me under him. I'm shaking and he's so heavy I can't breathe. Then—you burst into the room and stare the monster in the face. The monster kisses me goodnight on my forehead and walks out the room. You smile at me, and say 'sleep tight baby' and close the door."

Kelly squeezed her eyes shut then spat in a menacing tone, "But you never did that! Every morning after he *raped* me, you made waffles." Kelly released a bitter laugh. "Was that your way of giving me hope? And what about my brother?!! What did Marcus get?" she asked as she broke down weeping.

"I love you. Always did, Baby Girl. I just kept loving you and your brother and your father with all of my heart, Baby. And I put you all in the Lord's hands!"

"Mama for heaven's sake, *you* were the Lord's hands!" Kelly, surprised at her outburst, turned from her mother's ashen face. Tears streamed tracks down her face as she looked into the parking lot below, wishing she were outside and not having to confront her mother while she was in such a weakened state. The excuses were just too much.

"But I prayed for you," Nancy said. "Listen to me. Baby, every single day I prayed, and after years of prayer I came to realize that sometimes our prayers just keep you strong—keep you going."

"You prayed!" Kelly wrung her wad of tissues into small rags. *"Don't you think I prayed too!* Nobody's prayers worked. Do you hear me! The only relief I got was my summers with Auntie Di'!" Kelly swept a gaze across her mother's tear-stained face. "She couldn't have known what was happening to me."

Nancy's expression was frozen.

"Oh my God," Kelly whispered. "She *did* know. You all knew! And no-one helped me!"

"Sometimes people have sicknesses that can't be cured. Our family lived with a terrible disease all these years," Nancy uttered, looking directly at her daughter. "But we survived, Kelly. You and Marc grew up in a good neighborhood. You *know* what love and family is, and you have values. You and your brother are good, caring people who love The Lord. That's so—"

"—Who told you that, Mother?" Kelly spat. "I don't *love the Lord*! *Your Lord* was watching when your husband repeatedly raped both his children. I feel sick!"

Nancy adjusted her gown, grimaced and pressed the IV release for more pain medication. "Baby, who's to say how life's supposed to go? Me? You? Some things the Lord just asks us to bear."

Kelly paused, focused on her mother's movements. "Mama, are you hurting?"

She moved toward the door, intending to summon a nurse, but was stopped in her tracks.

"No! Baby, it's okay. I'll be fine. Just give the medicine a few seconds."

Kelly released the doorknob and eased back into the room, watching her mother settle back into the pillows.

"Kelly, I have prayed so often that you wouldn't hate me." She lifted her eyes to the ceiling. "The Master knows that I love my children—always loved you …"

Kelly staggered back to the bedside chair and squeezed her eyes shut. She repeated to herself, *God please give me the strength to forgive my mother—please give me the strength to not hate her.*

Thoughts coagulated in her brain as she regarded the wizened form that had taken over the body of the woman who was once her beautiful, vibrant mother, and her father's wife. Kelly reached forward, grasping Nancy's hand tightly within her own. She knelt at her mother's bedside, pressing her mother's hand to her forehead and then tenderly to her lips. Both women cried unabashedly, a cry that bonded their souls as never before.

CHAPTER 47

Joi sipped two fingers of Hennessy cognac, watching the ice cubes swirl around in the glass like horses on a carousel. She gazed at Russell. He placed his hand atop hers and gave it a comforting squeeze. He was ready. It only took one stiff cocktail to get Russell horny; she knew his rhythm by now. They had been partners for four years and lovers for eight months.

Helen had been in and out of the hospital for complications related to the progression of multiple sclerosis for the last five years, and up until very recently, Russell had been faithful. He and Helen had been together for fifteen years and he wasn't the type to abandon her when she needed him most. Joi had served as his sounding board after each of Helen's relapses, until one night, when Russell was in despair, they had found themselves in her bed making love.

She had already been his work-wife. The bond between police officers who partner together is pretty much like a marriage. Joi had worked hard to cultivate a good relationship with his wife. She often bought gifts for Helen and the couple's girls on birthdays, Easter, and Christmas.

Before Helen had gotten so sick, they had occasionally lunched and gone shopping when Joi was off-duty.

Joi hadn't planned to sleep with Russell, but somehow she rationalized that it was better that she and Russell were lovers. At least she cared about him and his family. She didn't need money from him and they both were clear that he loved Helen deeply and their relationship was strictly "comfort sex." Still it was a betrayal. Joi justified herself by thinking that at least in her, Russell had someone with whom he could safely unload emotionally, rather than some random woman who would seek to pull him away from his family altogether.

The revelation that Chad could be a suspect in the Gregg murder was an unlikely wrinkle that could end badly. What if Chad had actually gotten pissed off at daddy Gregg and popped him?

He didn't strike her as capable of murder, but then no one connected with this case did, and somebody was lying. Chad claimed to be driving back from a late meeting in Lisle on the night of the murder. Kelly used working late as her alibi, and the mother claimed to be drugged upstairs; her reason for not discovering her husband's body until the next day. Joi wondered who else, besides Marcus, could have been in the house that night.

As Joi watched Russell stagger into her bedroom, she had a pang of guilt, she realized that she needed to cultivate a real relationship with a man who was free to do more than occasionally scratch her wild itch.

Once they were both naked in Joi's king-sized bed, Russell stretched out under the satin sheets and propped himself up on his elbow. He hands began playing with the soft hair on the nape of her neck which escaped the twisted locks that caressed her chin. Then he cradled her tenderly in his arms.

"Damn Joi, I'm sorry about Maze leaving you."

"I'm not," she replied too abruptly.

"You sure?" said Russell, looking directly into her brown eyes for truth. "I think different. You been down the past couple days."

She exhaled. "Go to hell, Russell. The Gregg case is what has me worried," she lied smoothly. "Some things stack up and some don't. At face value, I'd say it's *gotta* be Marcus. He was in the house the night of the murder, arguing with his father. He has marks on his face from a fight. The stone from his ring was embedded in his daddy's face."

Russell sighed as he always did when she switched from sharing anything deeply personal to something work-related. His penis shriveled.

"He says he was there around eight p.m., and Devin established the time of death between eight forty-five and eleven p.m." Joi lay face down under the covers and Russell gently massaged the tight area between her shoulder blades as she continued. "Marcus is family. He would have known where his father kept the gun."

"Sounds like you got it figured out pretty much," he said sliding his hand down the small of her back.

Joi responded by snuggling closer.

She felt his penis growing.

"But you know when it's that neat, it's rarely *that* neat." Looking up at the stark white bedroom ceiling, she surmised, "There's more."

"Okay Joi, how about this? They argued. Possibly the gun was in the desk drawer and perhaps his father even reached for the gun first. But Marcus was too quick and strong for the old man. They struggled and the gun went off."

"You really are horny, aren't you?" she said, her sarcasm evident. "I admit I like Marcus for the killing, but Russell, what nags at me is the fact that the ME says Gregg was shot from a distance. So if they were wrestling, would he take the gun from the desk and back up ten-to-twelve feet before firing?" She shook her head. "Nah, I don't think so. And I'm even thinking that if they were fighting, the way to go would be just to give it to him up close and personal," she said, turning back to Russell. "Something about Marcus just makes me think that he's the kind of guy that could definitely kick his ole man's ass, but not the kind of guy that would kill him. Especially not by shooting him."

She moved her hip over to maintain the warm contact of his muscular body. "And then there's the matter of the second shot."

He lightly ran his fingers across the hairs around her vagina, teasing entry. "De-tec-tive, you are working on our personal time. What's up with that?" his voice elevated.

She placed a hand under the cover atop his. She felt him growing again and her body wanted to gain the advantage.

"Sorry," she laughed peevishly. For a few more seconds her thoughts lingered with the murderer.

You know the more I think about this, a woman could have shot him from behind ... a woman afraid that if she saw the man's face, looked in his eyes, she wouldn't be able to pull it off ...

"Russell, you know I was just—" and her next words were muffled by his kisses.

CHAPTER 48

Tuesday, October 26, 2004

The door opens and a faint stream of light from the hallway accompanies the hulking hairy form. Suddenly his body is over her bed. The little girl is a fly frozen inside a party ice cube. The monster turns the frozen form over and rubs it between the palms of his hands. "Please baby Jesus, keep me frozen, please. If I am frozen the monster will let me sleep."

The monster holds the frozen form in his hairy hand, examining it on all sides. He places the form back in the bed and lies atop it. The trapped child screams as she turns from ice to water. The heat rushes inside, overtaking her. The next scream is frozen inside.

❖ ❖ ❖

A fitful Kelly Gregg rolled over, quickly opened her reddened eyes and tugged her brother's sweaty tee-shirt down over her hips. Sitting up on the warm sofa, she was glad she slept over at Marc's instead of driving home, considering all the Rolling Rock beer they drank after her visit to the hospital. After her mother's admission of knowing that her husband was incesting their children, and her sick rationale for staying ,made Kelly queasy. She had needed time with Marcus, hoping that together they could process the sordid information.

There was so much ground to cover but when she got to his home she found him barefoot, in jeans and a paint-splattered tee-shirt, grooving to a Lenny Kravitz CD, and somehow the words never came up her throat. She was, after all was said and done, her mother's daughter. And he was her mother's son.

Instead of bringing up the abuse they had suffered at the hands of their father, she had made herself content with the fact that his girlfriend Milagros wasn't spending the night.

Tonight, at least I have my little brother to myself.

They had eaten Marcus' homemade guacamole with Sun Chips, and curled up on his brown leather couch drinking beer until she lost consciousness.

She heard Marcus shuffle out of his bedroom into the bathroom, followed by the sound of him peeing. When she heard his bedroom door close again, she scrambled into the bathroom and emptied her own exploding bladder.

Her watch read six fifteen a.m. She rinsed her mouth, gargled with Listerine and splashed warm water on her face. She had just enough time to dash home and dress for work. Darting from the bathroom, she hurriedly dressed and slipped into her soft brown loafers. She considered leaving Marcus a note but he knew her schedule better than she did.

She walked to her parked Camry and slid in the driver's seat.

Kelly agonized over how stupidly self-centered she had been. Marcus had somehow managed to bury his pain and move on, or at least try. Now it all made twisted sense; Marcus's unexplained fits of rage at everyone—including her. She had always been perplexed about his refusal to be around their father, and the darkness that expressed itself in the somber hues of his paintings.

She reflected upon how Marcus totally disconnected from her during her summers with Auntie Di. Kelly always sent him postcards and letters, but he never replied. Colorado had been extra special and she remembered excitedly writing Marcus one night as she looked out at the stars. When she returned home, she had called him on his lack of response and had been surprised by the way he had snapped back at her.

"Marc, I wrote you from the Grand Canyon. Did you get the letter and the photo?"

"Uh-huh, I got it," he'd responded without looking up from the bottle of Gatorade he was chugging as he sat on the back steps after one of his track meets.

"Pretty cool, right?" said Kelly, trying to engage her younger brother in conversation.

"Look, it was alright." He cocked his head and squinted at her. "Your hair looked weird in that picture. Did you even comb it?"

"What, you sound like, Mother. Could you not see past my hair and see that at my back was one of the seven wonders of the entire world?"

"Do YOU not see that you have all the fun every summer!" he had responded contritely.

"Marcus, don't you have fun while I'm gone? You have our parents to yourself and I bet you get everything you want all summer long," she teased.

Marcus hollered at the top of his voice, "No I don't! You just want to think that. I bet that makes you happy, to leave me here all alone!"

The back door had opened and out walked their apron-clad mother. "What is going on out here? Marcus, WHY on earth are you hollering at your sister like that?"

"Nothing, Ma, just nothin'," he had responded, bending his head to avoid her burning gaze.

"What have I told you about word endings? Let me hear you pronounce the 'g' Marcus. Nothinggg," she'd said in a tone that was both corrective and intimidating.

"Nothing!" he pronounced at the top of his voice, hopping from the step and tossing his drink into a metal garbage can outside the door. He'd avoided his mother's gaze as he walked past her into the house.

Now Kelly realized that while summers had been her respite, Marcus had been trapped. Her soul ached for her baby brother.

She sat in her Camry, sobbing from the frustration of her missed opportunity. Flipping open the glove compartment, Kelly found a rumpled yellow napkin, wiped away her tears and blew her nose hard. At that moment she remembered her grandma saying, *Ignorance is Bliss*. True wisdom, she thought.

Learning about Marcus had plunged Kelly back into hell.

She could never have remained faithful to a man that had dirtied his children the way daddy had contaminated his all these years. She wondered how her mother had stayed. What if she secretly hated him. Could her mother have been lying about clinging to her wedding vows even in the face of the most horrible test by fire? God forbid if she was in some way gratified or even aroused by her husband's disgusting acts.

Conflict ripped through Kelly Gregg's heart as she fought for composure before speeding away from her brother's home.

CHAPTER 49

Joi and Russell, along with two other detectives, were closing out the day's paperwork. Joi had barely slept two hours last night. Maze had called at midnight with an eye-opening request. "Baby, the landlord say he gonna put me out if I don't give him the right money. I just don't have it."

The "me" was probably Maze and the jerk she had left her apartment to shack up with. The rent had likely gone where it always did—alcohol and weed.

Opening her desk drawer, Joi downed two Excedrin with the last of a large 'to go' cup of lukewarm coffee. The medication was no match for the throbbing headache that had stolen her sleep.

She felt defeated because moving Maze in simply had not worked. And as much of a screw-up as her mother was, she had the audacity to be a proud screw-up, moving out while Joi was at work.

Hell, Joi thought to herself. *I know we cramped one another's style.*

But she admitted to herself, if not to Russell, that she missed Maze, missed her a lot. During the ten days she and Maze had shared her two-bedroom apartment, she had learned that Maze worked crossword puzzles like a champ and was addicted to the *Judge Judy Show*. She appreciated that her mother had respected her enough to smoke her weed after she left for work; the lingering smell of incense was the giveaway. In the evenings, Maze only drank beer.

Joi closed her eyes, still reflecting on their short time together. She had not imagined being warmed by her mother's admiring glances as she prepared for work and there was no mistaking the look in Maze's eyes when Joi walked through the door in the evening with 'take-out' for dinner. It was a look of relief, the relief a mother feels when her only child is momentarily out of harm's way.

She wanted to tell Maze that she didn't give a damn where she lived and that if she couldn't get the money on her own, then she could go to a women's shelter. Again. How else was Maze gonna get her shit together unless something happened to jolt her into reality? Joi had spent the entire night wrestling with thoughts of Maze being homeless. In the morning, she arose exhausted, stumbled into her kitchen, opened the freezer and parted a fortress of chicken breasts, butterfly chops and ground sirloin, to retrieve a plastic zip lock bag. Sliding the zipper top, she peeled four one-hundred dollar bills from her cash stash.

This is the last time.

However, instead of giving the money to her mother, she had stopped into the McKee and Pogue's 83rd street office and dropped off the rent balance, getting a receipt from the receptionist before doubling back to the police station for Roll Call.

Why was it her job to clean up her mama's mess? There was a saying, "Insanity is doing the same thing over and over again and expecting different results." She was ready to enter a plea of insanity.

Joi glanced across the room at the wall clock. It was a quarter to five. She had fifteen more minutes before she could head home and take her tired butt to bed.

"Russell, we've sifted through all the evidence," Joi said, shifting her weight off her cramped left hip as she sat cross-legged in the leather chair in their cubicle at the station.

Russell closed the file drawer, walked over to the small electric pot on the table next to the fax machine and poured himself another cup of coffee. He seemed to be drinking it like water lately. She glanced at her partner's butt. It was high, tight and well-muscled under his navy blue slacks.

"Want a cup?" he asked, interrupting her naughty thoughts.

"Nooo thanks," she crooned, holding her hand up. "I've had enough of that stuff."

"Nobody's given up anything." Russell rubbed the warm tan-colored ceramic cup with the bold electric blue words 'SUPER MAN' in between his palms and swallowed. "Not Chad, Marcus or Kelly." Then he shook his head. "With the mother being sick and all, she's no help."

He nodded to the open file on Joi's desk. "Here's a guy that gets the shit shot out of him—I mean face blown away—every one of them had opportunity, but no one seems to have a real strong motive." He sat the cup down on the desk blotter and continued his train of thought, "Damn, the nonsense in the paper about a home invasion or a botched robbery is a reporter's fantasy. Robbers rob. There wasn't a damn thing stolen."

"What did you learn about the boyfriend?" Joi asked, trying to keep her voice neutral.

Russell grimaced as he gave her a long look. "His alibi checks out."

She nodded, almost relieved at that bit of news. Chad might be a cheater, but she hadn't pegged him as a killer. "Ballistics said that the gun used to kill Dennis Gregg was his, so let's keep it in the family." Joi scanned the documents once again. "I can't tell you how I know—but—Kelly's the killer."

Russell narrowed his gaze at her.

"If we can get enough circumstantial evidence together to show that she could have been the killer, we might rattle her enough to get something we can work with."

"If she didn't do it," he said slowly, "she knows who did."

Joi nodded, still avoiding eye contact with him. "Squeeze her a little and see what she gives up. That way we have a couple of options."

"But what reason would she have for killing her old man?" Russell asked.

This time Joi locked gazes with her partner. "I wonder if maybe the old man was messing around. Did he have one of the pretty young sisters of the church stashed away? Maybe the daughter got wind of it. You said yourself she was devoted to her mother. Check on that for me, will you?"

Russell looked through reports that he had carefully arranged on a pressed wood clipboard. "You know, I keep wondering why Marcus, the so-called black sheep, even went over there that night. The number of his prints on the end of the desk, the leather chair and on the sliding glass panel leading from the house into the garden makes me wonder."

"Let's tighten up the circle, Russell." The phone rang on Joi's desk and she spun around to answer it. She quickly responded to the caller and returned to her partner. "Talk with Marcus again. This time you press him hard about Kelly, who she is and what issues she might have with their daddy. I'll question Kelly about Marcus' habits and see if she lets anything slip that would give baby brother a motive for killing their dad."

Russell took a final swallow of his coffee and suggested, "Then let's play the psychiatrist. Let Dr. Snowden know that we intend to pound on Kelly until she breaks. I trust you to menace the good doctor into giving us something we can use. Tell her that we have new info on the night of the crime. We kinda do." He leaned back in his chair chuckling.

"Riiiight," said Joi, stacking the paperwork in her desk and packing her belongings. "That way we get the shrink to spill the beans on the content of the sessions. My gut tells me *that* girl has some issues!"

"All the fine ones have issues," he said in such a matter-of-fact tone that it brought her up short.

"Seriously?" she said. "Do I have issues, Russell?"

"Joi, you *are* the damn exception to the rule," Russell quickly amended, using an exaggerated falsetto voice and grinning as he jumped from his chair just in time to avoid the yellow legal pad that whizzed past his face.

"Oh, I thought so!" Joi laughed pulling the strap of a Coach purse across her shoulder and throwing her army green blazer across her arm.

Russell stooped to pick up the legal pad and dropped it on the desk. "I'm gonna be in a little later in the morning. I've got to drop Helen off at her mom's for the day."

"Hey, give her my best," Joi said, instantly sobering as a stab of guilt hit her gut.

Russ gave her a lopsided grin. "Yeah, she actually has been lookin' a little better. We keep hoping. You never know."

"They say God hears prayers, Russ," Joi said, and winced at the fact that she had even mentioned God.

Everything in her life told her God didn't hear prayers. At least not hers.

Russell bent over and planted a kiss on her cheek as he headed out of the door. The scent of Joop cologne lingered briefly in the air. She scanned the area and was glad they were alone.

CHAPTER 50

THURSDAY, OCTOBER 28, 2004

Kelly stared through the floor-to-ceiling windows toward the calming view of Lake Michigan. The sun had risen and the water, though too cold to swim in, shimmered in its light. When she had begun apartment hunting, her mother had commented that Hyde Park was a pricey neighborhood and she had encouraged her daughter to find a larger, safer, less expensive apartment in the south suburbs. But Kelly had ignored her advice. She craved the feeling of peace she got losing herself in the timeless ebb and flow of the water.

She looked eleven floors down to the semi-crowded parking lot. The mixed-income building was full of young singles, families and seniors, yet there was no one in her building with whom Kelly could share the things that burdened her heart. Who can you tell while folding clothes together in the building's laundry room or while sharing a cup of coffee that you might have done something wrong? Something evil.

Kelly backed away from the sealed windows and plopped down

among the plush cushions on her soft velour sofa. Against her will, the thick blue haze of memories of ill-fated moments that changed her future intruded into her mind. Kelly shook her head. *No!* She would not be dragged back there, not now. She rose to dress for the hospital. She needed her mother.

❖ ❖ ❖

As Kelly passed the nurse's station she noticed a plastic jack-o-lantern spilling orange wrapped candies. She was reminded that Halloween was in three days. She needed to stock up on candy. Kelly cherished fond memories of Halloween when she and Marcus were always dressed up and taken to Trick-or-Treat. She remembered her favorite pink ballerina costume, complete with pink tights and satin slippers and holding onto her mother's hand as they skipped along happily beside her. She loved pretending.

"Good morning," came a greeting from one of the nurses.

"Oh, hi, how is she?" replied Kelly, removing her thick sweater and throwing it across her arm.

"Kinda quiet this morning. She'll be glad to see you."

Upon entering the private hospital room Kelly looked over at her mother, who lay quietly acquiescing to her pain. Nancy Gregg had lived a public life of dignity and generosity, but when the truth came out, it would end in disgrace. Nevertheless, Kelly felt obligated to tell her mother the truth, and with it she would unleash a landslide that she was powerless to stop. Once she uttered the words that clawed at her throat for escape, she would deal her mother a blow more devastating than pancreatic cancer.

For over a week, Kelly had argued back and forth with the voices screaming in her head. One minute, *What difference would it make to let her live out her final weeks in peace?* The next minute, *Tell her; just tell her the truth!*

There had to be a way to tell the truth and to give her mother something to hold onto if just for a few days, weeks or months. *When mother dies, I'll be an orphan.*

Kelly kept a daily vigil at the hospital now, spending as much time as possible at her mother's bedside. Her manager at Citibank was supportive and Kelly's attitude softened towards Grace, her former nemesis, who now absorbed much of Kelly's workload. Kelly worried because Nancy stayed dehydrated. Her body was unable to absorb fluids as cancer raged through her.

She peered through the hospital windows, searching for the sunlight hidden beneath the bilious clouds outside. She squeezed her mother's hand inside her own. There was no grip.

Kelly sat down on the small high-backed chair, quietly gathering her strength. Sleepless nights and emotional turmoil had taken their toll. She was as hollow as a drinking gourd.

"Mother I've thought about our talks and I want you to know that … that I have already forgiven you. I think I've been waiting all these years to have my feelings validated."

Nancy was silent and Kelly looked immediately at the instruments that monitored her mother's vital signs, for assurance that her mother was still alive. How much longer she would be was anybody's guess. Her eyes were half-open slits. Her words were morphine-slurred but when she parted her lips to speak her thoughts were surprisingly lucid.

"We wronged you, and Marcus. We were selfish, terrified of losing our family life and of being humiliated."

"Hush Mother, please don't waste your energy talking like that."

"Pumpkin, if there was any way, any way at all that I could take back what happened, I would do that. I'm so sorry," Nancy said, tears streaking the sallow complexion that seemed paler with each visit.

Kelly leaned over and clung onto her mother, burying her head in her chest.

"Mother, I'm the one who … did it. I didn't mean to … but he hurt me."

"What are you saying, child?" Nancy recoiled from Kelly, finally realizing what her daughter was disclosing. "Dear God in heaven ... It was you!"

CHAPTER 51

OCTOBER 28, LUNCHTIME

Detective Sommers looked at the wall clock over the Desk Sergeant's area as she headed upstairs to the division office. She was returning from a McDonald's run and juggled a tray with one large strawberry and one medium chocolate shake, two extra-large fries, a Big Mac, a cheeseburger and one piping hot apple pie. Her mouth watered for the hot oily french fries.

As she cleared the top step, she nodded at a pair of detectives headed for the break area. Before beginning their afternoon assignments, the detectives often watched the soaps or caught a few minutes of *Judge Judy*, Maze's favorite show. *Speaking of Maze, I haven't heard a single word of thanks from her.* This was definitely going to be the last time Joi bailed her out.

Walking down the narrow hallway toward the door with the opaque glass door, Joi tapped the wooden frame of the closed door. Her partner let her in.

"Russell, grab your food," she playfully cried out, almost losing control of the precariously balanced load and her handbag. She glanced at the flashing red light on her desk. "My message light's on. I'm just gonna eat at my desk."

"Cool, I'll be in the break room with Bailey and Williams. Join us when you're done."

"Watching Judge Judy, not you too!" she groaned, and he gave her a sheepish grin.

He grabbed his McDonald's bag, drink and several napkins from the stack Joi had placed on the desk, and was off to join the crowd.

Joi tore the yellow wrapping from her cheeseburger, then punched the blinking red button on her phone and entered her voice mail code. She picked up several long golden fries and nearly burned her lips as she listened to the message.

"Detective Sommers," came the raspy voice. "This is Mrs. Geraldine Crayton. You talked to me at my daughter's. I know something about poor Mr. Gregg's murder."

Joi carefully placed the sandwich on the wrapper as the message rattled on. "I know something about the night poor Mr. Gregg got killed. I heard gunshots that night and when I went to the window, I think I saw a woman in a white tank top running out of the Gregg's back gate."

Joi replayed the entire voicemail twice in order to decipher what the caller was saying.

Gulping down her chocolate shake, she flipped open her notebook and contemplated what this meant.

A woman in a white tank top ...

Hunger took a back seat to curiosity. She hurried to the break room. The place was crowded and she interrupted an officer near the entrance cramming a hoagie down his face, asking him to tap Russ on the shoulder.

Russ gave the man an irritated look before following his pointing finger. Joi beckoned Russell over.

When she whispered that they had a lead on the Gregg case, Russell stuffed the last of his sandwich into his mouth and grabbed his jacket from the back of the sofa. Moments later, both detectives were in a squad car heading towards Geraldine Crayton's home.

❖ ❖ ❖

As soon as they rang, Mrs. Crayton opened the door, almost as if she had been waiting for them.

"My daughter's at work," she said, ushering them inside. "The kids are at school."

Joi swept a look around the home before laying eyes on the elderly, obviously troubled woman. "Thanks for your call, Mrs. Crayton."

"You remember me," then she gestured toward Russell, "my partner Russell Wilkerson."

Russell nodded respectfully.

"Everybody calls me Geri, you can too."

"Thanks for calling ma'am," Joi said as she and Russell followed the older woman inside the home.

Geri Crayton turned to them and said, "It took me awhile. I got a lot to lose."

Russell shared a look with Joi before asking, "Why's that?"

"I'm a recovering drunk," Mrs. Crayton said sheepishly. "I slipped that night and had a—um, *some*—drinks."

Joi glanced knowingly at Russell.

"I *was* drunk but I know what I heard." The Crayton woman paused as though gathering her emotions. "You just don't know. My baby girl's been so good to me, better than I deserve. I love my grandkids. They noisy and they wild but I love 'em." She had a look of resolve on her face when she said, "I've taken my family through a lot and I don't want to piss Asia off. I'm scared she might kick me out."

"What made you come forward?" Russell asked, giving the older woman's hand a reassuring pat.

"My sponsor. I told Arlene and she said I'd never be able to keep my sobriety if I held this secret. You know, what goes around ..." She let the rest of the phrase trail off.

They talked with Mrs. Crayton for another ten minutes, with Joi asking the same questions she'd asked before, but this time in a different way, to look for inconsistencies.

Her partner took notes. Two gunshots, a small woman running out the back gate, soaked because of the sudden downpour but wearing a tank top. Mrs. Crayton couldn't exactly tell the woman's complexion. "If it hadn't been so dark and rainy maybe I woudda noticed her whether she was light skinned or dark. Sorry."

After the detectives spent twenty minutes talking with their only known witness, she saw them through the front door.

❖ ❖ ❖

Inside the squad car, the two detectives sat together, discussing their notes.

"The old girl seemed relieved," Russell said, flipping through a small black pad he pulled from the inside pocket of his brown sports coat.

"Yeah, I felt sorry for her. The guilt of falling off the wagon was eating at her."

Russell looked at Joi. "I saw it in her eyes when she said she didn't want to disappoint her daughter."

"Russ, I know where you're going with this. Just stop please." But Joi couldn't help silently wondering whether Maze ever felt guilt over repeatedly falling prey to her weakness. Her emotions wouldn't let her go down that slippery road. "Let's just stick to the investigation."

"Okay," he shrugged. "Let's look at what we've got. We did a lot of digging, and most of the members of the church we interviewed mostly saw Elder Gregg as a wonderful father, church elder and mentor. But several of them kinda beat around the bush, telling us they didn't trust him." He drummed his fingers on the console between them. "Chad had no love for him. He and Marcus had a love-hate relationship. Kelly seemed to be daddy's little girl, and if she was, why would she kill him?"

Russ opened up his notebook to a conversation he had with the former choir director, an openly gay man who had finally left Christ's Victory Apostolic after twenty-two years for a Unitarian Church that welcomed gays. He remembered the conversation vividly.

"The man I spoke with said, 'Call me crazy Detective, but I always thought something was going on between Elder Gregg and that cute little girl of his. I seen the way he looked at her, and she seemed to be able to do-no-wrong. I cain't put my finger on it, never saw nothin, but I am an empath and I feel things between people…'"

Joi put the squad car in drive and pulled out into the street. "Russ that makes sense, but we can't take that into court." She headed toward the China Star Restaurant on 162nd. She had a taste for egg foo yung. "Kelly is bullshitting us. She could have just as easily have killed him as anyone—and if he had been abusing her as a child…"

Russell smirked and slapped her leg affectionately. "Damn, Joi, I think we've got her!"

CHAPTER 52

OCTOBER 28, 6:30 P.M.

Normally elegant, Kelly looked woefully unkempt in her edgy ensemble. The strain of her father's murder had taken a toll on her. The ten pounds she had dropped showed in the rumpled avocado slacks and caramel-stained scooped necked blouse that exposed her shrunken décolletage. The thick green and brown sweater hung cloak-like from her shoulders. Her normally perky short hair was covered by a blue jean baseball cap. She rambled, tripping over her words, looking for the right combination of linguistic pairings that would explain.

"Mother I came to the house because … because he kept calling me and hanging up the phone before speaking. I couldn't stand it! I just … I had to confront him." Kelly literally shook as she uttered, "I needed to get him finally to admit it and tell me he was sorry!"

She sat back in the chair and closed her eyes. "When I got to your house, I saw Marcus was leaving and he looked mad. He didn't even see me, but from where I stood, I could almost smell his rage." She shared another truth that her mother had always chosen to ignore. "Daddy always talked so bad to Marcus, I just knew he had done it again. I know you're going to hate me. Mother I never wanted you to hate me. But I shot him."

"No, no honey," replied Nancy Gregg, straining her voice.

"Mother, I'm so sorry, I didn't go there to kill him. How it happened is … I hardly remember. After all the years, all the lies, all the … *everything!*

She covered her eyes, ashamed to look at her mother.

"Mother, I promise, I didn't go there to kill him I just wanted to … I thought he would apologize."

❖ ❖ ❖

Kelly had barely parked when she had seen Marcus leave. He left quickly and sped away. He must have been in his own thoughts because he never saw her car near the back gate. It was for the best. Her business was with Dad.

She had entered through the garden doors. He turned around the moment she entered. He seemed dazed and from the apparent upheaval around him, it was obvious that he and Marcus had tussled.

He was massaging his neck and she glimpsed a reddish, coppery blotch on the side of his face. She felt no compassion for him. She had rehearsed this scene over and over. Now she would finally get what she needed from her father.

She had planned to say, "I'm not your little girl anymore. Why didn't you treat me like other daddies treat their little girls?" Then he would respond, "I beg your pardon young lady."

"Yes, you should beg my pardon. Is that why you've been calling my answering machine and hanging up?"

His response was supposed to be, "I have. I admit to calling you because I wanted to hear your voice. I know you were upset after our conversation at brunch, but I didn't want to talk with you in front of your mother. Can you understand that? She's not well. I wanted to speak with you privately. I wanted to tell you that for all the pain I have caused you, I am deeply sorry. I have asked my Lord and Savior Jesus Christ for forgiveness, and now I ask you."

But her father had turned into The Monster. Huge, with matted hair, The Monster had ranted at her, then turned his back to her, the way he always did after he spat his venom down her thighs, grunted and turned away, leaving her with only her rag doll Polly for comfort. He had turned his back to her and triumphantly walked away. In the next instant a splinter of light blinded her, engulfing her in a blue haze, sending everything in the room spinning. She must have somehow walked to her father's desk drawer and removed the shining weapon he kept to protect his family, but she didn't remember.

BOOM!!!

The gun exploded and The Monster collapsed.

Kelly desperately needed to see his face. She had to get closer so The Monster could not turn its face away and pretend not to see her crying. She staggered over to The Monster and turned the heavy beast over.

BOOM!!!

The Monster was gone from her life forever.

When she came to herself, a body lay on the floor and a bloody sardonic mask glared at her.

She was holding a gun. Her clothes were splattered with blood and pieces of skin. The fresh taste of his blood splash on her lips gagged her.

Kelly ran through the garden door and into the darkness of the night. Her mind was a blur but she dug her way deep into the soft compost heap. She unbuttoned the bloody white cotton top. The warm, decomposing, soil received the blouse. Her white tank top would be enough. She fled to her car, unconsciously holding the gun.

As she drove away a small lamp flicked on in a back bedroom of the house next door.

Hot tears streaked her face.

Moments later a flash of lightening, followed by a loud crack of thunder opened the heavens. Heavy droplets formed a broom of water that swept South Holland clean and tamped the blood-spattered blouse further into the depths of the compost heap.

Kelly fumbled for her keys, unlocked the door and had barely stepped inside her apartment when vomit sprayed all over the lemon yellow entry wall, just missing Jomo, her lone surviving ceramic giraffe.

Her fingers skimmed the surface of her father's weapon. The weapon she had used to end his life. She crumpled to the floor trembling, oblivious to her surroundings.

❖ ❖ ❖

Kelly grabbed at her mother like a forlorn child, but the woman did not have the strength to catch her. She toppled over, landing on her mother's lap, a sobbing heap. Nancy somehow found the strength to pull up and away from her daughter for a moment, and Joi looked up at her to gauge her reaction to the news. Horror flickered in the older woman's eyes only briefly as she swept a gaze across Kelly's face. "Hush child. I know. Hush, hush."

"Mother, I'm *so* scared. I can't eat, I can't sleep. Can you forgive me, Mother, can you?" she sobbed. "Before I knew it, I fired the gun! I just fired it and he … fell! I wanted to talk to him but I knew if I let him look at me, he was going to change things and make them *his* way, just like he did all the time. I just didn't want him to change things this time!"

"Kelly, bend down," her mother said in a voice that was stern, almost commanding. "This was a tragic accident, nothing more."

"What's going to happen to me?"

"Have you told Chad?" Nancy asked, struggling with her pillows to sit up straighter.

"No, he would hate me," she whispered. Her eyes shifted as she said, "I haven't even told him my other news."

Nancy's eyes squinted as she fought the medication to focus.

"Other news?"

Kelly exhaled, "Mother, I'm pregnant."

CHAPTER 53

Nancy Gregg was dumbfounded. Her daughter had confessed to her own father's murder and in the next breath shared the news that she was carrying her grandchild! Her brains felt scrambled. Having such a tragedy bound to a miracle gave her heart palpitations.

She had lost her Denny. Kelly was the murderer. And cancer would deny her the blessing of ever holding her grandbaby.

Nancy had stood by her husband, upholding the sacred marital vow of "forsaking all others," including her own children. It appeared that everything she had ever lived for, dreamed of, lay in ruins.

No! Her primordial instincts took control. She had two wonderful children that would outlive their shame, and new life would be born into the Gregg family. She was a grandmother! She would protect her grandchild's future.

Her constant pain faded into the background as she murmured, "Kelly, give me a little time to think. Promise not to speak a word of what you have told me to *anyone*, not to Chad and never to Marcus." Nancy

Gregg summoned all her wits before saying with all the force she could muster, "Promise me. You must promise me right now. Right now."

"How can I keep this a secret? That detective is going to arrest Marc. I just know it!"

"Kelly, baby, I don't deserve your trust but I am begging you now. I know what I'm doing."

Realizing that her daughter was grappling with her moral dilemma and her concern for her younger brother's safety, she said, "We wronged *you*, darling. Please give your father and me a chance to make it right."

"But Daddy is gone."

"Yes, Daddy is gone, but I lived with him all those years and believe me, I know his heart. Please say you'll trust me. Don't go to the police or share what you have told me. Not yet."

"I'll wait if you say so, Mama," Kelly surrendered.

Her mother's weak brown eyes pleaded with a humility and urgency Kelly had never seen before. "Just for now, this has to be our secret. *Everything* depends on it my dearest Kelly. Know that I love you. I've always loved you and your brother." She took Kelly's chin in her hand. "Sweetie, no matter what else happened, you were loved."

Kelly nodded. "I believe you, Mama."

"I'm so tired. This medication is taking over," she whispered. "Make sure your brother knows that I love him, so very much."

Kelly peered at her mother for a moment. "Huh? But mother, you can do that yourself. He'll probably come by tomorrow; he's working a double shift today."

Nancy's lips lifted in a small smile. "Just in case he gets busy, when you talk to him, make sure he knows I love him too."

Kelly bent over and planted a warm kiss on her mother's forehead. Nancy clung to Kelly and said, "Goodbye, my sweet baby."

CHAPTER 54

OCTOBER 29, 2004

At five forty-five, Russell left the station to run errands before heading home. Joi had hit the locker room for a quick hot shower, changed into a pair of form-fitting jeans and her running shoes, and drove twenty minutes to O'Malley's Blue Island Gun Range.

Spending a couple of hours at the gun range killing targets after her shift served as Joi's second favorite release after a tension-filled day. She owned several guns, her department issued Smith and Wesson and several automatics, including a German Glock 9 mil and a Mac 10.

Although she was off the mean streets now, working homicide still had its risks. It was an unspoken practice within the Department to take a backup gun.

My extra life insurance policy.

Joi had just finished her third round of moving targets when Gordy

Jorgenson, the scorekeeper, came in and motioned for her to remove the headphones protecting her ears.

"Joi, you got a call from Russ. Says it's important."

"Shit," she whispered, hoping with all her heart that it wasn't bad news about his wife. She followed the short pot-bellied man into his office and grabbed the phone from the counter.

"What's up," she asked him, then listened tensely while he spoke. "Okay, I'm there." She disconnected the call and retrieved her pistols. "Gotta run, Gordy."

"Everything alright?"

"Just got a break on my case is all."

CHAPTER 55

Kelly pressed her keychain and locked her Toyota as she approached the main entrance to her high-rise. The police cruiser sitting in front of the building immediately alarmed her and caused a knot to form in her gut. She noticed that the squad car was white instead of the Chicago Police Department's blue and white. South Holland Police. This was it. They were here for her. There were two figures inside the car talking. She slowed up. Her feet felt like they had kickstands, but she willed herself toward the entrance.

Seconds later, a familiar voice called her name. "Ms. Gregg."

She trained her attention on the driver's side door and saw Detective Sommers. Her hair was covered by a tan and brown print bandanna.

As she got closer to the car the detective said something to the man in the car who she vaguely remembered seeing at her mother's house. She exited the car and stood directly in Kelly's path.

She looked 'off-duty' in jeans and a short, brown jacket that looked a little small on her. This was not a good sign.

"Oh, Detective Sommers, I almost didn't recognize you," Kelly lied.

Joi paused and drew a breath. "I have information on your father's case." She nodded toward the entrance. "Can we speak privately?"

"Yes, of course." Kelly replied, struggling to stifle her mounting fear. "Let's go upstairs to my apartment, shall we?" Kelly said, without waiting for a response. She suppressed nausea, opting to face her fate in her own apartment rather than be humiliated in the lobby of her building.

She felt her pulse rise in her throat and thump so hard it drowned out the sounds of traffic rushing behind them. Suddenly her head was light and her face was hot.

Please don't let me pass out in front of this woman.

She struggled to appear poised, forcing her feet, one before the other, along the curved walkway leading to the high-rise entrance. She fought the urge to simply break for her car to escape what was about to happen. She had confessed everything to her mother, received her forgiveness. That was all she needed. She wasn't sure why her mother told her to wait, but she would not involve her mother in any of this anymore. She swallowed to hold down the hot liquid boiling in her gut.

It was all over and she was glad the truth could come out. She would cling to that, no matter what happened.

❖ ❖ ❖

They rode the elevator in silence. Kelly was unable to speak, having summoned all her reserve not to scream. Her head pounded, hands trembled, and she was in danger of losing control of her bowels.

It was 10:50 p.m., after another late night at the office. With the weight of the conversation with her mother reverberating in her mind, she had barely gotten through her pressing assignment. She let out a long, slow breath, relieved when no one else boarded the elevator with them. They arrived at the eleventh floor and Kelly led Detective Sommers down the carpeted hallway to her apartment.

When she opened the door to apartment 1106, she instantly flashed back to the night she had fled her parents' home. Tonight she was sick to the stomach, just like she was the night her father was killed. It wasn't the greasy smell of Harold's Fried Chicken wafting down the hallway that had brought on her nausea that night. It had been the realization that she was a murderer.

CHAPTER 56

Kelly Gregg's apartment was exactly as Joi expected. This was the apartment of a neat, organized and creative woman.

Like mother, like daughter Joi thought.

Everything was unique, yet it all fit together in an overall theme that produced an atmosphere of elegance and calm.

Too bad. Joi looked over at Kelly, who had plopped down on the couch. Her face bore a puzzling look of resignation. Joi took a seat across from her, planting her bottom in a wicker throne chair. Kelly was wound tight, as though waiting for something awful to unfold.

Joi looked at Kelly and jammed her hands deep inside the pocket of her jacket. There was some news that she never liked to give.

"Ms. Gregg, did you get a call from the hospital?

"No, I left my cell phone ...," she spun around and spied her flip phone sitting on the kitchen table, "there!" she pointed. " I couldn't figure out whether I left it here or lost it. Why is something—"

"—We received word from the hospital. I'm sorry Ms. Gregg, but your mother passed this evening at 7:42 p.m."

Kelly's head dropped. She sank back onto the orange cushions on the sofa.

"They've been trying to reach you for hours. Where were you earlier?" Joi asked, narrowing a gaze on the younger woman."

Kelly winced, trying to focus in on the question. "What? I was at work. I have after- hours access, and after seeing Mother ..." her voice trailed.

She refocused on the detective's comment, "She what?" Kelly whispered, shaking her head from side to side. "Oh God no! You must be mistaken. I was *just there* this afternoon." She was blinded by tears that flooded her eyes. "She looked better. I knew she was ill, but I thought ... I thought she had more time. We all thought—"

"When I got word that they were trying to notify you and were unsuccessful, I thought I'd take a ride over."

Kelly replayed the last few minutes in her mind. "Detective, why are you the one telling me this instead of the hospital?"

Joi took a breath and poised herself. "Your mother didn't die a natural death."

"But you just said she ..."

"She did expire," Joi said, and her tone was measured. "But it looks like she overdosed on a combination of the pain medication she was getting intravenously and some sleeping pills. Her death, as it stands, will probably be ruled suicide."

Kelly failed in an effort to get to her feet. "That's impossible! My mother hated pills. She gagged, sometimes vomited when she had to take pills. What ... what kind of pills?"

"I don't know." Joi's phone vibrated and she could see it was Russ calling from his cell. She ignored the call. "It doesn't really matter, does it?"

"Of course not, but I'm confused—I just don't understand, Detective."

"It seems her physician had prescribed pills to help with the pain before she was admitted. Your mother kept them with her in her purse, and for some reason took all of them at one time. That, along with the pain medication being given to her intravenously, killed her."

Kelly shook her head. "But that's absolutely impossible. My mother hated pills! Whenever she had to take pills, we had to grind them on a spoon like she was a baby and put them in water or tea."

Joi gave Kelly a patient smile. "Yes, I hear you, but from the white residue around her mouth and teeth it appears that she chewed them up. A few were almost whole." Joi looked directly at Kelly. "They pumped her stomach and examined the material they collected. Most of them were not ground up, but enough were ground up to get a lethal dose into her bloodstream."

Kelly walked to the window. She seemed to be fighting for control. "God, when I saw her today she seemed ..." She covered her face with her hands. "Today was the last time I'll ever see my mother alive." Her voice trailed and tears streamed down her face. "If I had known that ..."

"Was she distraught today when you saw her earlier?"

"Detective, she wasn't in any pain." Kelly blinked to clear her vision. "Toward the end of our visit, she was very focused on ..."

"On what?"

"On making sure we knew she loved us. She was anxious to see Marc. He had my father's fear of hospitals. I ... I told her not to worry, told her he'd come, so she would rest. I just don't understand ... I can't believe she's gone."

Kelly opened a cubby hole at the bottom of a table, pulling out a wicker tissue holder and extracting several tissues. She blew her nose long and hard.

"Did anything happen to upset her—while you were there?" asked Joi.

She faced Joi, and without reservation said, "No, detective. When I left mother she was content. Yes, my mother was very content."

Joi took a deep breath and looked at the black covered notebook she carried like an anchor and then at Kelly.

"Ms. Gregg ... one final thing. Your mother left a note confessing to killing your father."

CHAPTER 57

Kelly thought about that last lingering look her mother had given her before she left the hospital. It had been round, warm and full of affection. She fought desperately to hold onto that look.

She forgave me. Warring thoughts clouded her brain and each clamored for her attention.

Today was the last time she'd see her… ever. Oh God, I wonder if Marc ever made it to the hospital.

Kelly looked away. The realization that her mother had planned this washed over her like a white foamed wave.

The words echoed off the walls of Kelly's apartment.

"Your mother left a note confessing to killing your father."

Kelly tensed. Her back became ramrod straight. Then, she slowly turned and leveled an icy glare at Joi. "Excuse me Detective, but that's not possible!"

The last conversation with her mother raced through her mind and her mother's insistence that she keep quiet about her confession. Suddenly, it all came together in a macabre way.

Joi toyed with the badge around her neck. "Uh-hmm, I know this is a blow. Did she say anything to you today or any other time to indicate that she was capable of murder?"

"Of course not!" Kelly rose and walked over to her round kitchen table. "What would make you say a ridiculous thing like that about my mother? She didn't kill anyone. She was ..."

Kelly's mind continued to flash back to her mother pleading with her to wait and not to mention their discussion to anyone. She had planned this from the moment Kelly had confessed.

"Your mother left a note specifically addressed to me, in what appears to be her handwriting, on the night stand in her hospital room. Ms. Gregg, the note was intentionally placed where it would be found."

Joi looked at the stricken Kelly. She stood motionless in the small kitchen. Continuing, she said, "She seems to have written the confession and *then* took the pills. When we contacted her doctor ... Crawford's records show that your mother could have had in her possession seventy-to-eighty OxyContin pills."

Kelly's head pounded as she thought of her mother choking down pills.

She wanted this.

Kelly snatched the blue jean baseball cap from her head and flung it down on the couch. She said softly as if she were replaying her last visit to her mother in her head, "Detective, Mother asked me to bring her purse before I left. Said she wanted to freshen up after she slept. I thought she was being vain. Just being her."

"And when you left?"

"She said she was about to take a nap," Kelly whispered. "She suggested I get back to work because of all the time I've had off lately. She sent me off to work knowing—"

Joi continued cautiously, "A nurse confirmed that she looked in on your mother after you left and that she was sitting up in bed combing her hair. It appears that she complained of being extra thirsty and asked for a pitcher of water.

"Ms. Gregg, I am very sorry for your loss. I know how hard it must be to lose your father and your mother in such a short time. And both in such unfortunate ways."

Joi injected a personal note that Kelly thought was well intended. "I still have my mother but I don't know what I'll do when she … dies."

In that statement, Kelly heard empathy in the detective's voice and almost reached out a hand to show she understood.

Joi continued her professional dispatch of information. "Of course, we may need a further statement from you and your brother, but this seems to bring the case to closure. I am so sorry that you had to find out this way."

Kelly shook her head. "Detective, I just don't understand."

"I'm sorry for how we staked out in front of your high-rise, but we didn't want this story to break in the news before you heard."

Joi gave some advice. "Because your father was such a big man in the south suburban community, this'll probably hit the morning news, so you might want to stay away from watching the news for a few days."

"Thank you, Detective. You've been—kind."

Joi moved toward the front door, "Our office will be in touch with you and your brother. He's where?"

Kelly checked her watch. "He'll be getting off work soon. He and Mother were especially close. I'll page him 911."

"Good idea."

Somehow, amidst her colliding thoughts, Kelly managed to say, "Thanks for coming over. Goodnight, Detective Sommers."

"You're welcome, Ms. Gregg."

Kelly undertook her painful mission. She paged Marcus, and minutes later when he returned the call, she delivered the news of their mother's death as simply as possible.

Then zombie-like, she removed her clothes. Reality struck her hard as she touched her empty belly.

She stumbled into the shower, inviting the beating the hot water gave her. The words to Celine Dion's song "Because You Loved Me" ran through her mind. She had never been able to hear that song without weeping. The lyrics had always been inspirational. She had never felt so deeply loved. She turned the lyrics around inside her tormented mind.

You were my strength when I was weak, you were my voice when I couldn't speak ... I'm everything I am because you loved me.

❖ ❖ ❖

Kelly came to herself on the floor of the shower, unsure how much time had passed. She vividly recalled the smells and sounds of the moment that she had become a murderer.

She had been permanently silenced. If she confessed, her mother's sacrifice was meaningless. The little time Nancy Gregg would have had left free of the burden of her husband's dark secrets had been squandered. Kelly had to honor her mother's sacrifice. Nancy Gregg died comforting herself that she was paying for her grandbaby's happiness with the final ounce of her life.

Kelly squeezed her eyes shut, remembering the morning she had taken the home pregnancy test. The minus sign had been highlighted. The results were crystal clear, she was not pregnant. She had lied to her mother to give her hope.

She hastily wrapped herself in her towel and stumbled to the living room, leaning against the floor to ceiling windows. Oddly the movement of the waters of Lake Michigan served to stabilize her. Kelly was not the card player her mother was, but she knew that this was a hand she had to play out.

CHAPTER 58

Stunned by the news of his mother's suicide, Marcus powered-off his cell phone and left his cubicle without uttering a word to his coworkers. How could he explain the devastating news he'd just received? He would call back to explain his abrupt departure later, when he wouldn't have to see the look of pity in everyone's eyes. He had only told Milagros about his mom's terminal illness after she had fainted at the funeral.

His beer buddy and coworker Jed was the only one at SBC that knew his mother was dying. He had only recently shared that information over beers a couple of nights ago. Back then he thought he would have more time with Mom. Time to say goodbye. Time to tell her he loved her more than anyone in his life.

He was in his truck and headed for Kelly's in a matter of minutes.

"Goddammit!" he hollered, slamming his hand into the steering wheel. Guilt overtook his sorrow. *I was supposed to go to the hospital today. I promised her I was coming. I promised.*

Kelly had pled with him to skip working the double-shift today. He was ashamed to admit that he was afraid of breaking down at the sight of his lovely mother dying in increments. Dying long before she should. It wasn't fair.

I should've listened to Kelly. Moms is gone and I'll never get to tell her how much she meant to me.

When he got to the apartment, Kelly answered the door, her eyes red and swollen. She grabbed him and clung to him. Instantly, the long dammed emotions released. He cried, joining her in a silent sorrowful tribute to the woman they both loved. They sat on the couch for a few minutes before either was able to regain composure.

"What time did she die?" he asked.

Kelly wiped her face with the back of a trembling hand. "Uh … 7:42 p.m. At least that's what Detective Sommers said when she came to tell me."

Marcus' head whipped to his sister. "She came over here just to tell you that Moms died? Was it a slow day or something?"

"No, she came because … Well, she came … she came because of the note Mother left."

Marcus peered at Kelly. She was chewing her bottom lip, something she only did when she was uncomfortable. "What *kind* of note?" he asked.

"Suicide note, Marc," said Kelly, as the tears flowed freely down her cheeks.

Marcus sprang to his feet. "*Moms?!!!!!* Moms committed suicide???? That's some bullshit!!!"

Suicide? Was the cancer's pain that bad?

Kelly reached for his arm and pulled him back down on the sofa. "The police said … said mother confessed to …" Her mouth opened and closed, then opened again, but no words came out.

"To what, Kel? Confessed to …" Then it hit him. "Naw!!! Naw, don't say that."

"Yes, she did Marcus." She buried her head in her hands, "Our mother confessed to killing Daddy!"

Marcus felt his brain swirl and then freeze the way it does when he had eaten a Popsicle too fast. What had he missed?

"But I was the main suspect. I'm sure of it! I was the one in the old man's face that night," he said, agitated. "How in the hell did Moms even get in the picture?"

His heart ached for his mother. He knew she had adored her husband, and for all his faults, she was lost without her companion. The cops thinking his mother was the killer was nuts. His head throbbed and he braced his elbow on the arm of the chair, supporting the weight of his head.

"Kelly, Moms grew things. *Grew things,*" he explained as if she didn't already understand that. Kelly wasn't even trying to defend their mother. "She made things beautiful. She couldn't kill a soul. So why would she confess to killing the old man?"

"They said she did," Kelly whispered.

"And you're just taking their word for it," he snapped.

"She left a note, Marcus! A note! She was there in the house."

"I was there in the house," he shot back.

"Did you kill him?" she asked, leveling a stony gaze on him.

"No! Did you?"

"Of course not." Kelly winced quickly looking away.

Marcus reflected on his last conversation with his mother a couple of nights ago. He had called her from work on his lunch break. She knew he hated seeing her in the hospital and she seemed so glad to hear from him. He scrolled through the call history on his Blackberry. They had talked for exactly twenty-seven minutes; reminding him of the conversations they used to have when he was in high school. On Fridays after school they would catch up on each other's whole week. It was her way of staying in touch with his life while he lived with Scott's family. No matter what, he felt that she loved him deeply. Theirs was a mother-son relationship lived in secret.

Marcus pictured their mother in her home, seated royally among the things she loved rather than in the sterile hospital environment surrounded by strangers. Without her beautiful, carefully chosen possessions around her, she was somehow out of context, a perfect picture without the frame. His heart sunk. He threw his head back, leaned back in the chair until his entire weight was on the back legs.

He rocked there for a few seconds before releasing his full weight and allowing the front legs of the chair to hit the floor. He remembered the last voicemail he received. "Marcus, I need to see that handsome face of yours." He should have spent more time with her, especially after Kelly moved out. Before they hospitalized her, he would take her for lunch or hang out in the garden with her. Often he simply drove her on a couple of non-essential errands. She loved his maroon 4x4, said she liked sitting up high. Again, royalty.

Having me take her on her errands was her way of having 'face time' with me, he thought wistfully.

"Marcus, I need to talk to you about mother," Kelly said, snapping him back to the present. Somehow, she had moved to take a seat in the rocker next to the window.

"That last day, the day she died, I had, something important to tell her."

Marcus remained silent, waiting for Kelly's explanation.

"Marcus," she said, pausing as she locked an intense gaze on him and placed a hand over her empty womb. "I was terrified mother would give up. Her spark … was gone. So I went in to the hospital to tell her that Chad and I are having a baby."

"A baby?" he said. And just for a moment, his sorrow took a back seat to his sister's happy news. "Are you kidding me?"

Marcus stood, lifted Kelly from the couch and wrapped her tightly in his arms. "So this is congratulations?" Marcus looked straight into his sister's eyes for a clue to her feelings.

"Yes, *it is,* but let's not spread the news," she said as he lowered her to the floor, "I haven't told Chad yet. I only told mother, because she … and now you." Kelly sniffled as tears overflowed the rims of her eyes. Marcus smiled, interpreting his sister's tears as symbolic of her joy.

Marcus was desperately grappling with the double blow of his father's brutal murder, and his mother's confession and suicide, but this news was a welcome respite for all the sadness that had shadowed his life. *I am going to be an uncle.* Kelly's smile disappeared as quickly as it had come, as Marcus continued mulling over the series of sudden revelations.

Something inside of Marcus couldn't accept the suicide note. He didn't give a damn what the note said, his mother was not a murderer, under any circumstances. The police had fingered him, but with his mother's confession, he wondered if they would ever find the real killer.

Marcus walked over to Kelly, who was gazing out of the window toward Lake Michigan.

If his mother had written a suicide note, taking the murder on her head, then she was protecting someone. Someone more important to her than her own life.

Reality stabbed him in the heart and he quickly clamped down on that line of thinking. The police might give up because things were neatly dropped in their lap. But he knew the truth. And he didn't have to look far.

Kelly is carrying our future. That thought distinguished itself from many that swirled in his brain.

Marcus stepped closer to Kelly and draped his arm around his sister's shoulder. They stood together, watching the receding waves.

CHAPTER 59

HALLOWEEN, SUNDAY, OCTOBER 31, 2004 WAS A BLUSTERY AFTERNOON.

The breeze off Lake Michigan was chilly and the afternoon was perfect for the throngs of Trick-or-Treaters accompanied by their moms, dads, siblings and caregivers. Ghosts, goblins and ballerinas, a Hershey's Kiss and a tiny lion tamer with a whip. A collection of the gorgeous and the ghoulish were slapping door knockers, ringing bells and knocking on locked doors of the 47th Street high rise, chanting "trick or treat" as they paraded up and down the hallways and from floor to floor.

Kelly looked over at the bowl of wrapped candy that sat on her dining room table. She had an arsenal of miniature Snickers, Pay Days and Reese Cups, and two bags of Hershey Kisses. A knock at her door prompted a move from the sofa.

"Trick or Treat!" came a chorus of small voices followed by a mom dressed as a queen.

"Who have we here?" Kelly said, grinning at the pixie dressed in a white tutu, white tights and pink ballet shoes.

"I'm a vall-e-rina," she announced.

"You are a ball-e-rina Sweetie," corrected her dark-haired mother.

"And I'm a big punkin'," said a little boy in an orange suit that looked like a huge stuffed pillow with a kid stuck in the middle. Cute.

"I can certainly see that," Kelly said, laughing as more kids swept past them and ran down the hall to the other doors. "And what a handsome pumpkin you are."

"Meow," purred the toddler dressed as a tiny black cat and perched in the woman's arms.

"And what a fearsome black cat," teased Kelly, reaching out to rub the cat between its ears. "I think you all need some candy."

She dug into the bowl and placed a generous handful of assorted wrapped candy in each child's bag.

Moments later, Kelly sat on the couch, looking through the window toward Lake Michigan. The water was rough as the tide ripped toward the shore. Water could boil, it could be snow, ice, but hot or cold its essence remained unchanged. Water brought consolation.

Kelly realized that life would never be the same for her, and yet something steadied her.

Everything had changed. In her mind she still heard Marcus' voice shatter with pain when their father had threatened him that night. How could her father be an Elder in the church and damage his children the way he had? *Man of God!* What did he think God thought of his molesting Mattie's son? Mattie had been his wife's dearest friend for over twenty years. They traveled together, talked every single day. Dennis had known Mattie's husband Emery. Kelly had to make it stop. He couldn't be allowed to hurt another living soul.

These were the thoughts that Kelly surrendered to on this cool morning that would begin the rest of her life.

The doorbell rang. On her apartment's security keypad, Kelly pressed the numerical sequence that unlocked the lobby door for Chad. He was moving the rest of her personal things over to his condo. She was relieved that he wasn't pressuring her to marry him. He knew she'd been through too much to commit, but he wanted her with him, so that he could protect her.

"Baby, I know you have a lot of healing to do. I just want you near me while you do it," was how he suggested that she move in with him.

"Yes," she had said after mulling over his proposal for a week.

She needed a new start. She wanted to leave the past behind. This apartment housed the memory of the last time she, her mother and father were in this very room—and the painful disclosure that unleashed a chain of events she could not have foreseen.

Kelly wanted to let go of everything that had contorted her life and created so much tragedy. Her mother had used the last droplets of her life to give her children a chance at happiness, to give her daughter a second chance. And perhaps some day Chad *would* have a chance to be a father. The kind of father she had never had.

The door opened. "Used my key. You don't mind do you?" said a sheepishly smiling Chad who entered wearing the black windbreaker that he wore when he jogged on the lake. He leaned over to kiss her forehead.

"Get serious, it looks like we'll be sharing keys for a while. You taste like salt," Kelly said, sucking her jaws in.

"I thought you liked me hot and sweaty," he said jumping back to escape an imaginary blow. Then, "Hey, got a present for you." Instead of handing it to Kelly, he opened the bag marked with the words 'WINDOW TO AFRICA,' removed a figure and held it up for her inspection.

Kelly reached for the sixteen-inch pinkish soapstone sculpture of a giraffe. The grain was absolutely flawless. She ran her fingers across the smooth porcelain-like figure, then held it up to be bathed by the daylight that poured into the large window of her soon to be vacated apartment.

"I thought you might try to rebuild your collection again. The lady that owns the shop said she brought it back from a trip to Kenya."

"It's beautiful, and so perfect. Yes, I do want to start all over again," she said throwing her free arm around his neck and savoring the salty taste of his kiss.

CHAPTER 60

Several days later

Early that morning, Russell drove to Joi's apartment in lieu of heading to the gym for his regular workout before going to the Station. Thirty minutes after his arrival they lay curled in each other's arms. His scent, a torrid mixture of sweat and Joop cologne, mingled with the scent of her Red Door cologne. The gold satin sheets of Joi's bed were tangled around them.

They were both relaxed—now.

"Joi, do ya really think the Gregg woman murdered her husband?"

"Hell no." She reached down to pick her fallen pillow off the carpeted floor. "The evidence we have points to either the stuck-up daughter *or* Marcus," she said, nestling back in her partner's arms.

"Remember that choir director said there was a rumor that the old man 'messed' with boys." Russell covered his lower torso with the sheet.

"I bet Kelly's shrink would've told us he messed with more than just boys."

Joi adjusted her head to tug at a lock entangled in her gold hoop earring. "There's a load of shit stinkin' under that sanitized surface."

"But the mother confessed *and* then conveniently committed suicide. In the eyes of the prosecutor, somebody paid for the crime-end of story," said Russell, thumbing through the October 2004 issue of *Ebony* magazine on Joi's bedside table. "You know they won't waste the taxpayer's money to pursue the case. What would the payback be?"

"Russ, how about the right person paying for the murder of the old man?" Frustration strained her voice.

"Look we took what we had to the Assistant DA," said Russell. "He said that the case would probably have been tossed for lack of evidence anyways. The crime is off the Village's books. Isn't justice about making sure the killer doesn't kill again? Somehow, I don't think this one will."

"Russ, you don't know that." Joi fluffed her over-stuffed satin-covered gold pillow and leaned back into it, wondering how much a woman like Nancy Gregg must have loved her kids to sacrifice what was left of her own life to protect them. Then she thought of her mother, but before any disparaging thoughts formed she reached over for her purse. Pulling a Virginia Slims from the deflated pack, she lit it, took a deep relaxing drag. The smoke curled about them, causing Russell to groan.

"You and your mom *both* need to be trying to quit damn smokin'."

"Will you keep your voice down?" Joi snapped. "She's probably outside the door tryin' to ease drop anyway. Besides, smoking is about the only thing she and I have in common. And thank God you're not my damn daddy. I'll never quit smoking while I'm working homicide. You can forget that mess." She flicked her ashes in an ashtray on the bedside table.

"Glad you went and brought her back here, aren't you?" he said, waving smoke away and coughing as though he was about to have a conniption.

"The jury is still out on that, but I sleep better."

Russell raised both his thick brows. Before he could continue his anti-smoking rant, Joi tossed the soft package in her purse. It was a slam-dunk.

"Sex, smoking and shooting, my three-legged stool." Almost on queue her cell phone rang.

"Yes, Detective Sommers here." She listened to the caller and interrupted. "Okay, I'll be out that way in about thirty minutes." Joi grimaced as she looked at Russell.

"Oh, I'll save you some time and make the call to Detective Wilkerson," she told the caller. Once she disconnected the call, she looked over at Russ and shook her head.

"Damn, so much for our active nap." She slid out of the bed. "Let's go Russ, homicide on the campus of South Suburban College. A female student—found dead inside one of the chemistry labs. Her head was damn near severed with a garrote."

Russell calmly reached across the bed and shorted Joi's cigarette in the bedside ashtray, "Another murder? You're freakin' kidding me. What is the Village coming to?"

"Trust me, I'm not kidding," Joi said checking the time. She removed her watch and laid it atop her handbag, then gave him a long look that swept across his hardening member.

Joi smiled and he hopped off the bed to join her, moving quickly towards the master bathroom to shower together as they often did.

SUSAN D. PETERS,

a native of Chicago's south side, is a graduate of DuSable High School and DePaul University. Always adventurous, Susan's curiosity lured her to Liberia, West Africa for eleven years. Her family's escape during the Liberian Civil War is the spellbinding account of her first book, a memoir, Sweet Liberia, Lessons from the Coal Pot. Sweet Liberia, received the 2010 Black Excellence Award for Non-Fiction by the African American Alliance of Chicago and in 2011 the book was awarded a prize for Non-Fiction from the Illinois Press Women's Association. A lifelong author of poetry, inspirational essays, short stories, and plays her writings will be featured in the IPWA's 2014 anthology, a collection of the works of twenty-three women writers.

Broken Dolls, Susan's second book, represents her foray into the mystery market and is the first of a series featuring Detective Joi Sommers as its heroine.

Susan currently produces a weekly talk radio program and manages community relations at a prestigious academic medical center. In addition to her busy career, she has raised five children and is the proud grandmother to a host of grandchildren.

visit Susan Peters on the web and social media
www.susandpeters.com
www.broken-dolls.com
find her blog at http://ahnydah-sweetliberia.blogspot.com/
and Facebook

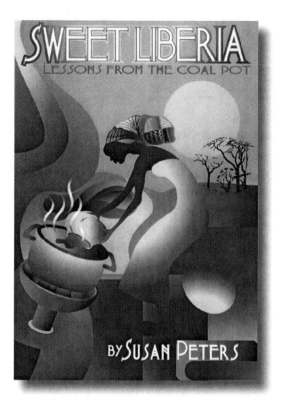

Sweet Liberia, Lessons from the Coal Pot is a delightful, painfully honest memoir that chronicles the thick slice of humanity sandwiched between Liberia's April 12, 1980 coup and the Civil War in 1989. Like many others who embraced Black Pride, Afros, African clothing and names in the 70's, Susan and thousands more took it one step further and immigrated to Mother Africa. This touching memoir is set against the author's personal growth, her cultural struggles, and her triumphs, and is an informative, personally revealing, and often-comical account of her family's eleven-year journey immersed in the rich culture of Liberia, West Africa.

Now, as Liberia stands on the threshold of rising under the leadership of Africa's first elected female president, Ellen Johnson Sirleaf, Susan writes about the wisdom, beauty, and resilience she witnessed during her sojourn.

www.sweetliberia.com
available in e-book and trade paperback wherever books are sold